40 Ways to Say Goodbye

TALES OF A MIDLIFE WITCH

BOOK ONE

DONNA MCDONALD

Dedication

This series is for the real life Peter Landerman, who is most definitely not a priest, but is definitely one of the nicest readers I've ever met.

Acknowledgments

Thanks to T. Beck for the edit. I appreciate your way with words. I'm so lucky to have you.

Thanks to my mother for showing me how tough some women can be.

Thanks to my sister, my niece, my daughter-in-law, my daughters, and my granddaughters for all the inspiration to write strong women heroines.

Book Description

How many ways do you need to say goodbye to your ex until he finally leaves you alone?

My formal name is Aran of The Dagda. I rue the day I became Aran Derringer, but soon I'll be changing it back to plain old Aran O'Malley. Most days it's not so bad being a forty-year-old witch from the lineage of the Tuatha de Danann. The last seven years weren't the best, but I don't have time to be regretting the past.

Despite what my demon hunter ex-husband and his demon hunter council told the world about me, I am not and never was a criminal. Before I could break myself out of prison, though, the demon hunter council made me a deal I couldn't refuse. A legit early release is costing me all my pride and a lot more trouble than a jailbreak would have, but I like the idea of not being a magickal fugitive.

I swear to Goddess Danu that to get my magical divorce from

Jack, I've become desperate enough to do just about anything, even if it means helping his stupid bosses.

40 Ways to Say Goodbye is an exhilarating new paranormal women's fiction tale from USA Today Bestselling Author Donna McDonald.

Chapter One

S even years ago...

MY MOTHER always told me that most of life's problems weren't hard on a woman, but that loving a man took everything. The last time I heard her issue that warning to me was the day Jack and I married. After that, Ma focused on the granddaughter I happily gave birth to at the end of my first wedded year.

Maybe Ma stopped hinting at the potential trouble I was in because she honored my marital commitment. Or maybe she simply wiped her hands of trying to get me to see the truth. Or perhaps moving from Galway, Ireland to Salem, Massachusetts changed Jack in ways I hadn't seen, even if the move had been at his insistence.

Today, though, I remembered Ma's warning and wished with my whole heart that I'd paid more attention to her then. Maybe if I'd thought about *why* she'd said those things about the man I'd chosen to tie myself to, I wouldn't be in my current situation.

What situation is that? Well, that would be the situation where a nice Irish witch married a selfish idiot. Most people were grateful when someone saved their life. My husband seemed determined to be an exception of the worst kind.

"Why are ya betraying me, Jack? We made a daughter together. I'm yer wife in word and deed. I don't understand why ya're doing this to me."

This was the demon hunter council room. I hadn't been in here before because I hadn't been allowed, but I could well imagine the pilgrim witches being brought here before being dragged away and burned. The stately space had a polished wooden table in the front for the ones who judged ya, and a few equally polished chairs facing it for those like me. Behind us were benches lining each side of the room like a church. They were for a missing audience, but not even my family was there.

Jack's gaze swept the room, but eventually landed on me. He seemed oddly untroubled about what was happening even though I was losing my mind wondering what he had planned.

Whenever I asked a question, Jack refused to answer. He just kept repeating that he was angry at me. Well, I was angry with him too. I could see no reason for my husband to bring me here to face the people he worked for. He hadn't even let me comb my hair or wash my face this morning.

Jack was a foot taller than me, so I had to glare up at him when I spoke. Confrontation was the only time in my life that I hated my shorter stature. "I've been the best wife I could be to ya, Jack."

"This isn't about you being a good or bad wife, Aran. This is about your magick. You called a demon from the Underdark

2

and commanded it to serve you. That goes against everything I believe."

Everything he said was a little true, but not exactly accurate. "Conn is my familiar but I do not command him. I simply ask him very nicely to help me with a specific problem and he does so. When he bit the mailman on the ankle for opening yer shaving club box, ya didn't complain about his help then, Jack. I would have thought ya would be grateful that he was willing to fight a demon from the Underdark to save yer life."

When Jack sneered at my argument, I knew it was a bad sign. He could be stubborn and belligerent when I proved him wrong. As he drew in a long breath to argue back, I realized I was wasting air trying to convince him of Conn's good intentions.

My husband had already decided that I was the one who was wrong.

"Conn was a *dog* when he bit the mailman. You didn't tell me your familiar was a demon, not once in all the time we were married. I thought Conn was merely a shapeshifter. How could you not warn me about what he truly was?"

I straightened in my chair, which wasn't easy when my feet dangled three inches above the floor. Such irritations made me grateful my daughter had inherited her father's taller height, but I was praying for all I was worth that my only child hadn't inherited his closed mind.

"Conn is a bound imp, Jack, and ya never once asked me for details about him in the time we've been together. I don't see how my familiar suddenly became a problem *after* he saved yer wretched life. Or don't ya remember that's part of the story? I notice ya keep leaving it out."

Jack glared at me with hatred, and it hurt my heart.

"An imp is a lesser demon, Aran. You don't have to be a hunter to understand the problem with him. Demons don't belong on this plane."

Still shocked by my husband's extreme reaction, I blinked at him. Had Jack always viewed the world through eyes not capable of seeing gray? How had I missed that about him?

Okay, yes. Technically, Jack was right about imps being classified as lesser demons, but that was only a label. Imperial demon history was far more complex than most could handle learning.

The bottom line was Conn had never done anything mischievous to Jack, much less harmful.

It was my cousin, Liam, who called real demons up from the Underdark. And those demons were the kind that caused all manner of trouble just for the fun of it. Why wasn't Jack worried about stopping him? Liam spoke the demonic language better than I did, and I'd studied hard to learn it.

The demons all liked Liam because they enjoyed being part of his elaborate schemes. Liam was also the reason I came to be Conn's keeper. My closest cousin had a penchant for using his demon-calling abilities for his own selfish purposes.

Da said I was the only magickal of my generation, on either his or Ma's side, that could be trusted not to misuse Conn. Had I been foolish to believe Jack also loved me for the innate goodness that made my family consider me worthy of our legacy?

I suddenly had a worse thought. What had Jack told our daughter Fiona about this situation? He'd taken me away this morning before I could talk with her.

I could handle the man I married thinking I was evil, but I refused to let my teenage daughter believe such nonsense. I had enough trouble keeping her outlook positive. As much as it pained me not to spew my hurt like lava all over my disloyal husband, I had to win Jack over before this went too far.

"Listen, Jack. The Dagda himself saved Conn from becoming a wicked demon many centuries ago. I know Da told ya about Conn's history with our family the first day the two of ya met. I heard the two of ya talking about it for hours. Do ya remember doing that, Jack? Ya have to remember it. I recall ya talking to Da like it happened only yesterday."

"Of course, I remember it, Aran, but I thought your father was exaggerating because you had said *absolutely nothing* about Conn being a demon. Everyone knows there are no good demons walking this plane of existence. You're being foolish to trust even a lesser one. If you freed him from being bound, he'd end your life with no remorse."

"No, ya're wrong, Jack. Conn would never harm me. Did ya not hear me when I said he'd served my family for *centuries*? We're not talking about a creature who got dragged through the veil yesterday. And he doesn't live in the Underdark. Conn belongs on this plane now as much as you or I do. He's belonged here for centuries."

Grunting with lost patience, Jack pulled me upright by the magickal handcuffs he'd put on me last night. I'd gone along with him snapping them on me because I'd been dressing for bed and thought his action meant we might be heading for a bit of sexy fun. Why had I been so foolish? Because I naively thought Jack was trying to make up for our fight about Conn.

What a fool I'd been about him all these years.

Ma would be ashamed of me if she knew I'd let any man so far into my heart that I'd trusted him with everything sacred to us. She'd remind me that Da never gave her a minute's worry in all their fifty-two years together.

Up to this moment, Jack had never given me any serious concerns either.

Or he hadn't until he'd seen Conn turn into a fiery red creature and grow a pair of black horns that curled back over his head. I assumed his true form had been necessary for Conn to sway the battle in Jack's favor. I'd never imagined there would be such fallout from him helping us.

Jack might not be grateful to Conn, but I was. My familiar had the right to refuse to help anyone but me. Jack had been out of his magickal arrows when the angry demon attacked him. Conn could have let the demon kill Jack. The only reason he hadn't was because I asked him to save my husband. How could Jack be mad at Conn—or me—when my familiar was the only reason he was still alive?

The realization of what Jack was doing hit me when the entire demon hunter council strode into the room dressed in black ceremonial robes. They took seats at the long, official table and looked at me the way a hawk watches a mouse about to run.

I was no common criminal and had done nothing wrong except save my husband's life, so I glared right back at them. I did nothing to thwart them either, no matter how I badly wanted to in that moment. Maybe I could have broken the magick of the cuffs, but I didn't try.

As angry as I was, my instincts warned that zapping the lot of them would not help my case or make me look like the innocent witch I was claiming to be.

Eventually, a female council member stood up and looked me in the eye. The one time I'd seen the woman before today had been at Jack's consecration when she'd handed my demon hunter husband an enchanted crossbow and a quiver of demon-killing arrows. Yes, I tried to tell Jack over the years that his demon hunting was in vain and that hadn't won me any points with the man I married. But I swear to Goddess Danu, it never crossed my mind Jack would ever use those arrows on any member of my family.

Now I realized that was precisely what he planned to do.

Last night, Jack said my possession of a demon familiar reflected poorly on him. For the sake of keeping peace, I let my husband's hurtful comment pass without spelling him to grow a squealing pig's tail. However, I did tell Jack where to shove his wrong opinions, because even the most understanding witch has to draw a line when faced with such unjust prejudice.

My head whipped around when I heard the female council woman speaking my name.

"Before us stands a witch calling herself Aran of The Dagda. She has confessed to the illegal possession of a lesser demon. The demon hunter council commands her to call him forth so he can be destroyed."

It's funny how drastically yer life can change in a single moment of time. That moment for me came when Jack forced me to protect Conn from him. Outside the crushing emotional pain of my husband's betrayal, choosing Conn over Jack wasn't as hard as ya might imagine considering only Conn had been loyal to me.

I lifted my chin. "Yer request is not even reasonable. My familiar is a member of my family. Plus, Jack would be dead if Conn hadn't saved him. How can the demon hunter council ignore those facts?"

Jack's hand disappeared into some pocket portal of his coat and then reappeared with a loaded crossbow in it. "Don't be a fool, Aran. Once your demon's dead, we can work on mending our relationship. Call him—let's get this over and done."

My husband's words worked on my temper like gasoline

when thrown on a blazing fire. The handcuffs were all that kept me from hurting Jack. In fact, I might have found a way to use my magick despite the cuffs, but it was my lingering love for the man and my confusion about his betrayal that restrained me.

Though I fought not to show the depth of my hurt, it was breaking my heart. I felt shattered and raw inside. His words made a mockery of our marriage, and nothing I said made a difference.

I turned away from Jack and looked at the woman. "Ya're all mad fools if ya think I'd help any of ya hurt my truest friend."

"Call him," the council woman ordered more firmly.

I shook my head, remaining as stalwart as the Irish cliffs I was named after.

"Call him or face the consequences," she said.

My instincts warned me that anything other than going along would not serve me well today. I needed to buy myself some time with compliance, even though the cost would be dear to my pride. Worst of all, Ma would no doubt remind me for the rest of my life that I'd brought this mess upon myself by marrying Jack in the first place.

Ever the optimist, I tried one more time to reason with the man I married. I was never going to forgive Jack, but this madness could still be stopped. "Use yer head for something more than a hat rack, Jack Derringer. If ya think so poorly of me and mine, how can we ever have a real relationship? Where is yer loyalty to me?"

Jack sneered at my refusal to obey the woman's orders—*his orders*. Why would he ever think I would? He should have known better. It was like he was suddenly a stranger instead of the man I'd lived with for thirteen years.

"The demon you're protecting will die one way or another, Aran. No one would convict me for killing you to get to him."

My heart bled at his words until pain filled my chest. "Goddess, one minute ya want to reconcile, and the next ya're threatening to kill me. Make up yer mind at least. This is a shameful way to treat yer wife."

Jack frowned at my calm statement. "Controlling a demon is one secret I can't let you keep from the world. You're protecting the wrong person, Aran. Can't you see that?"

"No. What I'm doing is protecting myself and all I hold sacred. I'm fulfilling my duty to my family."

Jack glared back at me. "*I'm* your family, Aran."

"No, ya're not—not anymore, Jack. Not even the worst drunkard among the O'Malleys ever threatened to kill a family member for no good reason."

It was a hurtful thing for me to say to the man I promised my loyalty to, but Jack was making me choose Conn over him.

I lifted my chin and kept it high so I didn't look like a child standing next to him. Never in my life had I wished harder to be six feet tall.

I projected my energy as much as I could under the circumstances and glared up at Jack for making me do this. "If ya want to talk about magickal retribution, no magickal person in the world would arrest me for chopping off yer body parts to defend myself. Challenging me would not be a good idea."

Jack's lips formed a sneer. "Are you willing to lose me and our daughter because of your demon? Because he's going to cost you both of us."

Heartbroken at the idea of losing Fiona's love, my voice was quiet when I spoke this time. Any threat concerning my daughter pushed my heart as far as it had room to break.

"No matter what ya tell our daughter, Jack, one day she'll learn the truth. Yer lies and deceit won't stay hidden forever."

"These circumstances are your own fault. They're not mine. I'm not the villain here, Aran. I don't even want to do this. You're giving me no choice."

I held up my wrists to make sure Jack and his council saw I was still bound with the cuffs he'd placed on me. "Ya're the only one here with any sort of choice. So kill me if ya want, husband. At least then, we'll be truly done with each other. Conn will pass on to another in my family line. Once that's done, though, ya better watch yer back. There won't be anywhere on this planet where ya can hide from my family."

Jack's yell was that of a man being tortured. "*Why are you trying to make me into the villain?*"

I blinked up at a man I no longer knew. "If not a villain, then what are ya, Jack? Ya're not being a loving husband. Ya're not being the caring father of my child. Killing a demon in self-defense is one thing, but killing a bound creature would be flat out murder."

"Fine," Jack reached into a small pocket and pulled out a copper chain with a glowing black stone dangling from it. "I'll just use this amulet of yours to call him here. If Conn believes you're in real danger, I'm sure he'll come to your aid."

My heart sank into my stomach when I saw what Jack held in his hand. Whatever little love I had left for him died the cruelest of deaths in a single dark moment of clearing seeing him for the man he was.

Once again I lifted my chin and glared. "Ya've already broken my heart a hundred times yesterday and today. Did ya have to steal The Dagda Stone as well? Ya can't use it for anything. Not even my own kin can do that. The Dagda Stone is mine and mine alone until my death. Ya've betrayed me for nothing. Connlander of the Fir Bolg has nothing to fear from the likes of ya. He won't come no matter what ya do."

Jack sighed and hung his head. "Why can't you side with me instead of against me? I can't save you from yourself, Aran."

Snorting at his condescending tone, I spat the truth at him. "Until today, I thought ya were the one person who would stand by me through everything life threw at me. Ya can't imagine how it feels to learn how wrong I was."

Jack pressed his lips together. "No matter how difficult this is for me, I will do what must be done. One day you'll thank me for having the strength to do the right thing."

"No, I won't because I'll be too busy hating ya for doing me wrong. I've been the best wife I knew how to be. In the past, I bowed to yer wishes instead of doing what I knew to be right, but I won't be giving into yer demands today. I can't let ya murder someone in my family. I'd die myself before tainting my soul with such an act."

"Nonsense!" the council woman said as she waved a hand. "Demons do not belong to families. They do not feel loyalty."

The Dagda Stone necklace disappeared from Jack's hand and magickly appeared in hers. Apparently, the demon hunter woman was also some kind of witch.

"Aran of The Dagda, you are to be magickly incarcerated for a term of twenty years, which should be enough time for you to reconsider your stance."

I drew myself up to a stiff five foot one. "I don't know what authority ya believe ya have over me, but it's not as much as ya think. And to be blunt, council woman, I've been reconsidering all my life choices for the last several hours. Divorcing my traitorous husband is now at the top of my to-do list, and getting even with ya for helping him steal my private property is next. Consider yerself warned, council woman. Ya better take superb care of my necklace while ya have it. The true owner of it is a Celtic god who's not as merciful as I tend to be."

Jack frowned at my threat before defending himself again. "I don't want a divorce from you, Aran. I love you and the life we made together, but I can't let you run around calling forth a demon all the time. You are not above the rules."

I swung to glare even more fiercely at him. "Whose rules, Jack? Are they yer rules? Are they yer council's rules? The only rules I follow are the ones sanctioned by the Goddess Danu. And I'm pretty sure she's okay with Conn getting to live or he'd already be dead."

Jack glared again. "Humor won't change the seriousness of your infraction nor keep you from being incarcerated for your refusal to cooperate."

I sneered at Conn's would-be murderer for daring to chastise me. "Yeah, well, using big words to describe locking me up won't change how wrong ya are in using yer authority for this purpose. There will be consequences for yer behavior today. My family does not take betrayal lightly."

"My *job* is to remove all demons from the Earth permanently. Why can't you let me do my job without fighting me every step of the way? You have never supported my work."

My disappointed sigh was loud and long, but no tears fell. Ironically, I considered not weeping over my heartbreak to be a small win for my pride... and I desperately needed one. My future looked very bleak for the next few years.

"So what happens now, Jack? Are ya planning on torturing me in hopes I'll change my mind? Will I have to wear yer magick handcuffs forever? This is a modern-day witch hunt and ya know it. I'm innocent of any wrongdoing."

Out of the corner of my eye, I saw the council woman who took my amulet wave her hand at some nearby guards. Her voice carried with almost no effort. "Deliver Jack's wife to Asbury Cottage. It's warded against her Celtic magick. She can have visitors there but won't be able to leave until she changes her mind. If she calls up her demon, the house will alert us. For extra insurance, we'll keep her family heirloom."

Jack bowed his head to the woman when her gaze landed on him. I guessed it was to show his agreement with plans for me.

That nod finished us as far as I was concerned.

For now, I would go along with their incarceration for Fiona's sake. I had no choice but to protect her from Jack until she was old enough to deal with her father on her own terms.

I would not serve a sentence I did not deserve in some demon hunter prison. When the time was right, I would leave, and Goddess only knew Jack better be ready to deal with my wrath.

Chapter Two

S *everal years later, also known as today...*

THE SEVENTH SPRING of my incarceration caused the same
wishing in my witch's soul as the other six springs at the
cottage that passed before it. After being alone for so many
years, I knew longing for the impossible was hopeless.

Those who'd imprisoned me would not be experiencing
some miracle that would change their minds. That hope died
during the first year.

My official enemies now included the entire demon hunter
council and the self-righteous, deceitful demon hunter I'd
foolishly married and bred a witch daughter with.

Not only had Jack sided with strangers when I'd refused to
help him murder Conn, but he also stole my family legacy for
Goddess only knew what reason.

It had been five years since I last wept at the unfairness of it all. But I hadn't seen the man I married in the entire seven years of what they called my *magickal incarceration.*

His total absence from my life seemed normal to me. If he had shown up after all this time, I might not have been able to contain my wrath, and I imagine Jack suspected that.

I was very proud of myself for never accepting the injustice the demon hunter council did to me. With Da gone from this life, Ma returned to Ireland during my prison years. I hadn't been allowed to see her the whole time. Despite their promises that I could have visitors, Fiona had been the only one they allowed.

My parents had encouraged me to use my inherited powers for the good of people on this side of the ocean after I married one of its citizens. Jack and Fiona were the only reasons I stayed here in America, especially when my heart longed for cliffs and the sea.

My family plans hadn't exactly worked out for me, though. Instead of using my gifts for good and training others to do so, my powers had been questioned, betrayed, and hidden away for the last seven years.

But there were good reasons my mother had named me after the Aran cliffs near her original home. A diminutive witch named after towering rock surfaces could not be broken by the opinions of others, especially when they were flat wrong.

The day marking my fortieth year of living on this earth was less than two weeks from now. With that celebration would come an additional burst of power not constrained to the family heirloom necklace Jack stole from me.

Not that I needed its power to get out of this place. I never had.

If Fiona had been willing to follow me back to my family's original dwelling place, I'd have returned to Ireland long before now. There I could have raised her in a land where magick was respected and our family was honored.

Fiona had been thirteen when they sent me to the cottage and she hadn't wanted to leave her friends. So I'd stayed and dealt with my imprisonment for her sake.

They let me see Fiona as often as I wanted, which was a powerful motivation to not become a fugitive. Obviously, I couldn't escape and leave her behind. No way was I letting Jack raise my daughter to be a traitor too.

My goals changed, though, after Fiona came into her own. She was twenty now. Whatever choice my adult daughter made about where to live, I'd already decided not to serve out the remaining years of my unjust imprisonment.

Monitoring Fiona's life at a distance was not reason enough to go without seeing the rest of my family. No, my celebration plans for my fortieth birth year involved gaining my total freedom.

I'd always possessed enough power to break their so-called Celtic magick wards, but it was instinct that held me back. Something told me life would be easiest if I stayed a while longer. I hadn't listened to my gut back when my instincts warned me about the shadier side of the man I married, but I was listening now.

Planning to escape instead of actually doing it always made me restless, though, so I rose from my seat on the porch and walked out into the yard as far as the warded boundary allowed without setting off the blasted alarms.

I'd done that multiple times—all accidental—during my first year here and what a mess that had created. They'd almost put Jack's handcuffs back on me.

Standing at the edge of their boundary now, I stared resentfully at the road I wasn't free to walk down before I strolled back toward the porch. Maybe it was the line of blooming pink azaleas growing on both sides of the porch that had me wishing things could be different.

I headed to sit on the swing that Fiona had helped me lower enough that my feet touched.

The house was perfectly pleasant. I hated my prison for what it represented—Goddess knew I did—but I also understood the Victorian cottage pleased most eyes with its pale yellow exterior trimmed in bright white scrollwork. Given the world's current infatuation with all things "vintage", the quaint Victorian kitchen made the cottage a realtor's dream. It didn't appeal to my aesthetic tastes, but feeling trapped in it certainly didn't help my opinion.

In all honesty, the only real negative was the too modern living room. Rumors from food deliverers and the guards assigned to check on me was that the warlock previously imprisoned in it requested the large masculine furniture that dwarfed my petite body.

Sure, I'd spent a few nights sleeping on the monstrous couch in the living room when I was feeling depressed and too lazy to climb the stairs, but never once had I sat in any of the matching over-sized chairs. Instead, I'd dragged a reasonable-sized wooden rocker from the master bedroom downstairs. The rocker wasn't the most comfortable seat for lounging, but at least my feet touched the floor. That was my usual requirement for furniture.

I sat beside the fireplace during lonely winter nights and rocked myself into a state of calm.

Long ago, I was told everyone imprisoned here got to redecorate a room or two, but I'd found that offer too ironic to take them up on it. Why bother changing the contents of my prison cell? I was neither tenant nor guest in the cottage. The mismatched furnishings kept my situation from feeling normal, and my discomfort reminded me that this was not my true fate.

I refused to adapt any further to this farce.

The only reason I hadn't tried to escape was because they'd allowed Fiona to visit me over the years as much as she wanted. Using her as my excuse not to change my situation had reached its expiration date, though. At twenty, she was a child no longer... and thank the Goddess for that. I mean, I loved my daughter madly, but being stuck in this place was more maddening than an innocent woman should have to endure.

Time had passed faster for me when she came to visit. Even with several bedrooms to choose from, my daughter had favored the weirdest one in the house. Its dark purple walls were adorned with posters of boy bands from the 80s. I hadn't tried to find out if some incarcerated teenager chose the furnishings. Anger simmered in me still. Learning that Jack and his demon hunter council had imprisoned a teenage witch would have only made it worse.

Fiona said she liked the feeling of the furry black rug by the bed on her bare toes. Goddess knew she'd not been a simple child, especially for me as a part-time mother, but I loved my daughter with my whole heart. Knowing she'd made it this far in her life still able to appreciate such minor pleasures as a furry rug made my heart happy.

There was no man in my daughter's life yet, nor did Fiona seem to want one. Life was funny, though, because I had been exactly her age when I met Jack. We'd married quickly, and soon I had gotten pregnant with Fiona. Like my daughter, I also had appreciated life's simple pleasures. Without a single doubt in my soul, I'd given all of myself to Jack believing the two of us truly were meant to be together.

On good days, the mystery that was my only child convinced me I hadn't made such a colossal mistake in sleeping with him. But on other days? Well, I suppose I preferred not to dwell on those.

When I finally grew tired of dwelling on the same old things I thought about every day, I rose from the porch to go back into the house. Last week Fiona had brought me a new book of spells. I couldn't perform the more interesting ones with the limited magick allowed around the property, or at least, I couldn't without revealing my powers.

Instead, I focused on memorizing the more intriguing ones.

One day soon I was going to leave this place and practice whatever spells I wanted. I had an entire list of what I would do when I left. The first and most important goal I had was to get *The Dagda Stone* back no matter how many dead bodies I had to step over.

Then I was going to do what I should have done the day Da gave it to me. The only reason I hadn't done the ritual was because Jack had been too fearful of the magickal cost. I wouldn't be incarcerated if I had fully accepted my legacy because the demon hunters would have known that their pitiful wards wouldn't have held me, not even a single day.

Many times in the last seven years, I'd asked the Goddess to apologize to my Da and The Dagda for putting Jack ahead of my other responsibilities. I'd vowed that I would fix things as soon as I could, and that it wouldn't be much longer now that Fiona was grown.

It had been Fiona who had explained to Conn all those years ago that they had incarcerated me because of my relationship with him. Calling him to me in my magickal prison was out of the question when that was precisely what Jack and the demon hunters wanted.

But I hadn't wanted him to feel abandoned either, so Fiona had arranged with my mother—her maternal grandmother—to keep my familiar until I got out of here. Da's mother was the last legacy witch in the family before I became one, but she'd passed long before Da did.

Ma was all I had left, and she hadn't batted a false eyelash at the request. She'd taken Conn in because that's what family did when ya needed help. Or it was what *real* family did.

Before I left this country and the unhappy life I'd lived here, I would track down my traitorous husband and magickly divorce him. It was a sad truth that I might not be able to take back the blood vow I made to him on our wedding day, but I refused to stay connected to Jack in any other way. Killing him was not an option because of the vow, but maybe I could watch while someone else did it.

Perhaps I'd leave this place the day I turned forty. Sure, I still had to decide what I was going to do with this midlife opportunity to reinvent myself, but I'd figure it out. For sure, I would not be spending the rest of my life with some other man who might stick a knife in my back. One of those in my life was enough.

THE MOMENT I crossed the threshold of the front door, I knew I was no longer alone in the house.

Feeling someone magickal, I made my way into the kitchen and found a stranger sitting at my kitchen table. Intruders were a common occurrence, and one I didn't dare try to prevent, so I didn't react to this one either. No doubt he was here simply to make sure I still was. They sent someone to check on me every day.

"Greetings, stranger. Do ya fancy a cup of tea before we get to yer business? I have a nice herbal blend that won't ruin yer dinner or keep ya up all night. I'm having a cup myself, so it's no trouble to make ya one."

"Is the tea your own magickal blend?" he asked.

"No," I said, chuckling at the thought of having that much control over what I ate and drank while at the cottage. "My daughter brings it to me when she visits. Her father checks it for poisons and hallucinogens before she does. Since I've been drinking it for years without issue, ya're probably safe. There's honey and milk too if ya have an urge for those."

"Just honey, please."

I got two big mugs down and the squeeze-bottle of cheap honey they provided. Food appeared in my kitchen every week like clockwork. I think the house reported how much I used because nothing ever got doubled. Either the house was magickal or it was spelled. Mostly I couldn't complain about the way they fed me, but the quality wasn't high.

Before my incarceration, I used to harvest honey from the bees living in my garden. Fiona reported that she'd tried to keep the hives up over the years but didn't have my touch for beekeeping. I grieved my bee loss years ago and set it aside just as I had all the other things I'd taken for granted.

Each loss only made me hate my demon hunter husband that much more.

After dropping a strainer filled with loose tea in each mug, I carried them to the table. On the second trip, I fetched honey, two saucers, and two spoons. There was something soothing about the ritual of making tea that never failed to make me feel slightly better, despite my deplorable circumstances.

"While the kettle heats, we can get yer business done. Are ya my checker today?"

The man was at least Jack's size, which meant he cleared six feet or more in height. Although he was seated, I could tell his height because our eyes met easily as I stood next to the table. His longish hair was pulled back in a ponytail streaming down to mid-back. It was charcoal black with a bit of silver showing at the temples, suggesting he was my age or older.

I was surprised. They usually sent younger ones to chat me up. The young ones were eager to tattle on me for whatever favors the demon hunter council promised them.

After spending the first year being mean and surly to visitors, I eventually forced myself to be nice. Revealing that I was still angry gave too much of my true feelings away, so it became my best kept secret. I even kept it from my visiting daughter because I didn't want my teenager rebelling against her father on my behalf. Also I didn't know what Jack might do to control her. Given the ease with which he'd betrayed me, I couldn't take any chances.

I returned to sit at the table as I waited for the kettle to boil, I caught myself imagining what my new visitor would look like with his hair undone and falling over his very wide shoulders. I imagined it would be as long as mine, but then I hadn't had a real haircut since I got here. Dye also was forbidden to me for some strange reason, so now I looked the way the Goddess intended.

When the silver grew below my shoulders after three years, I'd had the then sixteen-year-old Fiona cut the old half straight across with a pair of kitchen shears. Half my old hair fell to the floor that day, and along with it all the memories it carried. Fiona scooped the cut strands up and put them into the trash while asking me why I looked so sad when my hair looked much, much better.

There was no answer to give her that she'd have understood at that age. My imprisonment had become too normalized in our life. One day years from now, I'd remind her of that haircut and explain how it had felt to see a gray-haired stranger when I looked in the mirror. If she showed compassion for those feelings, I might also admit to her that I was ashamed of myself for not using my powers to change my fate.

Maybe she'd figure out that the reason I restrained myself was her. Or maybe she wouldn't. Ya couldn't tell what a young person was thinking most of the time. She was twenty now and I still couldn't tell.

My visitor's grin over my silent musings annoyed me, so I pulled myself back to attention. I met his gaze and waited until he finally answered my question.

"Maybe I am your checker today. No one used that term when they sent me to come talk to you."

The teakettle chose that moment to whistle loudly. I held up a finger for him to pause his comments as I rose from the table to retrieve it. After filling both our mugs with hot water, I returned the kettle to the stove and dug for a package of cookies in a nearby cabinet. I rarely indulged in eating sugar because it messed with my energy, but Fiona enjoyed them whenever she stopped by.

Since I had not invited this man, I didn't bother with a plate when I brought the cookies back to the table. I just slid the now open package in front of him so he could help himself when he was ready.

"My name's Aran. I'm sure ya know that already, but introductions make me feel normal, so I indulge myself with every new person. Now, who would ya be?"

He glared over my cheery greeting like I'd offended him somehow. I decided it was a peculiar reaction, but who was I to judge what his day had been like before I saw him?

"Why are you incarcerated, Aran?"

Before I attempted to explain, I removed the tea strainer from my cup, set it on the saucer, and added some honey to my tea. I gave the brew a slow stir to make him wait a bit longer.

"How is it ya don't know about my situation?"

His shoulder lifted and fell as he shrugged. "They say you're here because you control a demon who obeys you."

I lifted my hands and looked around. "If I controlled a demon like they say, don't ya think I would have burned this bloody house to the ground by now?"

He brought his cup to his very nice lips before he spoke again. I was too mesmerized to look away. That was what seven years of celibacy did to a woman. It caused me to fantasize about one of my jailers. Wasn't there a syndrome for that nonsense?

He smiled as he lowered his mug. "I'm a good listener, Aran. Why don't you tell me the truth?"

Was he really implying that I was a liar? I laughed at his nerve. "I didn't expect to be playing twenty questions with a stranger over tea today. Ya've caught me unprepared."

He shifted uncomfortably in his seat. "The council told me their side of your story. I came to hear your version."

Yes, I was sure that was true to some degree, but the real question was *why* he wanted to hear what I had to say. The man wanted something big from me. Even though I had no clue what that could be, I could feel him working his courage up to ask for it.

I sipped my tea as I gave him what he asked for. "Oh, my side of my story is very simple. I'm stuck here because the man

I married betrayed me. However, being betrayed is an old, old story, ya know, as well as a boring one. Don't ya find it hard to talk about personal things with a stranger? I know I do. Or are ya intending to eventually tell me yer name and why ya're really here?"

While he mentally wrestled with my insistent curiosity, I let my gaze travel over his face. I think my staring made him more uncomfortable than my verbal challenges because he lifted one dark eyebrow in surprise. The man who had yet to give me his name wasn't nearly as handsome as I recalled Jack being, but it had been many years since I laid eyes on the man I was still legally bound to.

Fiona hadn't even shown me any pictures. She said her father had asked her not to. I had my suspicions as to why Jack made that request of our child, but I chose to remain in denial until my suspicions were confirmed.

My mysterious visitor's mild scowl hinted at the sort of masculinity I'd found vastly intriguing when I was younger. The brooding sort offered a challenge that appealed to me— unfortunately. That was probably how I ended up with Jack. No one brooded better than he did when he didn't get his way.

Thankfully, I was no longer as stupid as I once was. Or maybe I only found him attractive because most people who visited were half my age. I admit I was lonely for company who could relate to me as an adult. I had too much time to analyze things in life these days and there was no one around to talk sense into me.

Over-thinking, which is what I called my tendency to dwell, did nothing but frustrate the saner parts of me.

My fantasies about the man's hair for sure were a sign that it was time for me to resume a life that included having some male company now and again. Grateful for the epiphany he'd provided, I sipped my tea and stayed silent when he still didn't offer to introduce himself.

Eventually, I had to speak because the silence was simply too awkward to stand.

"Ya don't have to tell me yer name, of course. Everyone magickal knows there's power in the label we receive at birth, so I understand yer hesitation."

He lifted an eyebrow again, like he'd forgotten he hadn't responded. I snorted but didn't laugh.

"My name is Rasmus."

His name sounded like the long rasp of a file as it slid across metal and hearing it told me my initial instinct was spot on about him. Since he appealed to me on some womanly level that felt ignored in the worst way, I suppose I secretly hoped to be wrong this once. But I was rarely wrong in intuiting what a person did for a living.

I lifted my cup to drink the last of my tea. The honey hiding at the bottom wasn't enough to sweeten the bitter conclusion I had to force down my throat before I told him what I knew.

"Ya're not a warlock, but power simmers along the edges of yer energy. It's sharp and deadly, just waiting for a chance to be released."

Rasmus grunted into his cup. "When you're done guessing, let me know and I'll tell you."

"Oh, I know yer kind all too well, demon hunter. I was stalling while reminding myself not to cut yer throat until I discovered why ya came."

He lowered his guilty gaze as he sipped the last of his tea. After a few seconds, his gaze lifted to mine again. His eyes reflected a sober unhappiness, and he looked resigned.

"Should I apologize for my entire profession?" he asked.

"Not for all," I replied, pushing my empty mug around with twitchy fingers. "Yer work probably serves a good purpose as long as yer original purpose is good. Despite my husband's threats to kill me and my family members, I don't consider all yer kind to be arses of the lowest order. But I find that powerful males like yerself are often incapable of comprehending the gray areas of life."

Rasmus shook his head. "That's quite a denigration of my character when you really don't know me."

I put the strainer with the tea leaves back into my cup and glared at him. "Guess we'll just have to agree to disagree on that point. My desire to know more about ya ended with yer confirmation of what ya've devoted yer life to doing. I haven't forgotten my husband put his work above my well-being. Surely ya can't be surprised by my mistrust."

Chapter Three

My patience with his wordplay was wearing thin. It was time for him to get to the point before I lost my temper. "Why are ya really here, Rasmus? My husband hasn't visited me in the whole seven years I've been trapped here. No demon hunter but yerself has darkened my door."

Not bothering to dunk his strainer again, Rasmus pushed his cup of hot water in my direction. "Thanks for the tea, Aran… and you're right. I came here to make you a deal. If you help us with a demon problem, the council will reduce your sentence."

Never in a million years would I say yes to that sort of deal because my freedom was non-negotiable. I wanted their acknowledgement of my innocence as much as I wanted my property returned.

"Help ya how and with what?" I asked.

Rasmus blew out a breath before taking in a deeper one. "Demons are showing up in greater numbers than we can destroy. We haven't been able to locate the Underdark portal where they're entering this plane of existence. Jack said you might help us if we showed you leniency."

"He's right that I *could* help ya, but ya've given me no good reason to yet. And I'm not in the mood to play word games with ya. Offering me leniency when I did nothing wrong is a joke."

Rasmus glared at me for all he was worth. "Demons are hurting some people and killing others. Why wouldn't you help us just because it's the right thing to do?"

I snorted. "Yer words and opinions can't be trusted. Didn't ya hear what I said about why I'm here? My husband threatened to kill me and someone else in my family. As if that wasn't reason enough to hate ya all, one of yer council women stole my personal property. So take yer pick of those reasons, Rasmus. My actual list is much longer, but those are the top reasons why I'll never agree to help ya for so little gain."

Rasmus slapped a palm down on the table. "Look, we've exhausted all our efforts to find the portal. Twenty-seven demon hunters died last month because we failed. A bigger infestation of demons might be more evil than all magickals working together could eradicate."

I softly chuckled at his dramatic claims. "Yes, well, I know only what the average magickal does about a demon's goals, but I'd bet my supply of sweet biscuits this portal problem of yers is limited to this side of the ocean. Do ya know why, Rasmus? Because all other countries in the world have their own methods of dealing with the Underdark. There's nothing for me in yer offer of alleged leniency except a lot of personal risk. So no thank you. I'll be returning home as soon as I'm able and leaving ya to solve yer demon problems on yer own."

Rasmus sighed. "Fine. Name your terms then. I know you have to want *something* badly enough to help."

I widened my eyes at the offer. "Seriously? Can ya grant me three wishes like a bloody djinn?"

He spoke through tight lips. "No, but I can take your wishes back to the council and argue that they grant them."

"Wow. I suppose I'll have to think about yer generous offer for a few moments then."

Pretending to think, I rose and walked to get the teakettle again. I carried it back to the table and filled our mugs to the brim with hot water that still steamed. His mug sat unattended, so I played the friendly host. "Do ya want some fresh tea leaves for your strainer, Rasmus?"

He frowned and shook his head. I knew letting him stew would convince him better than words would that I had little interest in his petty offer.

After returning the kettle to the stove, I plucked an amber and black stone from a bowl of crystals on the counter before I turned back to talk. Cradling the stone in my hand, I studied Rasmus and his frown.

"How desperate are ya for me to say yes?"

"Desperate enough to entertain your requests," he answered, glaring full-out at me.

Snorting at his irritated tone, I crossed my arms. A tingle of excitement crawled over my skin. This could be a chance to get my freedom to-do list done legitimately and in one fell swoop. How could I pass up a chance to make the council restore my freedom *and* to force Jack to drop his dogged pursuit of killing Conn?

Hope could do a lot to fuel my cooperation.

"Okay, demon hunter. Here are my non-negotiable requests. My familiar, Conn, is forever off-limits as a target for yer kind. Jack personally must swear to abide by that as well. Plus, I want Jack to retrieve my heirloom necklace from yer council and hand it back to me, since he was the one who stole it. He owes that much to my Da. Last, of course, it's only logical for the rest of this bogus incarceration to be dismissed as if it never happened. I want to be a completely free witch."

Rasmus chuckled low. "That's quite a list for a proven criminal. I don't know if they'll agree to all that."

I smirked at him. "Did I ask ya for reparations or money for the time I've been wrongly held here? No, I didn't ask for that, because I don't need to extort anyone for gain. All I want is for my rightful property to be returned to me and for my witch integrity to be restored. To do that, Conn needs to be safe from the likes of yer kind. Ya heard my deal. I want it all or I won't be helping ya."

Rasmus chuckled. "I find your negotiation-free stance surprising for a woman who's been magickly confined for so long. I figured you'd be desperate by now to get out of this place and willing to do whatever it took."

I tilted my head as I stared at him. "I only stayed here because I had reasons for staying. When those reasons are no more, I promise ya I'll be leaving when I please no matter what ya try to do to stop it from happening."

A sexy male smirk formed across lips that should have been used for much nicer purposes.

"You stayed because of the wards on this place. It's warded against Celtic magick. I know all about the details of your incarceration."

It was my turn to chuckle. "No, ya don't. Ya know only facts that aren't important. No one can ward against the power of the gods. It's infinite and changeable and blesses my family as it chooses. My heritage never lets me down when I call on it. I haven't yet made that call, but I've been rethinking the value of my cooperation with the likes of ya."

Snorting because he didn't believe my claim, Rasmus glared at me. "Are you saying you're a god, Aran? That's pretty arrogant of you. If you had that kind of power, they would have recruited you to help us long ago."

I rolled my eyes and counted to ten in my head before speaking. "Do ya know who The Dagda was?"

"Sure. I read mythology. He was one of the original leaders of the *Tuatha de Danann*, who were not gods as far as I know. They were extremely magickal humans with advanced skills in technology."

When I looked at Rasmus, my insides got warm and mushy, but when I listened to him, all I heard was another version of Jack trying to convince me he knew something more than I did.

"The Dagda was the first ancestor of my bloodline. I never tracked how many great greats exist between us, but Ma says he's always been around in some form. The tribe of Danu eventually became immortals. Goddess Danu allowed it."

"Do you have any proof of your claim to have the power of gods?"

I frowned at the question and pretended to be saddened by his rudeness. "I suppose ya require some extraordinary magick to convince ya, don't ya, Rasmus? I'd remove the wards on the house, but that would bring the wrath of yer snooty council down on my head, and I'm not ready to deal with them yet."

Even though I was still standing by the sink, Rasmus pushed his watery mug to my side of the table. "My tea's gone. You could conjure some hot tea for me with magick."

"That's way too easy for our purposes," I said, waving away his suggestion. Then I chuckled. What popped into my mind was a simple magick trick, but one I would enjoy inflicting on him for the rest of the day.

Raising my hand, I pointed one finger at his hair. *"Enchanta purpleanta,"* I announced. A stream of purple traveled to him from my finger and burst into a million sparkles in front of his face. My annoying visitor coughed and waved the sparkles away as I laughed at his new hair color.

While the spell took full effect, I turned and casually refilled the kettle at the sink, which was still nearly full. Filling it gave me something to do while I thought about what to say to convince him.

"This house restricts what the council thinks of as *real* magick, but that's because they understand nothing except their own limited view of things. Demon hunters are far more mortal than my ancestors ever were."

I turned and waved a hand at the stove. "This stove made by human hands works as much magick as any spell I could cast. For a simple exchange of energy, the teakettle heats all water we could ever want for tea. Science, technology, and mechanics are just as magickal as conjuring or sending forth a spell from yer fingers. My family taught me to respect all power... and all creatures. That's a life lesson the magickals in yer country could use."

"I'm still waiting for you to convince me of your god-like powers."

I rolled my eyes at Rasmus and his impatience. "Well, ya're doomed to disappointment today, then. I'm going for a walk in the front yard to check the wards. Why don't ya leave before I return? I refuse to eat dinner with a person of so little faith."

Rasmus rolled his eyes as he stood up. "If I wanted to stay here with you, nothing you did could make me leave."

One corner of my mouth lifted. "Are ya truly sure about that? I can be pretty forceful when I need to be."

"I'm a foot taller and outweigh you by at least a hundred

pounds. I would have a natural advantage in any fight, but I also know your magick is restricted here."

My sigh was loud. "Every confrontation comes down to some egotistical guy pointing out how short and powerless I am. I'm sick of people thinking they're smarter than me simply because they're taller."

I lifted my hand and squeezed my fingers into a fist while Rasmus continued to self-righteously smirk at me. My gaze bored into him as I moved my intention from my fist to his neck. Soon, Rasmus grabbed for his throat and fell back into his seat gasping for the air I denied him.

I smiled at his pain and shock. "Bullying is rude, and it's no way to say thanks to someone who served ya tea. I guess I'm going to have to post a 'no bullies allowed' sign in the kitchen. Now go away before I get even madder."

I slowly unfurled my fist to let my power wane bit by bit. While I did that, an explanation rolled out of me, even though Rasmus had done nothing to deserve it.

"The *Tuatha de Danann* belonged to the Goddess Danu. They were her chosen people. She gifted each of them part of her goddess power so they could do the tasks she assigned them. As her first born son, my ancestor got the biggest share. The ancients would have laughed at yer petty debate about whether or not they were actual gods because they always knew what they were and felt no need to label themselves. I refuse to tolerate yer disrespect towards me and my people. I had my fill of that with Jack. A forty-year-old witch deserves to be respected."

Rasmus gasped for breath as he dragged gulps of life-giving air into his lungs. I watched his struggles without feeling a drop of regret. When the kettle whistled once more, I turned it off and walked back to sit down across from the still recovering demon hunter. Maybe I missed his playful teasing a little, but I wanted no misunderstandings.

I was done catering to male egos. If Rasmus truly wanted my help, he was going to earn it by legitimately freeing me from this place.

After he started breathing normally again, Rasmus stared for a long time before speaking. "I'm sorry. I wasn't trying to bully you. I'm worried that we're wasting precious time when we should be hunting for that portal."

"Let's not get ahead of ourselves, Rasmus. Yer problem is a Demon portal. My problem is being punished unjustly. Until I solve *my* problem, I have no motivation to help ya solve yours. Do ya understand me?"

"Did you miss the part where you would get out of here? Even temporary freedom should tempt you after all this time."

I sighed, and it echoed in my kitchen. The man was dense and had a one-track mind. It lowered his appeal until even my hormones shut up their chirping about his wide shoulders, nice lips, and longish hair. I had no energy or time to give to another man like Jack.

"Let me see if I can clarify my position for you. Fiona was thirteen years old when Jack put me here simply for not letting him kill the familiar I inherited, and who once served The Dagda himself."

"Your familiar is a demon. Demons can't be trusted."

"Anyone ever tell ya that ya have a one-track mind? For the last bloody time, Conn is my familiar, a member of my family, and my friend. He saved Jack's life the day before I ended up here. He did it because I asked him to help my husband. Most of the time, Conn is a dog of one sort or another. But to fight the demon Jack battled back then, Conn had to assume his truest form. He revealed himself for my sake, and I will allow no harm to come to him for it."

Rasmus snorted. "And I suppose you've been protecting him further by never summoning him to help you escape here."

"Good Goddess, ya're a stubborn man, and the answer is no. I stayed where I was put so my daughter would have as normal a life as I could give her. It wasn't her fault she was born to a father who might one day lock her up like he did her mother."

"You're exaggerating," Rasmus said.

"No, I am not. Staying here has been a very hard decision for me, but in the end it all worked out. My daughter could have been the unfortunate child of two constantly fighting parents. Instead, Jack became an extra-good father to make up for what he did to me."

Rasmus nodded. "Okay, I get it. Everything was always about the welfare of your child. You've made that point very clear."

I shrugged before going on. "Accepting my priorities is a good start to yer understanding of me, but ya're still not seeing the big picture. When a daughter of the gods is ready to leave a place, she will leave, one way or the other. Ya don't scare me with yer bullying threats, Rasmus. If I was a restored witch and felt like my old self again, then I'd probably help ya with yer demon problem out of the compassion I feel for all mankind. But that compassion will never be felt by a fugitive witch once she moves out of yer council's precious reach."

He shook his head. "Are you seriously saying you're more than a witch?"

"I don't know why ya're so fixated on my ancestry. Jack

knows all about me. Da explained it to Jack before we ever married."

Rasmus frowned into his empty tea mug.

I glared at him. "Ya should ask yerself why Jack sent ya here to ask for my help instead of coming to ask me himself. Better yet, ask Jack about our pre-nuptial agreement. I took extraordinary steps to make sure Jack had no reason to fear me. Yer appearance to do his dirty work tells me that apparently, he still does. He's afraid to face me, and the reason why makes me loathe him."

Rasmus glowered before he spoke. "Jack's story is nothing like yours. He's a devoted husband. He's eagerly waiting for you to say yes to this offer."

I gave Rasmus the same look I gave Fiona when she tried to convince me her father still loved me. "Do ya think I'm surprised that ya trust Jack's words more than mine?"

"We're not trying to trick you. Why are you so suspicious? He's telling the truth."

"Well, I think it's *exactly* like that, and I will not be further debating the matter with someone wearing blinders. Go get everyone to agree to the whole deal, Rasmus, so I can help ya. I want it all, free and clear. Do not betray me."

Rasmus narrowed his eyes. "Or what?" he demanded.

I leaned toward him. "If ya betray me like Jack did and tell the council that I can leave this place on my own, I will make sure the demons aren't the only problem ya have. See? I can make threats too. I want my life back, and ya've given me a high road I can use to walk out of here. Ya know what I want. Be my hero and I'll be yer heroine."

He lowered his gaze from mine and rubbed his throat as he stared at me. "I get why Jack believed you could help us."

I rolled my eyes. "And just so we're clear about everything,

Jack gets nothing at all from me in this deal... or ever again. He married a kind witch, got a wife eager to please him, and a caring mother for the child we made together. He willingly threw me and that life away. Jack knows absolutely nothing of what I've become since he put me here or what I want out of life these days."

Rasmus scrubbed his jaw. "Jack still loves you, Aran. He tells everyone that all the time. Maybe when you see him again things will be clearer."

The irony had me chuckling and made me roll my eyes. "Yes, my husband loved me so much that he betrayed me and left me alone here—all for denying him the privilege of killing the creature who saved his life."

"He's living for your removal from this place. Everything he does is working toward that goal."

I held up a hand to stop him before I got mad enough to shut him up. "Believe his lies if ya want, Rasmus, but I'll not be doing so. What Jack should know by now is that I intend to divorce him first chance I get. If he's planning a reconciliation, he won't be getting one. He doesn't deserve me anymore. And I deserve better than him."

Rasmus shook his head at my answer. How was I less believable than the man who betrayed our marriage for his job?

"Look, if we end up working together on yer demon problem, ya're going to have to accept that I'm telling ya the truth. Maybe Jack's fantasy of me pining away for him soothes his ego and assuages the guilt he felt about his betrayal. All I can say is that the love I once felt for Jack died the moment he gave yer bloody council woman my family property. He betrayed me and my Da. That's not something I can ever forgive Jack for doing."

"Jack won't return the amulet because he thinks your

family heirloom will give you too much power. He fears it will ruin your life."

I laughed at that, but it wasn't truly funny. My heart was still broken over Jack's theft. "The Dagda Stone is a family gift I was tasked with guarding for the rest of my years on this Earth. I was supposed to do a ritual to bond with it, but Jack was afraid it might change me as a wife and mother—or so he said. I put off the ritual thinking one day Jack's faith in me would show him the truth of my power. These last seven years without him have made me realize I put off many things for him. Jack was afraid of my power because I have never allowed him to control me or it."

"He was your husband. Don't you think he had a right to worry about you?"

I shook my head. "No, and I don't know why I'm even speaking to ya about the matter. Ya weren't the one who married him, so it's none of yer business."

"Explain to me how Jack was wrong in what he did."

I lifted both hands palm up. "How could my magickal growth be a problem for a man who professed to love me as I was when we met? If ya truly love a person, don't ya by default believe the best of them instead of the worst? No, Rasmus, I'm done with Jack. In fact, I'm done with all men. But that won't keep me from helping ya solve yer problem if ya get the council to agree to everything. Like I said, mine is an all-or-nothing offer."

"In the years I've known him, Jack has never said a single word against you. All his stories have been flattering. All he talks about is how wonderful his life will be when you get out of here."

I snorted and looked away from the fool. "And yet Jack never visited the wife he told you he loved so much. Nor did he apologize for leaving me here to rot. That's strange behavior for a husband who says he loves his wife, don't ya think?" I blew out my breath. "Have ya ever been married, Rasmus?"

"Not that I remember."

"With the Goddess as my witness, I promise ya that Jack's stories about me haven't been true since Fiona was a small child. He's living in denial if he thinks otherwise. Don't be raising his hopes when ya get home. Whatever delusions Jack harbors, I refuse to be a pawn for him to move around on his demon hunter chessboard. If I help ya, I'll be working alone and reporting to someone other than Jack. Ya need to add that to the deal because I'm not giving Jack another moment of my life."

"I'd have a better chance of getting everything else but that. Jack is a Marshal now. He makes his own calls about who people answer to on jobs."

"Marshal? When did that happen?" The truth hit me in a flash and I rose to walk it off. "Of course—they *promoted* Jack because he incarcerated his own wife. I've been such a fool for that man."

I turned my back to Rasmus. Just when I thought the knife couldn't be shoved any deeper into my back, I discovered I was bleeding and in pain again.

"Aran, it's not as bad as you're thinking. He never meant your incarceration to last more than a year. Everyone assumed you'd do the right thing for Jack's sake."

That was because Jack saw himself as the victim instead of the wife he'd willfully betrayed.

I hung my head. "Yer words are nothing but wisps of empty air, demon hunter. Get out of my sight and don't return until ya can promise me everything."

Chapter Four

Rasmus didn't return to fetch me, but word that I was to present myself to the council came through one of the daily checkers. I had already decided never to return to this place no matter what they decided, so I sent my meager belongings home with Fiona and said my goodbyes to the cottage.

I learned Jack had told our daughter about my potential release, but I had yet to talk to him about the matter. The coward was keeping his distance, and I didn't blame him.

Fiona tried to talk me out of wearing the shimmering blue robe with my family's crest for my presentation to the council, but I wasn't hiding my truth anymore. I was proud of who I was and I would never betray that for a man's sake ever again.

The guards opened the doors to the hall where the council convened, and I walked through them without glancing to either side. The black-robed council members entered shortly after me, and each chose a seat at their judgment table.

Rasmus did not sit with the others. Instead, he and his ponytail leaned in a doorway watching the festivities.

"Aran."

My head swiveled as I sought the owner of the breathy male voice calling my name. A very distinguished and handsome man—I guessed him to be a couple of decades older than me—strode toward me with purpose in every step.

He was inches away before I realized who he was... and what his premature aging meant. My heart hardened against everything he was now and all the memories he evoked in me.

"Hello, Jack," I finally said, returning his smile with a glare. "I see ya didn't miss me much."

The man I married ignored my words and beamed at me. There was awe in his voice when he spoke. "Even with all those silver streaks in your hair, you look amazing."

I snorted at the praise. "Too bad I can't say the same back to ya, Jack. Ya look awfully old for someone who's supposed to be my age."

Jack laughed at my words and reached out to touch me, but I backed up to avoid his hand. Did he really think I was still willing to be his fool? If so, I was about to prove to him otherwise.

"I bet ya only let me out of prison because ya wanted me to fix yer aging problem."

"No. You made a blood vow never to kill me. I was never afraid of facing you. I was just busy."

I looked him over. "I stupidly made a vow not to take yer life, but it doesn't mean I can't make ya regret living. In hindsight, I should have asked for something more in return than just visible proof when ya cheated on me."

Jack shrugged and looked away. "I slipped up once during the first year you were gone, Aran. I was furious when you didn't change your mind about your familiar. There's been no one since then."

I lifted an eyebrow at such a bold lie. His deceit disappointed me worse than his marital infidelity. Talking to this version of Jack was truly like talking to a stranger.... or worse, to an enemy. I had to remind myself that I once stood and swore my fidelity to this male.

"Ya look older than yer own father, which means ya've kept yerself quite busy in my absence. It would have taken many women to age ya this much, so why are ya lying to me, Jack? I don't care enough for ya now to be upset by yer cheating. There's no reason for ya to fear me today."

Jack looked around and then straightened before he spoke again. "I was never afraid *of* you—I was afraid *for* you. You could never tell the difference."

I waved away his denial, which was the same old lie he'd been telling himself and me for years. "It's over between us, Jack. Ya betrayed me in both word and deed. Fiona will always be a link between us, but I want nothing from you today except my property."

"I never meant to keep it from you, Aran. I brought the amulet here to keep Fiona away from it. Even your father feared its power."

"No, Da feared my refusal of it and what could happen to our family if I did. Fiona could have worn it every day and nothing would have happened to her. The Dagda Stone is my legacy... and only mine. Ya stole it and that's something I can't ever forgive. And it was the primary part of this deal. So where is my property, Jack?"

I crossed my arms and waited when he didn't respond.

Then I held his gaze until he looked away. "Return the necklace or send me back to the cottage. And it better not contain a tracking spell. I'll know if ya tried to alter it."

"No one has done anything to it. It's been in storage."

I smirked at his words and wondered if that was a lie as well. I suspected Jack and his cohorts had passed it around among them to see if anyone could activate it.

"Hand it over now or I'll take it back the hard way."

Sighing at my threat, Jack turned and walked to the table of council members. I heard him whisper something to the woman he'd allow to take the necklace seven years ago. She frowned at what he said, but nodded as she handed it to him.

My heart beat loudly as Jack headed back to me carrying it. I hoped Da was watching me from the afterlife. I hoped he could see me making this right.

Whispering a silent prayer to my ancestors for strength, I remained stoic until Jack once more stood in front of me. Glaring down, he held out the necklace, dangling it in my line of vision because he was so much taller than I was. Snatching it from his fingers was tempting, but instead I made myself calmly take it from him. The stone glowed softly in my hands as it woke from its seven-year slumber without me.

I breathed out in relief at its response. It could have hibernated for the rest of my life after what I'd let happen to it.

The stoicism I'd worn for emotional armor slipped away. "Thank ya, Jack. What about the rest? Dare I hope ya will keep yer agreement with me?"

My soon-to-be ex-husband smiled widely at my soft, appreciative tone. "You get everything you wanted. Congratulations, Aran. You're a free woman once more."

I trembled in happiness on the inside but stared at him without even blinking. I would not be showing him my weakness ever again. "After the injustice done to me, that's good to hear. Swear to me Conn is safe from all of yer kind and I'll help ya as promised."

Jack shook his head. "I can't because Conn's a demon and

shouldn't be on this plane, but I will never harm him myself. That's the best I can do, Aran."

I looked at the council. They watched me as closely today as they had when I appeared here seven years ago. I stared back until several of them looked away.

"I don't think they can hear our conversation clearly. Let's move closer so yer council can be a part of our discussion. There are no secrets I care to keep from any of ya."

I could tell he didn't like my demand, but Jack calmly turned to walk alongside me.

"It would help them trust you if you would officially agree to contract with us. Your skills are... unique."

"No, I'll not be taking a job with yer kind," I said, chuckling at the very idea of working for my enemy. "I can't believe ya're arrogant enough to even ask. I'll help ya find the demon portal because I gave my word to do so, but then I'm done. Fiona is a grown woman who can make her own decisions about life. I've lost seven years of mine, thanks to you. I won't be losing any more to yer obsessions."

"Aran..."

"No, Jack. Save yer lies and worthless apologies for the women sleeping with ya. My ears don't want to hear them."

I turned and faced the demon hunter council. My gaze raked all of them as I slipped The Dagda Stone on over my head. "Before we discuss the details of our arrangement, I need to tell ya something. Jack's already sworn to leave Conn alone, but he said he couldn't vouch for the rest of ya. So hear me in this... if any demon hunter tries to kill my familiar, that person will become my enemy. Do ya understand the seriousness of what I'm saying? Raise yer hands to confirm that for me, please."

My gaze went up and down the group. I didn't know if

these were the same members as the ones who sent me to the cottage, but slowly the proper number of hands were raised.

When I saw it was all of them, I nodded in approval. "Good then. I've got a little personal business with Jack to finish up, and then I'll help ya find yer demon portal. Bear with me."

Jack turned and smiled down at me. "We've got all the time we need to work out our issues, Aran. I'll hunt the portal with you."

"No, ya won't. Assign someone else, Marshal. I'll not be spending time in yer company ever again."

Jack closed his eyes and sighed loudly. "Fiona told you."

My lips formed into a smirk. "No, yer daughter simply said ya got promoted. She didn't say when or how, or that ya had become a Marshal. Nor did she know why ya never saw fit to tell me yerself. Maybe if ya had ever visited me in my prison, ya might have shared the news in person. Oh... wait... ya didn't want me to see how fast ya were aging, though, did ya?"

The woman council member looked nervously between me and a glaring Jack before clearing her throat. "Demon hunting comes with many risks. We're still looking for the reason Jack is aging faster than he normally would."

I turned to her and snorted. "Jack is aging because of *my* half of the blood vows he insisted we exchange when we wed. He's aging because Jacks broke our vows and slept with other women while I've been in yer jail." I waved a hand towards him. "Since he looks older than his own father, it appears he's kept himself quite entertained without me."

Their alarmed gazes all shifted to Jack to study him.

Finally, I looked at him again too. His face was a dull red from me speaking the truth, but he held his tongue and didn't offer a denial. It didn't surprise me he hadn't revealed the actual source of his affliction to his co-workers.

Omission was just another kind of lie, though, and ya wouldn't catch me covering for the liar. Infidelity was nothing compared to him stealing my property.

Jack bent his silver-haired head to glare down at me. "I thought you were exaggerating the consequences of the spell."

I smirked at his nerve and glared back. "And I only asked for that because I never dreamed ya would ever replace me in yer bed. Guess we both learned our lesson the hard way, didn't we?"

Turning back to the council members, I muttered a master spell as I waved one of my hands. Their hands moved in front of them and went flat on the table as they became stuck there. They pulled at them in shock. I raised my hands to calm them.

"Forgive me for the binding, ladies and gents, but I can't have ya panicking when I share the same proof of my power as yer man Rasmus insisted on me providing to him."

As they struggled, I turned to Jack again. "Let's settle our personal business once and for all. I'm so ready for a fresh start."

Jack shook his head as he stepped away. "No, Aran. You vowed never to harm me."

"No, I vowed never to *kill* ya, Jack. Nothing was said about making ya suffer and wish ya were dead. The magickal effects of spells exist in the nuances of them, Jack. But what are ya worried about? Ya're the one who didn't keep yer promise. Despite the pleasure it would give me to see ya grow old and die from the consequences of yer cheating, getting revenge on ya doesn't fit into my plans."

I waved a hand and lifted Jack several feet into the air. Twirling one finger, I wrapped invisible ropes around him to hold him in place. He said my name over and over, pleading with me not to hurt him.

I snorted at his fear, but at least this time, I was giving him a good reason. "Relax yerself, Jack. I don't intend to harm ya physically. What I'm intending might even restore ya to yer proper age. Who knows? Goddess Danu often surprises me."

Jack calmed enough to ask questions. "What are planning to do?"

"Well, isn't it obvious, Jack? I plan to magickly divorce ya. And I intend to make it official today. I wanted to take this action the day ya betrayed me, but I waited all these years for Fiona's sake. She knows I'm doing this, though, so ya don't have to worry about breaking the news to her. No one is going to interfere with me having my way in the matter."

"Aran... no. Please don't do this now. At least talk to him first."

Sighing, I turned to Rasmus who was doing the one thing I told him not to do. "What is yer deal? This is my personal business and none of yers. I'm divorcing my cheating husband like any sane woman would do in my shoes."

Rasmus held out a hand. "You're too angry at Jack to make a life-changing decision like this. Maybe you need to wait until you're calmer. The council and Jack have done everything else you wanted. Can't you at least talk to him about the divorce first?"

"No," I said flatly, smirking at Rasmus for his defense. "Jack promised never to harm Conn himself, but he refused to make sure others of yer kind did the same. That means I have to be watching over my shoulder all the time for men with crossbows and magick arrows. If he gets the chance to order someone to kill Conn, I know Jack will do so because he told me he would. Now step back before I have to choke ya again.

I've been waiting a long time to sever this connection with my tormentor, and I'll not wait a moment more."

Rasmus put both hands to his throat and took several steps backward.

I glared up at Jack. "If ya insist I have a keeper while I'm helping ya find the demon portal, I'm willing to work with Rasmus. He and I understand each other."

Jack shook his head. His head and feet were all he could move.

"I want to work with you myself. We need a chance to talk things out. Nothing I did was to hurt you."

I snorted at his declaration. "Ya broke yer vows yet made sure I couldn't. Be grateful I'm letting ya keep yer balls. I have a woman's right to unman ya for keeping me out of the picture while ya had yer wicked fun. I've been with no man because of yer selfishness."

"Aran, you don't understand. My life wasn't like you're imagining. I missed you terribly. I knew you hated me. Why can't you see I was only doing my job? I was barely getting by while I waited for you to come to your senses."

My sigh was loud in the room because all ears were listening to us. "How could ya cheat when ya knew it would cost ya yer integrity, not to mention yer youth?"

Jack's silence only made me angrier. "Ya know, The Dagda told me he helped countless people over the centuries who later tried to kill him to steal the very power they'd benefitted from. He said I should never expect to be rewarded in life just for being a good person. He also said I should accept that all non-magickals are innately selfish and flawed with envy. Fortunately, there was nothing in his lecture saying I had to stay with a terrible husband forever, which relieves me greatly. I would hate to be disrespecting my ancestor today."

The council woman audibly gasped. "Are you saying that you're not fully human? Are you a demon too?" she demanded.

I briefly turned from Jack to glare at her. "No, I'm not a demon. I'm a descendent of The Dagda, which makes me a child of the *Tuatha de Danann*. That's the tribe of the Goddess Danu for ya non-Celts. I suggest ya educate yerselves about natural magick and stop being heathens about the power ya take exception to."

"Aran…"

I swung to face Rasmus who was still trying to defend Jack. I pointed a warning finger at him. "Stay away from me if ya know what's good for ya, Rasmus. I spent seven years planning this day and only Goddess Danu herself can stop me. This is the last time I'm stating this. Ya've no right to interfere in my personal business, so shut up until I'm done."

I looked back and saw that all council members had stopped struggling to free their hands. Their gazes bounced between me and Rasmus.

While their attention was elsewhere, I turned toward the only person in the room who'd seen me naked. I faced Jack as I unbuttoned my blue robe to my navel. I kissed the warm stone hung around my neck and chanted the words of the bonding ritual as I pressed it into my flesh.

The searing hot smell of burned skin and muscle soon filled the room. I groaned at the pain of accepting my responsibility for it at last. Now no one could take it unless they killed me first. Hopefully, taking the stone into my body in order to guard it was enough of a sacrifice to appease my ancestors.

I hissed as the chain and the stone sank deep beneath my skin. My fingers tingled as burned skin healed and grew over the entire necklace. Ignoring Jack's worried stare, I fastened my robe once more and restored my modesty.

Now that I'd corrected the biggest mistake I'd ever made, I turned to the council and blew across my palm to release them from their bindings. They all immediately lifted their hands and checked them for damage.

"I have one more personal thing to do and it requires willing witnesses. I need to see a show of hands from ya again, please. That's why I released ya. Only two or three are needed, so abstain if ya don't want to be involved. If no one wants to watch, I will take this ceremony elsewhere."

Hands shot up fast, even though their owners still gawked at Jack floating in the air. Not a single member abstained, but that didn't mean they believed my stories. No, they were likely doing what I asked to make sure I didn't change my mind about helping them.

Jack renewed his struggles to free himself, but it would do him no good. No woman had ever been more determined to change her fate.

I nodded to the council before walking toward my soon-to-be ex-husband. When I was a few feet away from him, I raised both my hands, palms out.

"Goddess Danu blessed us when our love was strong,
But what seemed right once, now feels very wrong.
What the Goddess bound together, I ask to be undone.
May Danu free us of all vows and efforts to be one."

I reached into the pocket of my robe and drew out my oldest ritual knife that had served too many years as my daughter's mail opener. Fiona had brought it to me when I asked her to, even though she was sad about what I'd needed it for. I hoped we'd be able to talk about this woman-to-woman one day, but hoping for that would have to do for now.

My concern today was getting it over and done so I could be at peace and put past mistakes behind me.

A quick thin slice across my palm provided all the blood I needed to finish the undoing of my marriage. With the stone's power flowing through me now, I could probably have done the whole ritual without the blood, but it was best not to take any chances. I never asked the Goddess for anything without offering something of value in return.

The man I was divorcing certainly couldn't be trusted with me or my family. Ending his hold on me was a matter of self-preservation. Plus, I wanted this divorce to be official before I went to Ireland to live.

I hadn't shared my body with anyone in seven years. Celibacy hindered my ancestral magick, but there wasn't time or an honorable way to prepare my body. There was only one way I could rectify my situation and still be able to face the woman I saw in the mirror every day.

I walked closer to where Jack floated. Knowing my intentions and disagreeing with them, he struggled even harder to break my hold, but he was not getting his way this time. The deed was partially done, and I was eager for it to be finished. The love I once felt had left my heart long ago. All I wanted now was to feel free in body as well.

"Aran, I'm begging you. Please don't do this to us. I don't want a divorce from you. I swear on Fiona's life that I want us to be married. I want things to go back to the way they used to be before our arguments over Conn. If you'd just let me explain myself, I'm sure we could make things right between us again."

I snorted at his pleas. "It takes two people wanting and valuing the same things to make a genuine relationship. Ya had seven years to explain yerself to me, but ya never bothered to even visit the cottage, probably because ya hoped to hide yer infidelity from me for as long as ya could. Be thankful I don't consider ya my enemy and send my family to punish ya for yer betrayal. Ya need to accept that our marriage is over, Jack. I'm divorcing ya with no regrets."

I rubbed the blood into both my palms and slid his pants up far enough for me to grab the bare skin of his ankles above his socks. Touching him again caused no longing in me, but even if it had, feeling the energy of his lovers would have instantly quelled it. His wrinkled face and gray hair merely offered me validation of what my spirit had known would happen the moment he sent me away.

Nothing broke marital trust any quicker than infidelity.

"May our child not be harmed by what we sever.
I accept yer defection—be ya restored forever.
I offer Danu my blood as proof I mean what I say.
Thrice, I state my wish to divorce ya today."

A softly pulsing pink light suddenly surrounded me and soon it extended to Jack. For the first time in many years, I felt a welcome peace filling up my soul.

Goddess Danu's presence liberated me, but I knew I needed to finish this to make it official. Performing a magickal divorce was necessary for those like me. My connection to Jack was too tainted to keep, and it would affect me if I didn't rid myself of every bit of our connection.

I released my physical hold on Jack and backed up just in case he got his youth back and broke my bindings. I doubted he could do it at his current age, but why take any chances?

I raised a bloody palm and lowered him slowly until his feet touched the floor once more.

Jack no longer struggled against my restraints. Instead, he simply looked at me like he couldn't believe I was actually going through with breaking our bond.

What else did the man think I would do except divorce him?

His infidelity was one thing, and Goddess help me, I might have forgiven him for that, but his disloyalty to my family had broken my heart.

"I divorce you, Jack Derringer.
Today, I call back all the magick I shared with ya when we wed.
With Goddess Danu's permission, let it be returned to me
without malice or harmful intent.
As I will, so let it be done."

I raised the other palm and let the invisible bindings around him loosen. As they faded away, I found I could breathe much easier. And I felt lighter—so much lighter. I couldn't remember the last time my marriage to Jack made me happy. Maybe the day Fiona was born, but that was twenty years ago. After everything I'd suffered for last seven years, everything critical in my life had narrowed to this single moment of undoing my marriage. Like I'd said to him earlier, I had no regrets.

"I divorce you today, Jack Derringer.
Before these witnesses, I declare I am no longer your wife and you
are no longer my husband. I willingly return to you whatever
magick you shared with me when we wed. May our families and
all who know us accept this division as well.

Go away from me in peace. As I will, so let it be done."

I held both hands out to the side and pushed air behind me with bloody palms. Wind lifted my robe and my hair as all remnants of my connection to Jack were swept from me.

Weak from losing the energy I'd reclaimed from him, Jack wobbled in place before dropping to his knees. He grew younger as I watched, and I told myself not to resent his restoration.

Soon Jack would look like his forty-year-old self, instead of someone's father or grandfather. The Goddess had decided his fate, and I would abide by her decision.

Gasps from the council told me they'd also noticed.

I knew Jack's slowly changing face lent credibility to my tale, making it clear why he had aged. But I couldn't care about Jack's fate anymore. And I didn't have to care.

In a few moments, we would no longer be a couple.

"I divorce you in all ways, Jack Derringer, Marshal Demon
Hunter and keeper of secrets from me.
I free you from the penalty of our blood vow and ask the Goddess
to free me of the one I made to you.
May the will of Danu be done between us.
Go away from me in peace. As I will, so let it be done."

I clapped my hands together creating a shower of red sparks and rubbed them until the blood disappeared from my skin completely.

The room was utterly silent as I turned to the council once more. "I thank ya all for witnessing my divorce. As soon as I find the demon portal, Rasmus can let ya know. Despite the injustice ya did to me, I do not count any of ya as my enemy. Or at least, I don't see ya like that yet. But if ya ever try to incarcerate me again, it will be at yer own peril. Consider yerselves warned because a child of The Dagda makes a terrible enemy."

I waved a now spotless hand over my body. Normally, I didn't do such magickal grandstanding, but today was a special occasion. For a moment, I became as naked as the day of my birth. Listening to the gasps in the room, I conjured my favorite outfit, right down to the heeled black boots Fiona had gifted me. Given the soreness of the stone's new hiding place, the v-neck shirt had been a good choice, even if it put my boobs on display more than I wished.

I turned and lifted an eyebrow at Rasmus who appeared dismayed by my actions. He stood with his hands in his pockets, staring daggers at me. Maybe I'd made him afraid of me. If so, I didn't regret it.

"Okay, demon hunter. I'm ready and highly motivated to get this done. The sooner I find yer portal—the sooner I can go home."

Jack's younger voice caught my attention. Danu had wasted no time. "You can't work with him, Aran. Rasmus retired from demon hunting several years ago."

I heard the council woman clearing her throat to assert herself into the debate. "Let Rasmus go with her, Marshal. We'll make a contract to pay him for his work with her. Whatever it takes to find that portal must be done."

I paused beside Rasmus and looked at him. Even in my new boots, the man was still a foot taller than me. I felt pretty sure he was even taller than Jack, but with my ex-husband still sitting on the floor, that observation would remain nothing more than conjecture on my part.

"Ya don't look old enough to be retired, Rasmus. Were ya

forced out of action? Or did ya just tire of all the senseless killing ya were doing?"

Rasmus snorted. "I was wounded in the line of duty. Now I help only when I'm needed."

I nodded like his explanation made complete sense, but whether or not it did really didn't matter. "Were ya helping the council when ya came to see me? Or was that Jack's idea to send ya? I admit I'm curious about that."

Rasmus turned to look at the council. They all nodded at him slightly, but none of them really met his gaze. Finally, he looked over at Jack on the floor, but Jack said nothing. While Rasmus grappled with his decision, I studied his profile. All I saw reflected in his expression was more worry about the secrets he was still keeping from me.

Rasmus should have been happy. He'd gotten his way, hadn't he? I'd kept my word and was helping him. Maybe I'd messed up a scheme he'd cooked up with Jack, but for now anyway, I couldn't change the retired demon hunter's beliefs about my now ex-husband. Working with him might become a problem, though. I didn't have time to drag his dead weight with me as I searched.

I fisted both hands on my hips. "I can see ya have some reservations about working with me. How about I just call ya when I find the portal?" I stuck out my palm. "If ya have a pen, write yer number on my hand. Surely by now ya know I keep my word when I give it. Yer reluctance won't be of any help to me."

Rasmus blew out a long breath and seemed to deflate before my eyes. "My reservations are not about you, but I guess I have to tag along since the council will pay me to do so."

"Good. So, um... can I crash on yer couch tonight? My ex

got our house when we split. I don't have a place to stay out here in the free world."

My snark about Jack's life without me roused him from his silence.

"You can go home any time you want, Aran."

I swung to glare at him. "*Yer* house hasn't been mine in seven years, Jack. I'd rather sleep on the street than under yer roof ever again. Get some therapy for yer denial. We're divorced."

Rasmus ran a nervous hand through his hair and knocked the tie from his ponytail. He looked like he wanted to run away from me and the others too. I looked him over and wondered how much of a liability the secretive man was going to be.

I sighed in frustration because what I wanted now was to put some hard-earned distance between me and Jack. "Look... I don't know what makes ya side with my ex-husband so much, but I don't need ya to get the search done. I also don't need yer charity. It may surprise everyone in this room, but I have a few friends I could ask to put me up for a night. I just thought ya might want to keep tabs on me and discuss my plans."

The council woman's voice rose above the other noises in the room to reach us. "We'll book two adjoining rooms at the Fairmont Hotel for tonight. During your search, Rasmus can phone in your locations and we'll find you places to stay as close as we can. We're willing to pay all expenses."

I smiled at her. "That's very kind of ya and much appreciated this evening."

She nodded but didn't smile back. "If you find what we're searching for, it will be worth it."

I nodded again and gave her a thumbs up. "I'll do my best."

Then I turned and walked out of the room. The way Jack glared at both me and Rasmus was getting on my nerves.

Maybe I should have left him old and decrepit. Just because I divorced him without chopping off some of his body parts didn't mean I was over being mad.

It was going to take me a while to master feeling neutral about how much Jack had wronged me.

Chapter Five

The bar in the hotel restaurant had Guinness and crinkle fries. I happily dug into my feast when it arrived. No one paid me much mind while I ate my celebratory dinner.

I was nearly done eating when some good-looking guy in a suit sent me another Guinness. After sending my thanks to him via my kind waitperson, I smiled. Maybe forty and single wouldn't be so bad after all. Maybe I'd leave my hair gray and see what happened.

I smiled at the fantasy of taking the drink buyer to my room for the night, but casual sex wasn't my style.

Who was to say the man wasn't married and cheating on his own wife? I'd have to spell him to be sure. What a mood killer that sort of magick would be.

No, I'd best keep to myself until I'd settled into being single again. I had time and freedom now. Indulging my urge for male company could come later. At forty, I wasn't in the market for another long-haul relationship, but gaining some regular bed company wouldn't be a bad thing.

I felt it the moment my admirer found the nerve to approach my booth. Before he made it, a scowling Rasmus stopped him in his tracks. Apparently, scowling was the demon hunter's superpower because the guy grinned, shrugged, and returned to the bar.

I pursed my lips to keep from chuckling when Rasmus turned his glare my way. "Ya're a glass half empty kind of person, aren't ya? He was only being friendly."

Rasmus kept scowling as he slid into the other side of the booth. "You don't have time to be picking up men."

I snickered at his complaint. His irritation was grumpy-old-man funny until I realized that whatever Rasmus believed about me had come from believing Jack's lies.

"Yeah, I'm a real femme fatale when it comes to attracting men. Not that it's any of yer business, but unlike my ex-husband, I've been celibate for the last seven years. Now that my divorce is official, I can sleep with whoever I want. And I will when I want to."

"Not until we're done with this case," Rasmus said, waving to the wait person.

Using my power to punish his arrogance could become a daily routine if I let him get on my nerves all the time. I politely nibbled on the rest of my fries as I waited for Rasmus to place his order.

When we were alone again, I pushed my plate toward him. "Ya seem hangry, Rasmus. Eat some of my fries before I'm tempted to do something to ya I might regret. My power is a little restless since I bonded with The Dagda Stone. I need to stay as calm as possible until I adjust."

"You could have waited to do your ritual. And you could have talked to Jack before you divorced him. Why couldn't you have at least granted him a final say in the matter? You may be the most impatient, unreasonable female I've ever met. You were on a diva roll today, and somehow I got stuck with dealing with you."

I ate another fry as I considered his outburst as neutrally as I could. Then I just had to know. "Well, I think ya're most naïve man I've ever come across. Do ya owe Jack a life debt or something? Other than yer possession of similar man parts, there must be some other reason ya keep haranguing me over my decisions about him. He's a cheater *and* a liar. I proved that beyond any doubt today."

Rasmus squirmed in his seat. "It's not a life debt, but yes, I owe Jack for keeping me from spending the rest of my life in a cozy cottage like the one you were stuck in. Jack and I were working on a job five years ago and things went wrong. He kept the situation from becoming worse than it already was."

So Rasmus considered Jack to be his personal hero. At least I'd traced his dislike of me back to the source.

I sipped my Guinness and sighed at the delicious bitterness sliding across my tongue. It was truly the small things in life that brought a person the greatest joy. "If ya think Jack is such a wonderful catch, why don't ya marry him yerself? Fiona told me same-sex relationships are legal in some places now."

"You're mouthy and disrespectful. I don't know what Jack ever saw in you."

I set down my drink and looked him in the eye. "If ya keep harping on his wonderfulness and how awful ya think I've been to him, I'm going to spell yer mouth shut. I've been on my best behavior so far with ya. Some women would have neutered Jack for his cheating. Despite the mercy I showed my ex, I don't take betrayal lightly. Yer comments are leaning too much in that same ugly direction for me."

I watched Rasmus frown at the beer deposited in front of

him. Who frowned at a beer? Sir Grumpus did, of course. The wonderful food that arrived shortly after didn't make him smile, either. In fact, the only smiling I ever saw Rasmus do was at the cottage when he thought he knew something I didn't.

I shook my head at the possibility that Rasmus and Jack were simply two of a kind, but even if true, there was nothing I could do about them. I'd find the portal as quickly as I could and then be done with all demon hunters. Today was a marvelous day, and no one was going to ruin my I'm-finally-divorced-and-happy buzz.

I sighed and let his attitude go. "Let's agree to disagree about Jack and change the subject. I don't know if ya remember me talking about my cousin, Liam, but I want to look him up tomorrow. Liam's the sort who walks that fine line between doing good and doing evil. When he crosses to the dark side, though, he occasionally calls up a demon to help him carry out his misdeeds."

The only answer Rasmus gave to my comments was a grunt. His food was getting cold while he brooded, but that wasn't my business. I rolled my eyes at his non-reaction and pressed on with my story.

"Liam saved a demon princess when he was a kid and has had the loyalty of her entire clan ever since. No, I don't think my cousin opened yer portal to let them come here in groups—mostly because he's not that powerful. Plus, my mother would have told me that by now because she and Liam's mother tell each other everything. The bottom line is that Liam is pretty good at tracking down information. Plus, he owes me a big favor. I'm willing to collect it to be shed of yer kind."

Rasmus scratched his nose, squirmed in his seat some more, and finally drank his beer.

Worse, he did all that without responding to what I shared.

Finally, the man sighed and ate his food, totally squelching my attempts to be friendly. There was no gusto in his appetite, nor did he take any joy in his meal.

Everything pointed to one reality, which was that he wanted nothing to do with me. Honestly, it boggled my mind. I'd done nothing to scare him personally. Or at least not that I could remember. He saw Jack grow younger, and I knew he'd heard the story in my divorce spell. So why was he being so hard on me?

I sipped my drink and tried to decide whether the truth of his discomfort was worth digging out of him. The possibility existed that Jack had hired someone to spell Rasmus to do his bidding and be his supporter.

Would I be able to tell if that was the case? Would Rasmus know it about himself? Or was hating the world simply his normal setting? Curiosity didn't only kill cats. Ma used to say I could be the poster child for anyone wanting to prove the perils of nosiness.

I set down my drink and lifted an eyebrow. "Did Jack spell ya to be his freaking champion?"

Rasmus choked on his burger as a bite went down wrong. He swallowed and coughed... and then had the nerve to glare at me like I'd shot his dog. "No, Jack did not spell me. He would never do that."

My mouth formed a smirk at his indignant tone. "Never is a very long time, Rasmus. I didn't think my ex-husband was the cheating sort, either. Nor did I ever in a million years think Jack would steal from me. I'm not saying he's evil incarnate, but Jack is way more conniving than he looks. I'm not willing to be his fool again and I don't care what ya think of that. Men seem to stick together when they find something—or someone —to hate."

Rasmus waved the uneaten half of his burger in the air between. "What am I supposed to believe after what I saw you do to him today?"

After thinking about my actions for a minute, I shrugged. "Maybe ya could offer me a compliment for ending my marriage without hurting anyone, especially Jack. That would be a friendly sort of thing to do for someone who's helping ya of her own free will."

Rasmus stared at me. "You assaulted the man you married and extorted the council. You even threatened *me* for simply trying to reason with you."

I leaned on the table and glared up into his chiseled face. "Today was personal between me and Jack. I restrained the council so no one would interfere. And I extorted no one. I demanded the return of my rightful property as part of a bargain I didn't have to make. I could have taken it back any time I wished."

"How do I even know your story is true? Jack told me you were the one who pushed him away. The other women helped him survive being left alone."

I narrowed my eyes at his complete ignorance. Could he really believe Jack was the victim? "What I did today was liberate myself from the mistake my marriage to Jack turned out to be. I don't need yer approval or acceptance. All ya need to do is decide if ya're going to give me some credit or keep touting Jack's lies like a cult follower."

Rasmus firmed his mouth and glared. "I owe Jack my loyalty. I don't owe you anything."

I leaned back in my seat to sip my drink again. "I've got no problem with that since I haven't asked ya for anything except to be the messenger yer council is paying ya to be."

"If you won't listen to Jack, why should I listen to you?"

I laughed at his belligerence. He sounded like a teenage boy. "I could have taken my property back by force, but no, here I sit wasting my time, sharing ideas ya have no interest in hearing. Why am I bothering with ya? I guess I thought sharing a meal might help us find some common ground so we could work together more easily. Don't worry, though, it won't take me seven years to learn my lesson with you. I'm done being friendly with yer kind."

"You should be working with Jack on this—having dinner with Jack—and not having dinner with me. Your attitude toward him is unreasonable."

"And your attitude toward him is naïve. Yer acting like I stabbed Jack while ya watched, but the truth is I divorced my betraying bastard of a husband exacting no revenge on him at all. It feels amazing to be free of that connection, and ya're not ruining that for me. I won't let ya."

Rasmus went back to eating without responding to my lecture. Giving up my lame attempts to get him to like me, I signed the meal check with my room number and slid from the booth.

"I'm going to go call my daughter. She's picking up my mother at the airport this evening. Enjoy yer meal, demon hunter. I'll see ya at breakfast around eight. Ya might want to work on yer attitude tonight because I'm already tired of yer negative shit and we've barely started."

I walked to the bar before leaving and thanked the man who sent me the drink. We chatted for a few minutes before I excused myself and headed to my room—alone.

Da always said even the good things in life came with their own set of troubles. Maybe Da was a glass half empty kind of person like the demon hunter. Either way, I was stuck working with him for now. For Da's sake, I was going to be nice to Rasmus, no matter how irritating I found him.

Besides, I made my bed by insisting to work with only him. Well, I made my metaphorical bed. My real bed would be empty a bit longer.

Chapter Six

It was barely seven in the morning when I hit the dining room looking for breakfast. I thought I'd risen early enough to eat before having to deal with my demon hunter shadow, but Rasmus was sitting at a table drinking coffee when I got there.

He looked a little rough around the edges. The scruff he'd decided not to shave off that morning softened the sternness his body radiated. What was that old saying? Oh, yes. Rasmus was wound so tight he could shove a piece of coal up his arse and make a diamond.

I sighed at my ongoing bad luck when he spotted me, but I bravely headed to his table. Normally, I'd have led with saying *good morning*, but I'd discovered the hard way that being polite was wasted on him.

"Are ya feeling civil enough for me to have my meal in peace with ya? Or should I find another table and pretend ya're not sitting here?"

Rasmus set down the mobile phone he'd been scrolling on

in order to give me his full, glaring attention. "I guess you think I deserved that remark."

I shrugged as I glared right back. "Let's not get into what I think ya deserve. We didn't agree to socialize during our task. If ya set a work time for an hour from now, I'll make myself available to ya then."

"I see you're one of those people who *really* need caffeine in the morning," Rasmus declared.

"Yes, I am. Are we going to fight about coffee and tea today? Can ya at least wait until I've a cup, so things are more even between us? I'd consider it a favor."

Both of us were surprised when Rasmus chuckled at my sarcasm. My smile refused to be held back as I slid into the seat across from him.

He waved a hand at the table. "I think we can agree to be civil until you've had some coffee."

"Good. My family will be stopping by to see me soon. I haven't seen my mother in seven years. My daughter was the only personal visitor I had while I was at the cottage."

Rasmus looked off but nodded. Any time we talked about my jail time, he got completely uncomfortable. Before we parted company, I intended to find out why.

I turned my cup up to let the waitperson fill it, then thanked him profusely. I took a couple of bracing sips before giving Rasmus my attention again.

"Instead of meeting her at the hotel, I asked my mother to come here. I'm hoping Ma can tell me where Liam is hiding out. My mum is really tight with Liam's mum, who's my Aunt Maura. She told Ma that Liam laughed his arse off when he found out I was being locked up. He was the career criminal of the family before then."

Rasmus eyed me over the rim of his cup as he talked.

72

"Right. Liam's your cousin who saved the demon princess when he was a kid."

He reminded me of an absent-minded professor with the beginnings of a beard. "I see ya were listening to me despite yer surliness."

Rasmus gave a half-shrug and looked off again. He seemed to be in an oddly congenial mood. It was like he was trying to apologize without actually apologizing.

Or, in other words, he was being male.

I started to ask if he was one of those people who simply couldn't utter "I'm sorry" without breaking out in hives, but he asked me a question before I could get it out.

"Are you still thinking your cousin is our best lead?"

I opened my mouth to reply, but then my food arrived. It was the first breakfast meal I hadn't cooked for myself in ages. I clutched my chest in delight.

"Thank you so much. It looks so beautiful."

After the wait person left beaming, I dug into my fluffy eggs and ate a few bites before addressing Rasmus again. "Why don't ya bring me up to speed on what yer kind has been doing about the demons? Ya told me there were a lot of failures. I'd like to hear about those."

Rasmus dropped his gaze to his plate. "I was one of those failures and the only member of my team who didn't die. Talking about that failure won't bring them back."

I paused eating to look at him. "I'm sorry, Rasmus. Why don't we wait until after breakfast to talk business?"

He started eating again, so I took that as a yes.

I was half-finished with my food, and sipping my second cup of coffee, when I heard Bridget O'Malley's distinctively loud voice outside in the hall somewhere. She eventually appeared in the doorway of the dining room and I lifted my hand to wave to her. Behind her, a yet to appear Fiona called out "Gigi, wait!" over and over.

I could have told my child she would have had an easier time stopping a tsunami, but today I was too happy to see my mother to speak a word of complaint.

Ma looked around for me, and I rose to meet her.. She pulled me in close and hugged me so tightly that tears instantly sprang to my eyes. She must have felt my emotion because she pushed me away to stare into my face.

"As proud as I was of ya standing yer ground on Conn, I hated every moment ya were in that place, Aran."

I chuckled. "I hated it too, Ma. But it's over. And I mean that. I have no reason to let it happen again, so ya can stop worrying about me."

"I know ya only stayed all that time because of Fiona."

I nodded and let my head drop. "It seemed the best strategy to keep Jack from taking things out on her. I was hoping my tolerance did not disappoint ya."

Ma stood six inches taller than me. She and Da both had. Neither of them were tall, but they hadn't known why I stopped growing when I did.

Ma reached out and lifted my chin up. "I understand yer heart is as good as a person gets, and I'm a proud mother. Who's the guy at the table, the one who's glaring at me? He reeks of the Underdark."

Demon hunters all reeked of demons. It came with their job. "That's the smell of a successful job well done on him, Ma. His name's Rasmus."

My mother stared at Rasmus over my head and it made me nervous.

"He's harmless," I added to be sure she knew.

Her gaze came back to me. "No man is harmless. I know I

taught ya better than that. Couldn't ya have picked a better sort to celebrate yer freedom with last night? He's another bloody demon hunter, isn't he, Aran?"

It took me a moment to realize what my mother had wrongly concluded from my cozy breakfast scene with Rasmus. "Ma, I'm not sleeping with him. Rasmus and I are business partners—sort of. I'm helping locate a demon portal. Once I get Liam to help me find it, I'll be halfway to shedding myself of him and his kind."

Ma's face wrinkled. "Didn't ya hear? Liam's nowhere to be found. Maura told me she hasn't spoken to him in a month. That's not typical, but since the boy has gone silent on her before, Maura hasn't looked into it yet. She says Liam gets offended when she tracks him down. I swear, that boy doesn't use his head for anything worthwhile."

That "boy" was in his mid-thirties, but Liam missing was not good news. Now I had to track down Liam and extricate him from whatever mess he'd gotten into. I rubbed my forehead as dread washed over me. If Liam's absence was connected to the demon infestation that killed the hunters Rasmus mentioned, I would have to get far more involved than I'd intended.

"Does Aunt Maura know his last whereabouts?"

"No, but she sent me with this. She said something told her ya might need it for scrying." Ma dug into her tote and pulled out a stinky undershirt. "Liam dropped off his laundry at her house before he took off."

I held both hands up in the air when I caught the smell. "Dear Goddess, that's foul. I wish I had a bag to put it in. I don't want to touch it."

My mother rolled her eyes at my complaining. "He's yer cousin, not the boy down the street ya thought had cooties."

I grunted. "Liam probably does have cooties."

Fiona finally reached us and frowned. "Gigi moves fast for someone her age."

My mother turned to her granddaughter. "I move fast for someone yer age too."

Fiona ignored her to look at me. "Did you already divorce Dad?"

"Yes, I did." She sighed, and I reached out to hug her. I pulled my taller daughter close and held on as long as she let me. "Ya still have both yer parents, and we both love you, Fiona."

"I know, but it's not the same," Fiona said, backing away from my hold on her. "Dad's going to be here in five minutes. He texted me on the drive over here."

I turned to glare at Rasmus, who hadn't offered me a word of warning. His gaze dropping from mine said more than words, but I asked anyway.

"Did ya know this was happening, Rasmus?"

The stubborn arse went back to drinking his coffee offering no denial or explanation. My feelings got instantly hurt again. Why did I keep letting his actions disappoint me?

"I'll not be forgetting this," I told him, fisting both hands on my hips.

Ma yanked one of my hands free and shoved Liam's nasty smelling shirt in it before grunting in disgust. "Demon hunters can't be trusted, girl. How many more years is it going to take for ya to learn that lesson? Ya're forty, for Goddess's sake. Wise up."

I sighed heavily at Ma's chastisement. When Jack walked into the dining room, I closed my eyes and shook my head. So much for enjoying breakfast.

When I opened my eyes again, I glared at Jack, who was all smiles, thinking he'd outmaneuvered me.

Fiona looked between us and saw the reality of my angry discomfort. She stepped in front of her father to halt his advance. I'd never practiced aggressive magick in front of my daughter because her power hadn't bloomed fully when I last lived with her full-time. I hadn't wanted her to feel less powerful because of what I could do, but Jack was pushing me beyond all those noble promises I'd made to myself.

Judging from the determination in Jack's eyes, a confrontation was going to be unavoidable. Despite the boundaries I set about our child, he was mistaken if he thought I wouldn't retaliate against his high-handedness. I had far fewer scruples these days.

I stared at my ex-husband. "What do ya want, Jack? Why are ya here?"

"I'm here to relieve Rasmus of his shadowing responsibilities. I came to help you find the portal."

I looked at my daughter. "Yer father and I are about to have an adult discussion about what the word *no* means. Are ya wanting to be part of it? Or would ya prefer to drive yer grandmother back to her hotel and swim in the pool there for the rest of the day? I'll catch up with ya both later."

Fiona turned and attacked me with a hug. "I love you, Mom. Please don't hurt Daddy." She patted her father's shoulder. "You look better without all that gray hair. Don't forget to thank Mom for fixing you. Bye, Daddy. I told you it was too soon."

"Fiona, stay. No one's going to be fighting. Your mother and I are going to talk. That's all," Jack called out behind her.

I snorted in disgust. "Divorced couples aren't supposed to talk to each other, Jack. That's the point of getting a divorce."

"I'm packing a bag and staying with Gigi until Mom gets done with her task. Love you!" Fiona turned a bright smile in her grandmother's direction. "Come on, Gigi. We need to swing by the house so I can pick up my swimsuit."

But Bridget O'Malley wasn't leaving just yet. Oh no, she was fuming and waiting for her chance to give Jack a long-overdue piece of her mind.

I held up my hand and shook my head to discourage her, but I knew that would not help matters. She wasn't only mad at him for what he did to me. She was mad at him because he betrayed Da, who had once liked him.

Ma leaned as close to Jack as she could get. "If ya even so much as *try* to touch my daughter after being with all those skanks ya replaced her with, I'm going to send the vilest creature I can call from the Underdark to chew off yer arms all the way to the elbows. Ya're the worst husband a woman could ever have chosen and Aran is well shed of ya. Be grateful for Fiona because she's yer one saving grace."

Fiona grabbed her Gigi's arm and tugged. "Come on, Gigi. Mom will deal with this in her own way. It's between them."

Ma let Fiona lead her off, but she was grumbling something about a curse under her breath. I blew out a breath of my own when Ma and Fiona disappeared. The dining room was filling up with normal folks, so I walked back to the table where my now cold breakfast sat congealing.

Before I could sit, though, I saw the check for my meal and Rasmus's was already signed. I looked up at him. "Ya knew Jack was coming this morning, didn't ya?"

Rasmus shrugged and looked at Jack who was standing behind me. They gave me no choice except to deal with their duplicity.

"Do ya remember what I said, Rasmus? Do you remember my threat about what I would do if ya betrayed me?"

"Rasmus is not in charge, Aran. *I am*," Jack declared from behind me.

I turned and looked at Jack. "Even yer voice irritates me, Jack. Next time ya speak to me, oink like the pig ya are. Ya don't deserve to talk like a human."

Jack laughed at my statement. Then he opened his mouth. *"Oink, oink, oink, oink, oink..."* He grabbed his throat with one hand and made a grab for me with the other.

I stepped out of his reach and glared at him. "Oh, no. Stay where ya are, deceiver."

"Oink, oink. Oink, oink, oink, oink..." Jack said more quietly, trying to walk toward me and finding he couldn't.

"Stop throwing your power around. You're being childish," Rasmus said.

My gaze narrowed on my most recent betrayer. "Would ya rather I turn Jack into an actual rutting animal? Even his daughter knows that's what he is."

"Undo what you did to Jack."

"Or what, traitor? What will ya do to me for resisting yer manipulative ways?" I asked, crossing my arms while I waited to hear.

Acting true to what I was coming to think of as his default setting, Rasmus pulled a stun gun into his lap and pointed it at me. The table barely hid it. My arms unwound to drop listlessly at my sides. I was so tired of dealing with this crap.

"I should have guessed it would come to this. The two of ya have manipulated everything to get yer way." I pointed at Jack while staring at Rasmus. "I'm not going anywhere with that man and ya can't make me. Yer kind needs to deal with that fact before I get really mad and do something to the whole lying lot of ya."

"And you need to calm down and listen for once instead of ranting simply because you're not in control."

Glancing around to make sure no one was watching too closely, Rasmus lifted his gun and pulled the trigger. Instead of the electrical wire he expected it to shoot out and take me down, the barrel released a small burst of purple smoke.

If I hadn't been so mad at Rasmus, I would have laughed when he looked down at his weapon in alarm.

"Freaking amateur," I muttered, sweeping a hand, and making his weapon turn into a bouquet. "I was trying my best to give ya a chance, but ya're no more trustworthy than Jack. I was on the fence right up to where ya pulled yer stun gun out."

"Aran..."

I held up a hand and Rasmus went quiet. "No. I refuse to listen to more lies."

Rasmus started to get up from his seat and found he couldn't. It served him right.

I looked over my shoulder at Jack. "Unless ya want to *oink* all day, get yer arse into the seat across from yer lackey. I'm done being nice. Don't make it worse."

Jack stumbled free of the invisible foot restraints I placed on him, and then scrambled into the chair I'd been sitting in earlier.

"Good. Now stay there for a few minutes while I pack. I'm going to let Rasmus keep talking normal because the other folks in here having their breakfast don't deserve to have it ruined by the two of ya."

I counted to ten... and then to twenty. If I didn't calm down soon, I was going to make a scene that would ruin everyone's day. They'd made me too mad to be rational.

I turned and glared at Jack again. "If I could go back in time and find another man to give me my darling child, I would do that. Unfortunately, The Dagda himself told me time travel was forbidden. But I swear on my Da's grave that if ya keep coming after me, Jack, I'm going to do to ya what Da would have done... and what Ma still might do. So go on about yer other business until ya hear from me. I want nothing to do with ya."

Then I turned to Rasmus. "Ya've betrayed me over and over, not in big ways, but in a lot of small ones. I don't think we can work together now. I will finish the search on my own."

"*Oink, oink...*"

I turned to glare at my ex. "Shut up, Jack. I'm not talking to you. I'm talking to yer fan boy."

I put my attention back on Rasmus. "When the rules are fair, I play by them, but ya haven't been fair. Ya've been a pain in my arse since I laid eyes on ya. I'm done with being nice to ya, demon hunter. Don't come after me because I won't be as kind if I see ya again. Do ya understand?"

"*Oink..*"

I swung my head. "Ya're a pig, Jack. Ya're a worse pig now than the day ya betrayed me."

Rasmus gaped at me in surprise. "You're behaving worse than anything you've accused us of doing to you. You're humiliating us all in public."

"Sure, and this is all my fault because I'm not rolling over and letting ya have that last word on the matter. What kind of woman could find the two of ya scheming against her as embarrassing or hurtful? I mean, every divorced woman should be grateful for the continued harassment of the man who cheated on her. Is that what ya're saying to me, Rasmus?"

He frowned at my tirade. This time, I didn't care about his feelings.

"Expecting you to talk to Jack like a mature adult is not a crime," he said.

I lifted my lips and sneered. "Neither is expecting people to understand that I'm still coping with my former husband's total lack of remorse for all he's put me through. If ya knew how truly angry I was with my ex-husband, ya wouldn't be goading me to chat. Ya would advise him to keep away from me until I'd had some time to calm down."

"You control a demon, which makes Jack right about you. How are you not a criminal to mankind? Explain that to me."

I lifted my hand and rubbed my forehead. Rasmus was worse than Jack because he was too brainwashed to think straight.

"Goddess bless, I have to get out of here before I do something I'll regret. I'm getting déjà vu just talking to ya because I know we went over all this yesterday. So let's skip the redundancy and get to the bottom line. Breaking yer word voided our agreement about ya shadowing me. I'll not be going up against the forces of darkness with someone I can't trust by my side. I'm better off alone."

"You have no right to throw your power around and restrain us," Rasmus commanded.

"And ya have no right to trick me and bring my ex here without warning me. Everything I do concerning Jack is a matter of self-defense. Ya pulled a freaking stun gun on me only moments ago. I have every right to use my power to protect myself from the likes of both of ya. Yer restraints will fade away in thirty or forty minutes. I meant what I said. Don't come after me, Rasmus."

I assumed ending my agreement with Rasmus would also

end the council's agreement to put me up while I was looking. Well, no matter... I'd find the portal like I promised. And I might have to contact Jack to turn the location in. In the meantime, though, I was done dealing daily with people who couldn't keep their word to me.

I walked out of the dining room with no money, no place to stay, and no one to help me find the demon portal. The only bright spot was that I wasn't still stuck in the cottage. If I'd been younger, I'd have been weeping in frustration at my bad luck, but I'd outgrown that sort of complaining years ago when I'd learned wishing people were different was a waste of time.

I left my worries behind in the dining area and calmly went to my rented room. See? There were some bright spots to aging. Being older meant being less prone to drama. And I really enjoyed going about my business without the regret I might have if I'd maimed or tortured someone who annoyed me.

Maybe maturing would be okay.

For my first older woman decision, I was going to forget Jack and Rasmus for fifteen minutes and take a long, hot shower before I packed.

Then I was going to contact Conn. I hadn't seen my familiar in seven years either.

Chapter Seven

Before Conn went to live with my mother, he'd taken all my magickal stuff and put it in storage. He'd sent word by Fiona that he'd found a troll-guarded place in Salem that the demon hunters would never find.

Fiona told me on the phone that Conn was retrieving what I needed and said he would catch up with me.

Sure, I could call him to me and demand his presence immediately. As his guardian, I had that right. One call would bring him instantly to my side, but I only did that when it was a matter of life and death. In the last seven years, I had never called at all because it was his death I cared about preventing.

I'd barely hefted my bag to my shoulder when my inner alarms went off. There was a knock on my door at the same moment, but I felt no danger. Dropping the bag, I threw open the door, and then threw myself into the arms of the male standing there.

"Are we knocking on doors like strangers now? Ya haven't knocked on my door since I first got ya."

Conn hugged me and swung me around. "They don't

allow dogs in your hotel. I had to go the brother route for my disguise. I hope that was okay."

"Ya look wonderful to my eyes in any form. It's yer soul that matters to me."

Conn set me down and stood back to study me. "My true form was why you ended up rotting away in a cottage instead of being out in the world practicing your magick."

"I only stayed there for..."

"Fiona's sake—yes, I know. But you got sent there because of me and you stayed because of her. I'm still not sure that was the wisest way to finish raising your only child. What will she think when she figures out she was the reason you let her father treat you so horribly?"

"Children are innately self-serving. She'd think it was her due. Besides, I have years before she matures enough to think of anything but her own needs. Are ya well, Conn? Ya look well enough."

"How could I not be well? I've been staying in Ireland with Bridget all this time. She brought me with her when she came to see Fiona in person. I have to say living with Bridget was very entertaining, but not nearly as exciting as being with you." He pointed at my bag. "Checking out early?"

I glanced at my tiny bag and chuckled. "I'm running from a couple of idiots who keep messing with me."

"That's a funny coincidence. I followed one here."

I shrugged. "Then I guess ya already know about Jack surprising me today. His partner-in-plotting betrayed me and I fell for it. I think I went soft while I was locked up."

Conn lifted an eyebrow that nearly mirrored mine. He'd used my facial features to create his persona but had begged me to let him be taller. His modest five feet ten height seemed to suit him perfectly. No creature wanted to be as short as I was, not even those who were naturally small.

Conn picked up my bag. "I've been following Jack around since our plane landed. Let's go, and I'll catch you up as we escape his evil clutches. We need to cash out some gold coins so Bridget doesn't keep thinking you're some fugitive from justice out starving on the street. She's only one or two resentments away from going after Jack with a curse."

I chuckled before closing the door behind us. "Jack isn't important enough for Ma to worry about. I told her I wasn't destitute. It only appears that way at the moment."

"Do you have any cash on your person right now?"

"Well, no."

Conn smiled. "See? This is why you need me. You refuse to use your magick for anything to help yourself."

I lifted a shoulder and let it fall. "I'm not starving, nor am I intending to become a selfish magickal. I admit my life is easier when ya have my back, but I need ya most for yer company. Ya're the only man I know that isn't scheming behind my back."

Conn stopped, laughed, and then shrugged. "I'm flattered you see me as your savior, of course, but you haven't forgotten what I'm really like, have you?"

I chuckled remembering some things he'd put me through over the years. "No, of course not. I just trust ya're not feeling yer mischievous urges today."

"Oh, I'm not. I'm feeling vengeful instead. How long before Jack and the ponytail guy get free?"

"Were ya spying on them?"

He snorted. "I was following your ex-husband to see where he was going. When I got to the hotel, I felt your magickal signature and followed it thinking I would find you. Finding Jack glued to a chair did not surprise me. No man can damage a woman more than one who once shared her bed. Worse, no one—man or woman—is immune to it happening. Even The Dagda dealt with that."

I froze in place imagining what could have happened if Jack and Rasmus had been free of their restraints when Conn showed up here. Despite their promises not to act against him, they'd already proven themselves to be consummate liars. "Did Jack recognize ya? Tell me the truth, Conn."

A smirk lit his face before he spoke. "No, he seemed completely clueless about who I was. The ponytail guy eyed me hard, though. He knew *something* was not quite right, but neither of them screamed *demon*."

"Ignore the ponytail guy. Rasmus sees a threat around every corner, so ya're not special in that way. Ya look enough like me to be my twin, and if we were standing next to each other, even Ma would wonder if Da put a babe in someone behind her back."

I didn't mind that Conn chose me to emulate, but an angry Rasmus would have wanted him dead for it. I shrugged and then answered his original question. "They've got maybe another ten minutes until my binding on them wears thin. Packing took me longer than I thought because I took a shower. Since I wasn't sure when I'd be getting the chance to take another one, I thought it was a good idea."

"Bridget told me you were going to look for Liam. I told her not to worry because I would go along too."

I sighed as we walked down the street. "I want ya with me, but ya might not want to tag along when ya hear my task. In exchange for my freedom, I promised to find a demon portal stuck in open mode. Finding Liam was a means to an end. I figured he might know about it and point me in the proper direction."

"In my true form, I could probably help you find it myself. If that worked, we wouldn't need Liam."

"No," I said, shuddering at the thought. "I don't want ya running around with red skin and black horns curling backwards. Liam is no doubt in trouble that he can't get out of, anyway. Plus, demon hunters are out in record numbers looking for the portal the same as they sent me to do. Twenty-seven of them have died looking already. Rasmus told me demons killed everyone on his team but him."

"That sounds ominous... and unusually aggressive. Demons like doing things in secret and without drawing attention. Someone must have declared war. They hate being hunted."

"That was my thought as well. And I'd bet none of the hunters bothered to ask why the demons came here. I haven't heard that anyone except demon hunters were harmed."

Conn pointed at the coin shop. We disappeared into it and exited forty minutes later. My half-finished breakfast had disappeared and my caffeine buzz was totally gone. I needed to refuel.

"Let's find some coffee or tea. I need some propping up today."

Conn smiled. "I know this place close to here. I'll carry your bag."

"So long as the road isn't warded against me, I'm willing to walk anywhere."

Laughing, Conn reached out and rubbed my back in support. "Aran, I think you have magickal PTSD from being in jail."

My mouth twisted at the thought that Jack had damaged

me in yet another way. "Is that why my loathing for Jack Derringer burns hotter than thousand suns inside my gut? Should I be getting some therapy for it?"

Conn grinned at me. "I like your poetic description. In a couple of days, we'll revisit your need for therapy. It's only a fear I have for now."

"Got anything to tell me that might lessen my hatred for him a bit?" I asked because I was still a hopeful sort of person.

Conn laughed harder, which didn't bode well for me getting neutral about Jack anytime soon.

"Let's get coffee before we tell stories," my familiar advised as he hefted my meager bag of belongings onto one wide shoulder.

"Maybe we should go to a bar instead of a coffee shop," I grumbled.

"Bars aren't open this early. It's barely ten in the morning," Conn said with a grin curving his lips.

I rolled my eyes. "That's only the time here in Salem, *Connlander of the Fir Bolg*. Ya well know it's evening time somewhere in the world."

Conn laughed at my use of his name and title. He never seemed to mind that he was bound to me by it. "I heard your words, *Aran of The Dagda*. It's hard for me to believe that you'd use my magick to transport us to where we could have a drink at ten in the morning, while you refuse to use it to find your elusive portal. That has to be magickal PTSD talking. Maybe we need to re-examine your priorities."

I knew what he was getting at and why he found my teasing so funny. Before I went to prison, I was "disgustingly moral" as my mischievous familiar liked to point out. And it was true that I was very careful with both him and my magick when Jack was present.

"Get off my arse, Conn. I'm forty, not twenty. If I want a bloody drink for breakfast, I'll have one."

Conn stopped as I walked on. When I realized he'd halted, I looked back to see what was up now. Grinning, he pointed at the door. "Coffee and stories? Or are we going to walk the entirety of Salem until we find a bar that's open?"

"Very funny," I said, because it was funny. Well, sort of. I was definitely feeling off today.

Smirking at my capitulation, Conn opened the door and held it for me as I headed back to him.

Chapter Eight

We got coffee *and* pastries. It was deliciously decadent... and sorely needed. I'd only managed to eat a few bites of food in the hotel restaurant before being interrupted.

A pretty barista flirted with Conn at the counter before shooing us to find a table. We looked so much alike that no one ever thought we were a married couple. I always believed that was the reason Conn created his "brother" form when I suggested there would be times when he could not be at my side as an animal. His brotherly form was pleasing to strangers, especially the barista who giggled whenever he spoke.

"What form did ya have to use with Ma?" I asked once we'd taken our seats.

Conn sipped his coffee as he studied me. "I appeared like this at first and then had her choose a dog breed she liked. My only request was that she pick a smart breed."

"I remember you stipulated no tiny poodles or toy-sized terriers," I said, quoting what he once told me.

"That's right. We went with a good-sized Irish Setter."

"Nice. That's a friendly breed and very sharp."

Conn nodded. "Suffering hugs from strangers was the worst of it, but being her beloved pet was a pleasant way to spend those years. She fed me people food, and it was fine. For the plane ride back here, I insisted on being something small enough to fit under the seat in front of her, in case the plane crashed. Since she worries so much, I stayed close at her side unless she was asleep or in church or visiting her booty guy."

My coffee went down wrong and I coughed until the shock faded. "Booty guy? Who's that?

"Your father—rest his soul—has been gone for ages. Between worrying about Fiona and worrying about your incarceration, Bridget was a mess. I nudged Roy Finnegan after I caught him admiring her backside. Neither of them has marriage in mind, but they enjoy their bi-weekly distractions."

I leaned on the table and covered my eyes with my hands. "There's nothing wrong with it... truly. I just feel like I missed so much, that's all."

"Well, seven years is a long time to be isolated."

I uncovered my eyes and nodded. "It was, and it shouldn't have been over five. Fiona was a realist by the time she was fifteen. Staying in the cottage beyond her eighteenth birthday wasn't necessary, but every time I got ready to leave, some voice inside said to stay. I was worried that I'd gone mad until Rasmus showed up with his deal. Through it, I found the high road to wipe away what happened and not leave a taint on my child."

"Rasmus is the ponytail guy."

Nodding, I accepted a refill from the barista who was giving Conn her sweetest smile.

Goddess forbid I ever go back to being that silly around a man. Once the rush of desire wore off, a woman had to deal with things she hadn't noticed about the man sharing her bed.

For example, the young barista did not know that she was flirting with an immortal creature from the Underdark. Luckily for her, Conn was always on his best behavior whenever he was with me. I adored him, but my familiar was a randy male, and currently still unattached..

He'd had a wife when Cermait, son of The Dagda, was his keeper. Despite him being bound into service, Conn's wife lived alongside him because Celts appreciated a good love story more than they feared immortal beings.

He rarely talked about being immortal, but I think Conn secretly liked that I was interested in the stories of his past. I heard that his wife's eventual death had been a blow to the entire family. Being of two separate species, they'd had no children, so Conn moved on through time alone after that. I became his guardian many, many, many generations later.

"Stop worrying about me and the barista, Aran. I'm not in need of a female today. You're just projecting your own sexual desperation onto me. Do you regret leaving the ponytail guy behind? He seemed your type."

Talking about Rasmus depressed me, but not for the reason Conn teased me about. I couldn't believe he turned out to be such an arse, and it bothered me because I'd tried so hard to win him over. I could have manipulated him and made sure he favored me, but no, I'd been gut-wrenchingly honest. Even now, I still had no idea why Rasmus sided with Jack instead of me.

And I also hadn't heard Conn's stories about Jack yet. Sighing, I leaned back in my chair and pretended to have an interest I didn't feel. If I never heard Jack's name mentioned again, I would die a happier woman. My body ached with regret about ever choosing him. I would not make the same mistake with a man again.

I waved a hand at Conn. "Ya said ya followed Jack to see what he was doing. Tell me about that."

"He spent a lot of time talking to the woman heading up the demon hunter council—Hilda something, I think. Her name seemed Germanic."

That got my attention. Her almost pleased reaction to me severing my connection to Jack still puzzled me. It was more than a woman felt about a man she was merely sleeping with, which had me wondering how long they'd been sneaking behind my back.

"Were they fighting about me? She seemed happy when I divorced him. That was suspicious enough."

"Jack was holding the woman's hand and speaking softly to her. From what I saw, it looked like he was trying to reassure her about something, but that's just a guess. I couldn't get close enough to hear their actual conversation. The room was warded too heavily. I saw her patting her throat and chest as she talked."

"She's the one who had my necklace. Jack kept his promise to give it back to me, but I could tell she wasn't happy at that turn of events."

Conn's eyebrow lifted. "What did she plan to do with it besides wear it with her witch costume? She's not from a Celtic tribe."

I shrugged because I didn't know, either. "The necklace was the sticking issue for me. I can't forgive Jack for stealing it."

"Should I put it into storage?" Conn asked.

The corners of my mouth lifted. "I already put it somewhere safe. The ritual wasn't pleasant, but I still wish I'd never let Jack talk me out of it. What I'm trying to figure out is *when* he betrayed me. Those first few years were all about love and laughter between us and Fiona was this beautiful creature we made. It's like someone flipped a switch inside him and turned him into another man."

"When Fiona turned six and went to school, your father took Jack to task for keeping you from bonding with the necklace, as well as several other legacy things he felt you were putting off. He urged Jack to support you as a husband should support a wife with gifts like yours. He told him countless stories of how he supported Bridget."

I drew in a ragged breath and fought not to cry. "Da was a lovely man indeed. Why have you never shared this with me before?"

"Because you were too besotted to hear anything realistic about Jack before seven years ago."

"If ya tell me I was acting as silly as yer giggling barista, I'm going to get furious with ya."

Grinning, Conn linked his fingers on the table. "Okay, then I'll not point it out. A mature woman of forty is old enough and wise enough to reach her own conclusions."

I stared at Conn and tried to see him for who and what he truly was. He was an ancient immortal who'd seen a lot in his long life. "I forget ya watched many generations of my family fall in love, wed, and have children. When I chose Jack, I must have seemed incredibly naïve to someone like ya."

Conn spread his hands in acknowledgement. "Each person travels their own journey. Relationships come to us for reasons that only Goddess Danu understands. However, it amazes me how often history repeats within the same family."

"How do ya mean? Who did I repeat? Not Ma and Da."

Tilting his head, Conn studied me. He was silent for so long that I feared what he would eventually say. I could tell I'd asked something he'd wanted to tell me for a very long time.

"Your father was always a good person, even as a small boy.

It was no surprise that he grew into an honorable man. When your mother and father met, Bridget thought he was *too good* for her. I remember every delicious second of the magickal torture she put him through before finally agreeing to marry him. Most of her beaus had tried to make her use her magick for nefarious purposes. A witch specializing in curses could become quite the leverage over a man's enemies if a man successfully wooed her into doing so."

"I wouldn't turn my back on Ma if she didn't love me. She was threatening to curse Jack today, and I know she meant it. I begged her to let things go. Will she do that? I have no idea. My mother is an unpredictable sort."

Conn laughed. "The last person Bridget truly cursed was Peter O'Malley, your father's brother. Every time your uncle drank, he took a swing at his much smaller wife. Your mother cursed him to get sick as a dog from booze and simultaneously gifted your aunt an iron skillet meant for his head. After a few months of suffering in multiple ways, Peter joined his wife's church and became a better husband. Bridget left the curse in place because she said all O'Malleys except your father were notoriously mean drunks."

I smiled because I knew it to be true. Ma told me that story herself. But I always had a feeling there were more interesting tidbits about our family that my parents kept to themselves.

"When my magick first appeared, all anyone would tell me was that my powers were a family legacy. Da was smart as a whip but had no magick. So I naturally concluded I got them from Ma. That was made easier to believe because I grew up working with her and her coven. They made potions to heal the sick and helped bring children into the world. I thought I would grow up and do the same."

Conn shrugged. "Your father didn't trust Jack to know the

truth, and your mother went along. I wasn't passed along to you via some unknown uncle, aunt, or cousin as you were told. That was a well-intentioned lie meant to keep Jack from finding out the source of your power."

"Bugger the lot of them, Conn, because I thought ya came to me from Ma's brother. That's what they all led me to believe."

"It was your father's mother, feisty Muireann, who bequeathed me to you. I think your parents feared you would end up living her chaotic life, so they kept quiet about her powers and never let you visit her alone. Later when she took ill, though, your father felt guilty for never telling you the truth. I think he also felt a responsibility to see you got the magickal training his mother should have given you. She'd known you were meant to follow her but honored her son's denials out of love for him... and you."

I blinked in shock as I took it in. "The irony is knowing all that might have saved me from marrying Jack. I might have suspected his motives before we wed. I might have avoided my time in the cottage completely."

"But you also might not have birthed Fiona." Sighing, Conn went on. "So second-guessing the past is a waste of time. Jack told your father that you were his and that he was the man who would direct your magickal path. They never spoke intimately about you after that. Jack became an ambitious demon hunter and your life's work became nothing more than supporting him."

This time I blinked because I felt like someone had slapped me awake. "Ya should have warned me about my own powers, Conn."

"I couldn't because I was the one secret you successfully kept from your devious and controlling husband. He would have tried to kill me at every turn because together we are a force to be feared. I couldn't risk Jack finding out what I was until you were ready to own your gifts. When that time came, your father was already gone and your mother didn't know how to warn you any more than she already had. We were all holding our breaths until you found out for yourself."

I frowned at my coffee because frowning at Conn wouldn't do me any good. This wasn't the news I thought I'd hear, but no epiphany was ever comfortable. And the horrible things I kept learning about Jack seem to go on and on.

I looked at Conn as I explained my side of things. "Jack and I grew farther apart each year after the first ten. Maybe it was Da's death, or maybe I felt misunderstood. I loved Jack once, but he put emotional distance between us on purpose. Nothing I said made anything any better. Fiona was suffering from our arguing."

"When your daughter's magick blossomed, your magick changed. I think some part of you realized you weren't setting the example for her you wanted to set. You got defensive when Jack criticized your magick, and then you got aggressive with him. In short, my dear guardian, you became your paternal grandmother. She had married an unworthy man as well. Your grandfather left Murieann a month before your father was born."

I ran both hands through my hair. "Didn't ya tire of watching yet another female in our family let a man lead her away from herself?"

Conn shrugged before smiling. "You were traveling the journey you had to travel to figure this out. My role was to walk that path with you and decide what I could safely share. By then, I'd realized that I would have to see to your training. So I did what I felt sure Murieann would have wanted me to do."

"Is that why ya suggested we join the Shadow Breakers?"

"Yes. And that's why I brought The Dagda to visit you on this plane. I told him you sorely needed some godly illumination about your family's powers. He manifested as human only for the purpose of helping you. It had been a long time since he did that for anyone. I knew then that you were special."

"Goddess, if I hadn't met The Dagda, I would never have known much of anything."

"You couldn't have had a better teacher, Aran. He came to adore you. That's why he stays in touch. I doubt he'll go home to the ancients until you do."

Over the years, I rationalized all manner of reasons a god would visit me. He'd said he was family, and I could feel that blood connected us somewhere along the line. But the significance of his sacrifice to be physical on the Earth plane never once crossed my mind. I made a disgusted sound over at how much I'd fooled even myself.

"I only practiced what The Dagda taught me when Jack was away at work. I told myself he'd be unhappy with what I'd learned to do and it would be hard on his male ego. I suppose that much was true, but my reasoning was stupid."

"It was a blessing he was away a good deal of the time," Conn added.

I shrugged because it was the truth, but I hated feeling like a fool. What could Jack have done if he knew how much more powerful that training had made me? He couldn't have done anything. And I had many powers I'd never shown him. Why did I think that was a normal situation between a husband and wife?

I buried my face in my hands and groaned loudly. "I should

have figured this out sooner. I'm too old to be dealing with this now."

"I think this timing was always inevitable. You came into more power on your fortieth birthday. Why do you think Jack is so determined to reconcile with you?"

My hands slid away from my face. "Well, it's not because I'm the only woman he wants warming his bed. He looked like his own grandfather after seven years of cheating."

"Jack wants to control your powers, Aran. He wants to use you to accomplish his goals in life, which are all about his own fame and fortune. Have you seen the car he's driving these days?"

"No. I've been doing my level best to stay away from him. All I want to do is turn him into a toad or something. Goddess, how I wish I'd picked someone else to father my child."

"Fiona hasn't suffered for his behavior. She doesn't have your magick, but her child likely will. That's what happened to you and your father. Jack loves her as much as he loves anyone other than himself. He also knows *you* love Fiona. Fear of what you'd do to him has been a powerful motivator for him to be a decent father to your child."

"Divorcing Jack wasn't enough to get him out of my life, though, was it? How many more ways can a woman say goodbye?"

Laughing, Conn wouldn't hold my gaze. "Time will fix what you want fixed. Until that happens, all you can do is keep being you. If you absolutely need revenge, I suggest seducing the ponytail guy. It would solve two of your problems. Jack would be appalled, and you'd get your rioting physical needs met. He has that look of being good in bed."

I rolled my eyes. Whatever faint attraction I felt for Rasmus was long gone after his betrayal. "Goddess, yer lectures make it sound like I'm Fiona's age."

"Well, forty is the new twenty. Haven't you heard?"

"I'm not sleeping with Rasmus to make Jack mad. I might have done that at twenty, but I'm forty now. Mature women do not stoop that low."

"That's unfortunate because I think your ponytail guy might know where your demons are. He reeked of demons. Some demon caste had him and kept him long enough for him to absorb their effluvium. I was close enough for long enough to determine which one. Jack had a little of the same clinging to him, but nothing like your long-haired nemesis."

Maybe that explained Rasmus's blind loyalty to Jack. Maybe Jack did rescue Rasmus from demons, though that seemed unlikely. Jack usually let others do his dirty work. Rasmus had said all his team died but him. Maybe he only credited Jack with saving him.

"How would I even find Rasmus now? I ordered him to stay away from me."

"I'll find him for you," Conn said. "Go visit Bridget and swim with your daughter. Get a haircut or something. Goddess knows you need one."

He pulled a small phone from his pocket. "Here. I got us a family plan with unlimited text and minutes. I even pre-loaded some games and apps. There's one to order a ride whenever you need to go somewhere. Don't expend your magick on transport travel unless you have to. I put enough in your account to pay for them. Save your magick to fight the demons because you know that's going to happen."

I hated technology. I used it, but I didn't like it. It was too mechanical and impersonal. But it allowed me to conserve my energy.

"Thanks," I said, taking the phone from his fingers with a frown.

"Do you hate the color?" he asked.

I snorted. "I hate the freaking phone, Conn. Ya know I hate those portable things."

He sighed and shook his head. "You definitely need to get laid as soon as possible. I can't handle you being this hard to please. If this is what forty is like for you, I can't imagine how you'll be at fifty or sixty."

Chapter Nine

After multiple coffee refills and several trips to the bathroom, Conn and I parted ways. I used the app to call myself a ride to the hotel. My driver was a pleasant woman, and we had a nice chat on the drive. I was her last fare of the day and then she was off to collect her kiddos from school.

Fiona ran to confront me the moment I appeared poolside. Ma lay in a nearby lounger reading a torrid romance novel. Was she missing the booty guy Conn mentioned? Just thinking about that had me cringing. Maybe Conn was right. My celibacy was affecting my view of life in more ways than I knew.

"Did you kill Daddy?"

I laughed at my daughter's question. "No. Of course, I didn't kill him. I only made him oink like a pig for a few minutes to shut him up."

"What about the ponytail guy? What did you do to him? Not that I care, but I'm curious."

I searched her face. "Ponytail guy? Rasmus talked about yer father like they were the best of friends. Don't ya know him?"

"No. None of his work people ever came around. Dad preferred to hang out with his rich friends."

My mouth quirked at one corner. "Is that right?"

Fiona nodded. "Yes. But I never liked his rich friends, so I avoided their company."

"Why didn't ya tell me about his rich friends when ya visited?"

"I didn't want you to get mad enough to break out of magick jail and become a fugitive. It was hard enough living with my mother being a criminal."

I pushed away from her. "Is that what ya truly think of the situation? Has yer father actually convinced ya that I was the one who did something wrong?"

"You broke the rules," Fiona said, biting her lip.

One of my eyebrows arched in the air. "Whose rules, Fiona?"

Her answer was a shrug, and then an embarrassed, "I don't know."

I snorted and turned away from her. She had her head in the sand and until she pulled it out, talking to her would be a waste of air and time.

"Mom, wait…"

I spun around but didn't move closer. Instead, I gave her a hard stare. "We talked about this a thousand times. I know ya wish yer parents could get along, but that can't happen because yer father betrayed me. Did ya think a bouquet of beautiful flowers and a ride in his midlife crisis car were going to get me to forgive him? If so, ya're as deluded as he is."

"I can't pick between the two of you. That's not fair."

I could have told her life wasn't fair very often, but she'd find that out soon enough. "Whether or not ya pick a side is yer choice. Eventually, though, ya're going to have to figure out who ya're going to believe about the seven years I lost. I wouldn't blame ya for choosing your father and the wealth he gained from imprisoning me. The kind of money he makes now could make a young woman's life very cushy."

"This is not about Dad's money."

I stared hard. "What kind of car did he buy ya? Does it match his?"

Her wide eyes glanced at her grandmother. I couldn't believe I'd guessed right. If I'd picked her car, my child would have been driving something big, cheap, and safe... and my child knew that.

I glared hard at her. "Gigi didn't say a word. Conn was the one who told me Jack bought a midlife crisis car. The rest was easy to figure out since ya seem as determined as Rasmus that I reconcile with the cheating husband I divorced."

Fiona held up both hands. "I know you're hurt, Mom. That's understandable."

"No, I *was* hurt, Fiona, but I'm not any longer. The divorce made me happy. What upsets me still are people trying to force me back into yer father's life when that's the absolute last thing I want. I'm sorry, but ya can't think the best of both of us. I was protecting my family and my legacy. If ya think that was wrong of me, then fine. Go on and think of me as a criminal. It won't stop me from loving ya, but I won't be able to respect ya."

"I don't know what I think about either of you anymore. Why won't you at least talk to Daddy? Maybe this is all a mistake. Maybe there's something he can do to make this right."

"Can Jack give me back the years of freedom he stole from

me? Can he undo sleeping with those other women—the ones that turned his hair gray and made him look like your grandfather?"

I stared at her until her gaze dropped to concrete surrounding the pool.

"Do ya think it was fun staying in magickal prison for seven years? Do ya think it was fun to sleep alone while the man who vowed to be faithful to me filled his bed with whoever he pleased. I hope when ya're my age that ya don't have a daughter speak such an unkind thing to yer face. I hope yer child is wise enough to see the truth no matter how many fancy cars her cheating father buys her."

Fiona teared up and dashed off. I frowned and let her go. I was done putting up with people judging me unfairly. If she wanted to believe her father, she could believe him, but there was nothing he could say to make me forgive what he'd done to me. She needed to accept that.

And one day I would move on from this mess. One day I would find a new normal where I might find a man with the ability to make me smile again.

Ma snorted when I dropped into the lounger next to her and blew out a frustrated breath. "Ya made yer baby cry."

I rolled my head to look at her. "My *baby* is twenty years old and called me a criminal to my face. Ya don't see me crying and running off because of her insult."

"All she had was Jack for a long time. It's not like you can divorce yer father."

Resentment of my only daughter pushing me to reconcile with her loathsome father was too large to allow me to have sympathy for Fiona's life. She said nothing to me over the years about Jack's promotion, the women he slept with, or the money he made off what he did to me.

Maybe I'd understand her silence eventually, but that wasn't happening today. My daughter had been choosing her father over me for years, whether or not she realized it. My job as her mother was to point that out.

I turned to stare at the pool. It was a concrete pond full of chemicals. It held no appeal for me, but Fiona loved to swim in any sort of water. My one regret about arguing with her was that I'd ruined my daughter's fun.

"I know Fiona's had a tough time of things too, but Jack buying her fancy cars does not excuse what he did to me. I'm done being nice to people merely to keep from making waves. After the cushy rich life I hear Jack gave her, Fiona won't be able to understand my viewpoint for years. Hopefully, she'll pick a better man to marry than I did and won't have to learn the same hard lessons."

My mother clicked her tongue at me. That's what my mother did when she disagreed. She clicked her tongue.

"Are ya free of Jack or not, Aran? Every time ya get angry is proof there's something still between ya needing to be settled. Hate and love are often bed partners. Ya got to shoot for neutrality or apathy instead."

"Jack betrayed me for a freaking promotion, Ma. I want to cut off his man parts and hang them from the rear-view mirror of his expensive car."

Ma chuckled. "Good Goddess, Aran, ya need to let it go before ya talk yerself into acting on it."

"I'm tired of blaming myself for letting this happen in the first place, and I'm tired of people blaming me for Jack's bad behavior. This madness has to end. I divorced Jack, and Goddess Danu allowed it. I don't have to be nice to him ever again. That's the point of divorce."

"Then why are you so angry?"

I lifted my hand and pointed to the door Fiona ran out of a moment ago. "Because my daughter thinks her father is innocent of doing any wrong."

"This isn't only about Fiona, though, is it?"

"No, it's about Rasmus too, who also thinks Jack can do no wrong. Conn says Rasmus can help me find the demon portal. And since Liam is missing, I don't have the luxury of refusing to work with him."

Ma just stared at me. "Is that the name of the ponytail guy?"

"Yes," I said, closing my eyes. "Rasmus is on Team Jack. No matter how nice I've been to the arse, I've had no luck winning him over to Team Aran. He's being obtuse."

My mother laughed, and I don't think it was over my word choice.

"Well, men can be like that when they believe something strongly. Women can be like that too. Yer Da and I were both wrong not to tell ya how we really felt about Jack. We probably would have lost yer love for a time, but we should have risked it to plant the seed of truth. That's what ya did with Fiona just now, right?"

I blew out a breath and nodded. "I'm reacting fiercely because my feelings are hurt worse now. My husband cheated on me while forcing me to be faithful, and my daughter thinks I'm a criminal. What good is magick in those circumstances? None, Ma. None. No one feels sorry for me at all."

Ma's laughter had me giving her the side-eye. "I'm glad ya're amused by my pain." I yelped at the arm pinch I got for sassing my mother. Then I laughed too. "Sorry, Ma."

"Buck up, girl. I'm not laughing at yer pain. I'm laughing about the ironies of life. If ya want to win the ponytail guy over to Team Aran, ya probably should start with getting a decent haircut. Ya look like a madwoman who whacked it off herself."

"Thanks, Ma. Maybe a haircut will get Fiona to see me in a better light too. She's the one who hacked it off for me all those years ago. The prison didn't allow me to get my hair properly done."

"Well, then, that was the first thing ya should have set right when ya got out, don't ya think?"

I gave her a look I normally reserved for something disgusting. "No. I did things in the proper order. I got back The Dagda Stone, bonded with it, and then divorced Jack. Those were my priorities."

"Where did getting yer hair done fall on yer list?" Ma asked.

I tilted my head to one side, and then the other, cracking the bones to release the tension built up there. After my head moved more freely, I turned to my mother and smiled. "Since it bothers ya so much, do ya have any suggestions about *where* I should get my new stylish look?"

"Yes. Fiona took me to this shop over on Farrington Avenue. They do good work even though they're far from cheap. The shopkeeper is a magickal person. I suggest ya see if ya can get an appointment with her. Ya're going to need a true professional to tackle that mess on yer head."

I pulled out my phone and handed it to her. "Put in the shop's number and I'll make the call. Goddess forbid people have to look at me like this for another blessed day."

"Silver hair requires additional care, Aran," my mother sang.

So much for lazing by the pool and visiting with family. I ran both hands through my hair. Well, I tried. My fingers got caught in frizzy tangles. Okay, it probably wouldn't hurt to get it cut into a more manageable style.

Ma turned to me and smiled as she handed back my phone. "The world looks bright when your hair is right."

I nodded because I knew mocking her snarky rhymes might get me cursed with an uncomfortable rash in the wrong place. Bridget O'Malley didn't suffer disrespect from anyone, including her own daughter.

Chapter Ten

W hen I got there, I got the strangest feeling that the woman at the counter had been waiting for me. She took a good, long look, though, and then rolled her eyes.

My eyes sparked in irritation. Neither of us had spoken a word yet, and already I didn't like her.

"Hello. I'm Aran. I'm looking for Mulan."

The woman pointed at her face as she slid off her stool. "Do you see any other Asians in here?"

After noting she and I were nearly the same height, my eyes traveled the shop. It was as diverse as any other hair shop in Salem, Massachusetts. I looked back at her. "Is Mulan an Asian name?"

Muttering to herself in what I guessed was a Chinese dialect, the woman turned and walked away. She must have assumed I would follow her because she never looked back. Several stylists stopped snipping on their clients to wave me forward with their scissors. I watched Mulan disappear into another room without checking if I'd followed.

Wondering what I had gotten myself into—no, what Ma

had gotten me into—I walked through the shop trying to locate her. Eventually, I found Mulan standing next to a glass wash bowl in a small room full of hair washing stations.

She pointed at the seat, and I sat.

Seconds later I was draped in a hair cape, lying back with my head in the sink, and staring up at Mulan as she vigorously washed my hair.

"How long do you wear your hair?"

"Longer than this, but it needs a new style." I shrugged under my cape, but soon realized she was asking me a serious question and waiting to hear my answer. "I normally wear it as long as I can grow it. My daughter cut off the non-silver part for me years ago. I need a style that looks better than what I have, but that's also easy to care for. It can be long because I don't mind wearing it up when I need to."

Mulan grunted. "Your hair looks uncared for."

"I haven't done much to it for seven years," I said to her.

Mulan stared at my hair as she worked. "Women need good hair to walk proud. Why did you let it go?"

"My keepers didn't allow me to get a haircut while I was in prison." I chuckled when her eyes widened, but her fingers never stopped.

"Prison? Are you a criminal?"

"No, I'm a witch who picked the wrong man to marry. It's complicated. The net result is that I got incarcerated and he got a job promotion. I divorced him the moment I got out."

Mulan mumbled something under her breath. "Did you turn him into something reflective of his dastardly character?"

Ya had to appreciate a vicious woman. "No. I wanted to do that, but we have a daughter together. It would have upset her... and Fiona's a crier."

With that, Mulan's fingers froze on my head. "Now, I

remember. Bridget told me your story. You have a sweet daughter and a handsome husband. I saw pictures. He looked too old for you."

A stylist's chair was holier to a woman than a confession booth, but the reason for Jack aging still pricked my ego too much to talk reasonably about it. I closed my eyes to focus on what she was doing. "Ma talks too much. What's your story, Mulan? I feel your magick."

"I'm a Wu Shaman. I help crops grow and cast out demons. Not much work here in America for my magick skills. Doing hair pays bills."

I laughed at the way she stated her shamanism like it had been her major in college. What in the world was Ma thinking of sending me here?

Conn chose that time to pop into existence. He still looked like my brother. Mulan growled at him as she rinsed me, but she didn't seem overly surprised to see him. Conn must have tagged along when Ma and Fiona came here.

Mulan mumbled an incantation in a language I'd never heard before. After that, she wrung my hair out, wrapped it in a towel, and frowned at Conn.

"I cast you out of my life, Connlander. Stay gone."

Conn chuckled low and grinned. "You cast me out of your shop, but not out of your heart, beautiful Mulan. Your affection grants me special access to everything of yours."

"Behave with me or I cast you out again. Is this your witch?" she asked, pointing at me.

Conn nodded with his grin still in place.

"Figures," she said, before charging out of the room.

Conn looked at me as I stood "What did you do to make such a poor impression?"

I looked in the direction she'd run and shrugged. "I didn't know I had."

"My lovely Wu Shaman is tense and fussy. That means she's stressed."

My mouth twitched with the urge to laugh at how well Conn seemed to know Mulan. "Yer lovely Wu Shaman thinks I'm a criminal because I was in prison. She doesn't like me because I laughed when she told me about her magick."

Shaking his head, Conn chuckled again. "Seven years of not socializing took its toll on your manners."

I held the towel in place as I chased Mulan through the rooms again. Conn walked beside me. "She seems to know yer whole name. I thought that was forbidden."

Conn looked off and scratched his nose. "She knows a lot more than that about me. I have no secrets from Mulan. It's simply not possible."

So the Wu Shaman had a way with demons. That was interesting. "Has she ever tried to kill ya?"

Conn laughed. "Mulan's powerful enough to kill a demon, but I can't imagine what it would take to push her to that level of action. Unlike the hunters, Mulan doesn't seek my death. Her goal is only to make sure I'm not doing any demon mischief on this plane."

"Do ya mean like cursing someone's herb garden or blighting their corn crop? That probably would get her attention."

Conn laughed. "I missed your rapier wit."

I grinned at him. "Ya're probably the only one."

"Oh, I'm *definitely* the only one," he said, laughing harder.

Back in the main room of the salon, I climbed into a vacant chair two stylists pointed out to me. Mulan appeared by it seconds later. She spent two minutes swearing and pumping the chair to let it down as low as it would go.

When the towel was whipped away, long, wet strands tumbled over my shoulders and down on my breasts. I looked in the mirror, shocked as I touched the length. Somehow she'd coaxed my hair into growing at least six inches.

I smiled at her. "I bet this sort of thing always earns ya a good tip."

"Vines or hair—it's all the same to me. It wasn't like I trained to be gardener."

Was she telling me my hair was the texture of rough, twisted vines? I blinked but said nothing as she picked up the scissors.

With a last glance and headshake at Conn who lingered nearby, Mulan snipped at my strands until the floor was covered.

I was left with long layers that fell softly into place with only gently coaxing. After charging me a fortune and making me buy some styling gel, Mulan finally let me escape.

"Return and I will care for your hair again," she told me.

Given how much better I felt with my hair fixed, I probably would return.

"Did ya find the traitor who keeps telling Jack where I am?"

Conn eyed the piece of sandwich I'd cut off and not eaten. I reached over and exchanged my plate for his empty one. He dug into my leftovers before answering. My familiar had an appetite and immortality hadn't dulled it any that I could tell. Whether it was food, women, or the work I gave him, Conn seemed to enjoy everything equally.

"Yes, I found your ponytail guy. He's brooding in some tiny office tucked next to the demon hunter main building. They pay a special coven to ward their facilities. I'm sure you could get in, but they'd know you were there. Same with me."

I leaned back in my chair. The last thing I wanted was to put all the demon hunters on alert. I also didn't want Jack to know I was working with Rasmus after all. Once I won him over, I wouldn't let Rasmus communicate with anyone but me and Conn until the search was done.

The question was... how could I handle this without becoming the controlling magickal person Rasmus had accused me of being?

"Can ya kidnap Rasmus and make it look like a different demon did it? I'd prefer they didn't think ya were one."

Conn nearly choked on his last bite trying not to laugh. He finally swallowed, laughed, and then stared at me. "Are you serious?"

"Yes. I don't want to be fighting off Jack and the others while I'm working with the man. We'll leave a note that explains his absence. We have to make it good so they won't look for him."

"Like a fake threat?"

I nodded. "Can ya think of anything better?"

Conn snickered. "No. What do you want the note to say?"

My smile bloomed. "*Stop trying to find the portal or yer hunter dies.*"

Snickering, Conn nodded. "Maybe prison was good for you, Aran. You're a lot more fun now."

"No," I said. "Prison was terrible. I missed seven years of everything. Women sexually peak in their thirties and I missed that too."

"Witches don't peak in their thirties, and that's not true

even of human women. I will not tell you how I know that, but you can trust my words."

My smile was tight and disbelieving, but that was how it felt. "I feel like everyone went on without me. There's a shock around every corner I turn."

"That's just the hurt talking. It's only been a few days since you got out of your confinement. You're still adjusting."

Maybe Conn was right, but I still felt left out of my own life.

He reached over and patted my hand. "Jack was the only one who didn't miss you. I wasn't over here all the time, but Bridget and I visited several times a year. He lived like a single guy while you were gone. I still don't know where he got all his money. Being a Marshal of demon hunters doesn't pay enough to live the life he's been living. That part remains a mystery to me."

It was the same thing I'd thought when I heard about his fancy car, but then I felt like I was being jealous and petty. I hoped Fiona didn't suspect anything shady was going on. She'd lost enough of her childhood illusions lately.

Finally, I asked the question that kept running through my mind. "Do ya think Jack is on the take?"

Conn shrugged. "Either he's extorting people, blackmailing them, or he came into a large sum that he invested to tide him over while you were gone. I would say his insta-wealth came from somewhere other than work."

I thought about it. "He didn't sell The Dagda Stone because the bonding ceremony worked. Ma said nothing was missing from her belongings. Ya retrieved everything I owned of magickal value and tucked it away in storage. What could Jack have sold for that kind of money?"

Conn narrowed his gaze until it drilled into me. The answer was suddenly obvious.

"Maybe he sold you, Aran. Your witch powers are unique. You can call on your gods for help. And you have me."

"I miss working for the Shadow Breakers, Conn. I miss Ireland. If Jack hadn't insisted on coming to Salem, I would have happily worked for them forever."

He nodded in understanding. "None of the Shadow Breakers ever believed you did anything wrong. You could ask them for more work over here."

"Truly?"

Conn nodded. "Yes, truly. I looked them up when I lived with Bridget and went to explain your situation."

The Shadow Breakers were an unofficial group back in Ireland that hired magickal help to solve magickal problems. I'd joined them to keep improving my skills, but ended up loving the challenges they gave me. When Jack made us move, I made myself forget them as much as I could so leaving them and work I loved wouldn't be one more daily fight with my husband.

The mystery of Jack's wealth gave a whole new spin to why he wanted me back in his life. Did someone pay Jack to get me out of the picture? Who would have done such a thing? And more importantly, why? I didn't make enemies while I was in the Shadow Breakers. Or none that I knew. I'd all but stopped practicing before the demon hunters locked me up.

"So when are we kidnapping your ponytail guy?" Conn asked.

"Is it too late to do it today?"

"Write the note and I'll see it gets done," Conn ordered.

A thought occurred to me. It wasn't a pleasant one, and it was risky, but it would set the tone for what I was about to do.

"Show him yer true self, Conn. If ya deem it safe enough, of course. I'm not hiding ya from him. Just remember that no one but Jack promised not to kill ya."

"Ooo... a brush with death. I haven't had one of those in years." Conn tapped his fingers on the table. "Let's call Katie. She'll put us up for the night. It's going to take a while for you to get your kidnapped demon hunter to see the wisdom of your plan."

In Rasmus's case, it could take forever or never happen at all. It felt good at least, to be taking *some* action. There was nothing worse than feeling helpless.

"I'll make the call to Katie. I can pick up some supplies for a bribe and meet ya at her place. Should we put Rasmus in chains or in a cage? Both options delight me."

"Cage," Conn said with a laugh. "Using chains is too much like what Jack did to capture you. Don't project your feelings onto your hostage... and don't become your ex."

"Okay, that's good advice," I said with a sigh. "Good goddess, I can't even trust myself at the moment."

"It's okay. I trust you enough for both of us," Conn said. "Call Katie while I'm gone."

Conn disappeared from the table without a goodbye. I looked around to make sure no one had seen him evaporate into nothing. Normally, he walked out of a place and then disappeared discreetly.

I pulled my dreaded phone out of my pocket and glared at it because I didn't know Katie's number. A text from Conn came through before the thought even finished.

I added Katie's info to my contact list and made the call.

KATIE DIDN'T LOOK one day older, much less seven years older. Not only did she not have a single silver streak showing in her hair, but she also still looked as young as Fiona.

Oddly, the attractive woman I looked at was the only female I never saw Conn give a lusty glance to. She was blue-eyed, blonde, and perfectly proportioned. His reaction to her was like his reaction to me—very brotherly. His reaction to Mulan, though, was totally different.

Why had I never noticed Conn's discretion with women before? Maybe I was so besotted with my own relationships in the past that I never paid much attention to anyone else's. Maybe I was clueless back then like Fiona was choosing to be now.

I stopped musing about everything when Katie's lilting voice caught my ear. Unlike me, who never lost the Irish in my voice, she'd picked up a pleasant American accent with nearly no effort. She spoke like a New England angel, with proper diction and a total lack of idioms.

"You and Conn can use this room. It has two twin beds. I know it's not huge, but it's all I have free at the moment. A fairy family is coming tomorrow and they don't adhere to check-in hours. I need the rest of the rooms to be ready whenever they decide to show up."

I nodded to let her know I'd heard. "We didn't intend to disrupt yer business and appreciate ya putting up with us and our shenanigans at the last moment. I promise it's for a good purpose."

"The entire basement is yours to use as well, so long as your hostage is not a screamer. The ceiling and walls are soundproofed because I sing there, but vibrations still get through."

"We don't want to put ya out, Katie. We'll be as quiet as we can be."

She turned her flawless face my way and gave me a soft smile. Katie had chosen a virginal look for running the inn, instead of the grandmotherly one she used most when keening for the dead. I knew changing her appearance was something banshees could easily do, but she had mastered that skill to perfection.

I never asked Katie about her age or her history, but Conn had told me she had suffered a pain so great that she had to stop death singing. Mental damage happened to witches too, but it had never happened to me. Magick was like breathing, and I didn't give it any thought. If I needed to do it, I waved my hand or thought a spell into existence.

"I didn't mean I was put out, Aran. You and Conn are the closest thing to family that I have on this mortal plane. You've both made my time here tolerable. Another twenty years and maybe I'll be able to go home."

I hung my head. After being stuck at the cottage for seven years, I well knew what it was like to not be able to go home. Katie chose to stop keening and heal her mind, which led to her seeking another profession in order to make a living.

Conn told me Katie sang at a death that broke her mind, heart, and soul. He never said if it had been someone she'd personally loved and lost, or if it had just been one death too many.

Maybe Conn didn't even know because he'd clammed up after that. Her family considered her too weak to stay with them and sent her away. I knew she still missed her sisters because sometimes it would slip out in conversation.

I reached down and dug through my duffle to find the treasures I brought her. "I found the original music for that modern opera ya told me about. The man said he wrote this copy for an American mezzo-soprano with a beautifully smooth tone. I know it's in yer range. Hopefully, ya can follow the singer's notes."

"It's *Carmen* by the French composer Georges Bizet."

"I sure hope so because that's what I paid for." Her joy humbled me. Katie was a banshee without a tribe until her mental state rebounded. I didn't fully understand her gifts, but I understood that not using them would lead to voice atrophy. Any gift from the gods was worth protecting.

"I also brought ya some healing tea for yer throat. Astrid over at *Enchanted* said it would soothe yer vocal cords and not let them get strained too badly."

I was no death singer, but I considered myself a good friend. My alleged criminal status meant nothing to Katie. I knew she wouldn't take a penny from us for staying at her inn, so the gifts were the least I could do.

The inn lurched from side-to-side a bit, then settled into place with a thud.

"I believe your hostage has arrived," Katie said, reaching out and hugging me.

"Enjoy yer tea and music," I said. "I'm going to head to the basement and play good cop."

Katie's mouth quirked up at the corners. "Was Connlander playing bad cop? Oh, I bet he loved that."

Chapter Eleven

I squared off with the ginormous red-skinned, black-horned
being. He towered so tall over me that his head nearly
touched the basement ceiling, which was at least twelve feet
high. It was rare for Conn to go this large. He must have felt
like his size made a stronger impression.

"Katie called ya by yer whole name when she spoke about
ya. That's two people in less than twenty-four hours, Conn.
Who else knows yer name? Am I going to spend my life mind-
wiping people I like to save yer arse? Stop laughing at me. It's
not funny."

Conn's demon chuckle sounded exactly like a creature who
enjoyed bringing death. He vibrated with an ominous energy
like the kind that tormented a person in their nightmares. I was
immune, thank the Goddess, but I noticed Rasmus had
pushed back into the corner of his cage to glare at both of us.

Eventually, Conn turned away from me to walk off his
amusement. Getting his jollies had probably made my job a lot
harder. "Stop laughing, Conn. It's seriously not funny."

"No, it's hilarious."

Realizing he would not explain himself, I gave up and dropped my hands. Conn morphed from his demon form back into his "Aran's brother" persona and shoved his hands in his pockets as he turned back to me.

"Looking contrite changes nothing. People knowing yer name is a serious matter. I hope ya didn't tell them lightly."

His mouth quirked with humor. "Contrary to the way you make it sound, I don't go around passing out business cards with it written on it. And they would need more than my name to do any harm. You know that."

"Theoretical knowledge doesn't count. Mulan and Katie are both magickal. You should be respectful of their power."

Conn's grin was my undoing. I could never stay mad when he did that.

"Katie is a lovely soul, but Mulan is *delectable*."

I held up my hand. "I'm not taking yer bait and asking what ya're up to with Mulan. I don't want to know."

"I'm not up to anything," Conn said, putting a hand over his heart. "I like her."

"Katie or Mulan?"

"I love Katie the same as you. The Wu Shaman is in a whole other category."

Since I agreed Mulan was unique, I decided it was best to let my interrogation go. Pretty much every conversation Conn and I ever had was like this. If I'd had a genuine brother, I'm sure I'd have worked just as hard to keep him out of trouble.

Raising my hand to signal defeat earned me another laugh. I turned away from Conn to look at my prisoner. "Hello, Rasmus. Sorry for the abduction, but knowing yer penchant for betrayal, I took extraordinary steps to keep the rest of yer kind out of my business."

"You control a demon. I know that for certain now," he said from the corner of his cage.

I smirked at him. "Conn is a witch's familiar, just like I told ya. Controlling him would be a full-time job so I don't even try to do it. We're partners who share our life's work. That's how I think of him."

Behind me, Conn snickered. "I love that you defend me to people who lack the ability to hear you. It almost makes me mushy."

I glared at Conn. "This is yer fault. Ya said Rasmus knew where the demon portal was."

Conn raised his finger and grinned. "No, I said your ponytail guy reeked of demon energy and that he *might* lead us to the portal."

"What's the difference?"

Shrugging, a still grinning Conn found a wall and leaned against it.

I sighed and turned back to Rasmus. "In order to find the demon portal—and get both Jack and ya off my back—I need to know why ya reek of demon, Rasmus. Are ya willing to help me figure this out? Or are ya going to be yer normal belligerent self?"

Rasmus turned in the cage and looked at all the bars. "Why did you lock me in here?"

I stared at him in disbelief before my temper notched up. "Are ya tetched in the head? Why do ya think?"

Rasmus grunted. "I have no idea what that means. Try using English so I can understand."

I looked over at Conn who was studying the dirt on the floor. He thought I didn't see his shoulders shaking, but I did. Had he set me up for shits and giggles? If so, Rasmus would hate me even more after this farce. Not that I cared, but I didn't need more trouble.

Sighing, because I knew Conn would not help, I gave Rasmus a patient smile. "Humans naturally absorb demon effluvium. It clings to their auras, but eventually wears off. However, if ya're hanging out with one regularly, then ya reek of them. That is yer condition at the moment."

Rasmus crossed his arms. "You hang out with one. Do you reek?"

"No, as a descendant of The Dagda, I have a natural immunity to effluvium. And for the hundredth time, Conn is not a regular demon like the kind ya hunt. To emanate as strongly as ya do means you either visit with a demon regularly or one of the royals put a compulsion on ya. Which is it?"

Conn and I watched the demon hunter look down and scrub his face. He seemed to wrestle with himself over answering.

I turned to look at Conn. "Does a compulsion come with a silencer spell?"

Conn stroked his jaw. "It can, but it requires layering. Only a few can put a complicated compulsion on someone."

My head tilted toward the cage. "Do ya think they afflicted Rasmus with a layered one?"

"I never thought to check him for compulsions at all. He's a hunter, so I naturally assumed demons would avoid him. Why else would he be running around free and harassing you?"

"Fair enough," I said.

But I would bet money demons had put a compulsion on Rasmus. Believing it gave me an idea.

"Can ya teach me what to look for when we check him? Is that against the rules? I'd like to learn."

Conn shrugged. "Very little goes against the rules for you."

"Whose rules?" Rasmus asked. "What are you talking about?"

I turned back to him. "We're talking about The Dagda's rules. He was the one who bound Conn to my family. Ya know The Dagda was my ancestor. I told all yer kind the day I was captured and again the day they released me."

Rasmus blinked. "The Dagda was the son of Goddess Danu. He was first king of the *Tuatha de Danann*. I looked him up."

I snorted. "What ya mean is ya checked out my story after I explained all this to yer council. I'm sure ya just wanted to make sure I wasn't lying. The stone necklace Jack stole from me once belonged to The Dagda. It holds special powers and only Conn's keeper can use it. To everyone else, it's nothing but a pretty bauble."

"What does it do?"

Conn answered him for both of us. "It does lots of things you don't need to know about. In your case, it will allow Aran to also see which demon put a compulsion on you. We would need access to the spot on your body where the compulsion was placed. When touched, the compulsion owner should appear in ethereal form to all three of us."

"I don't want to see that demon woman ever again. She killed my entire team," Rasmus blurted out.

Conn shook his head. "I highly doubt that. She may have enslaved their minds and sent them to do some dirty work for her but killing them would cause too many complications. The Underdark has rules against demons killing humans outside of a sanctioned war."

Rasmus gripped the bars of his cage. "We hunted them and killed a few. They expanded their size like your sidekick and defeated us easily after that. When the fighting was over, I was the only human left. Bodies of my team were scattered about on the ground and never moved. Some were bleeding. Others had lost limbs. I can't see them still being alive."

I crossed my arms as I tried to think this through. Could the hunters really be dead? Sure, they could be. Whatever Conn believed, the galactic average demon from Underdark didn't shy away from killing a human unless specifically ordered to leave humans alone. And demons, unlike humans, regenerated. They rarely procreated from scratch, though not from lack of trying.

But I could be wrong.

Goddess knew those seven years I spent locked up had changed a lot of things in the world I remembered.

"We won't know the truth until we find the demons responsible. We won't know which caste ya dealt with until we look at yer compulsion mark. Are ya willing to let us look at ya or not?"

Rasmus scrubbed his face again. "It hurts to talk about this."

Conn spoke near my ear. "That's a definite sign of compulsion. Only the strongest mind can fight it off."

I nodded and pressed my lips together. "Would ya rather I knocked ya out, Rasmus? And I don't mean like punch ya in the face. I mean, I would spell ya asleep. If ya dealt with a royal demoness and walked away, ya've suffered enough."

"It's more than that," he mumbled, rubbing his forehead. "The she-demon who did this is carrying my child now. The last time I saw her she looked almost ready to deliver. She did something when I was captured to make me go along with her seduction. She came to visit me months later and showed me her pregnant state."

The demon hunter had given me plenty of reasons to

detest him, but my heart bled for what Rasmus incorrectly believed. It was a burden to carry misinformation in yer head and a torment to learn the truth after being wrong. Goddess knew, I was still learning that lesson with Jack's ongoing betrayal. He was still surprising me with his conniving ways.

I talked through the bars of his cage. "That can't be true, Rasmus. Humans and demons aren't biologically compatible."

"Actually," Conn said, raising his finger. "Before The Dagda conquered demon kind, it was sometimes possible, but only with the royals. The offspring of such pairings were born either as evil humans or lame demons. They deemed the mix bad for both our species, so the gods put a magickal restriction on such pairings. From then on, when demons and humans came into contact, the demons only enslaved the humans for their entertainment value. Humans lack the ability to eradicate a demon completely. Their attempts, such as those used by demon hunters, only anger them. But demons still find humans hilarious."

Rasmus made a sound I have no words to describe. It was obvious how distressed he was by the news. "Are you saying all the demons ever killed over the years are still alive?"

Conn lifted his hands in the air. "Alive is not a term those from the Underdark use. We say the person we know will be *gone for a while*. Regeneration varies with how they were dispatched. Missing parts grow back. Severed heads and limbs find each other again. A burnt demon's ashes incubate in total darkness until they replace the original form. The process takes time, whether a few hours or a few centuries. This truth is why the gods intervened between the two species."

Rasmus walked to the cot Conn had thoughtfully provided him with and sank onto it. He put his face in his hands and shook it back and forth.

I sighed at his misery while Conn laughed. "It's not funny," I said.

Beside me, Conn kept laughing. "No, it's hilarious. The man honestly thought he was killing demons. Do none of the hunters read? It's all in the ancient texts."

Ignoring the laughter of my own demon burden to carry, I walked to the cage. "I tried to tell Jack this when he became a demon hunter. Why do ya think I never hated him for doing that job? I knew he wasn't doing what he thought he was, but ya can't educate a man who refuses to listen to ya."

Rasmus grunted. "You could have forced Jack to listen. You had the power."

I let go of the bars. "Forcing my power on people is a new habit I've gained since my divorce. It was the only way I could get the two of ya to leave me alone."

Rasmus raised his head. "They did the same thing to Jack that they did to me. It was the price he paid to get them to free me."

I crossed my arms. "That's not true, either."

"I watched it happen," he said.

I grunted. "No, ya watched a show, Rasmus. No demoness would risk touching my husband while our energy connection existed. They would have waited until after our divorce. Jack married a witch born from the lineage of Irish gods. Jack might not have respected what that meant, but ya can trust someone from the Underdark would honor it. My family's reputation is well known there."

"How do you know they would honor anything?"

I narrowed my eyes and leaned forward, so he'd know I was serious. "Because I'm the only creature walking this Earth with the power to make sure they don't regenerate for *thousands of years*. When they return after that length of time, they don't remember who they once were. It's the closest thing to actual death that can happen to a demon. And yes, they know I've exercised that power before."

"But why would Jack be working with them?"

I looked at the wall to keep from grinding my teeth. I swear with Goddess Danu as my witness, if I found a compulsion on Rasmus to defend Jack, I would neuter my ex-husband.

"Ya know, I've been asking myself many strange questions after seeing Jack again. The first thing I want to know is where he got all his money. He's driving a car worth five years of his current salary as a demon hunter, even at Marshal level. Did he get money for locking me up? If so, who did he sell my extended absence to?"

"I can't listen to any of this. You're talking nonsense. Jack is not working with demons."

Rasmus and his blind spot made me willing to bet he'd received two compulsions. But I needed to know for sure.

"Do ya think a royal demoness—princess or queen—is going to let the alleged father of her child simply waltz out of her life forever? If birthing a demon-hybrid was her goal, then she's planning something big. Do ya think she's going to let Conn come in and get ya like he did? No, she'd be watching ya night and day, Rasmus. If she truly is carrying yer child, she's going to want more out of it than a one-time deposit of yer genetic material. She's going to need yer presence to provide proof of parentage."

Rasmus paced and rubbed his face. Finally, he came to the right decision. It gave me a little hope.

"Do what you have to do to me, then. I don't know what to think anymore."

Conn left the wall and came to stand beside me. He stared at Rasmus through the bars. "I need to be in my natural form to do this. Do you promise not to scream again? For your human ego's sake, I will choose a stature shorter than your own six-feet-three height to appear less threatening."

"Six-feet-two... and I don't care what size you are. Let's get this over with."

Conn nodded. "Very well. Remove your clothes then. It's easier to search you naked. The compulsion marks aren't visible through clothes."

"What do they look like? Maybe I could save you some trouble."

"Swollen red bug bites," Conn said with a snicker as he shifted. True to his word, he kept his size similar to the one he used as my brother.

Rasmus turned his back to us and pulled his shirt over his head. I stared at the width of his shoulders.

"Stop drooling," Conn whispered in my ear.

"Shut up," I told him and turned my back.

Conn laughed his scary laugh, and my face turned red. I was doing okay until he teased me.

"Aran's having some trouble with her libido. I'll restrain her if she gets handsy," Conn said in his gruff demon voice.

I suddenly knew what a fiery hell felt like. My face got so hot ya could have cooked on it. I knew it wouldn't hurt him much, so I turned and kicked Conn squarely on the leg. He'd yelped like I'd broken it.

I had no idea why he was performing for Rasmus... and truthfully, I didn't want to know. I just wanted him to stop.

"Ready," Rasmus said. "I'll remove the rest only if you find nothing."

Determined not to fan my face, I turned around and lifted my chin. It fell open the moment I realized how wrong I'd been about Rasmus. He looked twice as good as Jack ever had. I blinked and shook my head to clear it.

Conn snickered as he opened the cage. A stripped-down Rasmus walked out to face us. I reached across the room with my power and slid a chair over to him.

"Ya're too tall for me to see the top of yer head. Have a seat."

He looked down at me from his greater height, nodded, and sat.

I glared at a grinning Conn over his head. My demon friend might be reformed, but he was evil enough to enjoy my physical discomfort.

"Pull the tie from his hair. We have to check his scalp as well. The marks can be anywhere."

My hands trembled as I undid Rasmus's ponytail. I lifted the strands and fanned them out. "How will I know when I've found something interesting?"

Conn pitched his voice soft and low. "Come on, Aran. It hasn't been *that long* since you had a man. Seven years is a long time, but no one ever forgets what it's like."

I removed my hands from Rasmus's hair. "I swear by The Dagda that I will remove yer man parts if ya keep tormenting me, Conn. I'm having a hard enough time as it is."

Conn stepped back and laughed so loudly the basement walls shook, but he also held up two sets of sharp pointed claws and said nothing. It was all that saved him from feeling my wrath.

To my utter shock, Rasmus man-snickered, and then laughed out loud himself. The sound gave me butterflies in my stomach, but the vibrations reached much lower. My willpower was barely strong enough to keep my eyes from seeking his lap.

If he'd had a dad bod or a beer belly, I wouldn't have suffered so much. But no, the man had hard abs plus muscles above and below them, for Goddess's sake. What man with silver at his temples looked like that? I doubted any did but him.

Playing it as cool as I could, I parted his black strands and searched for anything resembling a bug bite. I worked from side to side of his head, careful to avoid stepping in front of him. I knew if I met his eyes I'd have to leave the room.

I griped while I worked to ease my discomfort. "Men are all alike—every last one of ya. All ya're good for is tormenting and teasing the woman trying to help ya. Those parts between yer legs make ya freaking idiots."

When I was done with his hair, I used the hair tie to give him a man bun. His hair was longer than mine, even after Mulan magickly grew it six inches.

I moved my gaze down his neck and nearly missed the red spot hidden behind his left ear.

"Is this one?" I asked Conn, folding Rasmus's ear so he could see better.

Conn walked around me, lumbering worse than a Big Foot impersonator. What on Earth was he doing? He was agile and quiet in any form he took. Normally.

"Rub the spot," Conn ordered.

I tilted my head down and glared at him. "Ya better be serious. I'm at the end of my patience."

"I'm serious," he said with a toothy demon grin, adding a rumbling growl to convince me.

Given his high amusement, his weird growling might have been just another type of demon laughter. We didn't have time for me to torture the truth out of him, but I would not forget this if it was a trick.

I rubbed the tiny spot and felt magick shoot out of it. An image of a beautiful brunette appeared in the air above our heads. She was in human form and stacked in all the right places, but not pregnant at all.

"Is that yer demoness?" I asked Rasmus.

His head shook under my fingers. "No. She was brunette like her but looked different."

Conn lumbered around us to face the image. His eyes blazed red, and the demoness gasped. "What compulsion did you place on this man?" he asked the ethereal form.

I thought he was acting crazy until the image wavered and eventually focused on Conn.

"This was not my compulsion, Great King," she said, kneeling down.

"Liar. Your signature sealed it. Answer my question," Conn ordered in his deepest voice.

"It belongs to Lilith of the Argosy Caste. She placed the compulsion. I merely sealed it for her."

"If you are lying to me about its creator, I will find out."

She rose in the image and held out both arms. "I would never lie to you. Take what proof you require."

I had no time to ask what she was offering him before Conn swiped at the air.

"Bah... go away," he ordered.

The woman and the image faded from our view.

Conn turned to me with glowing red eyes. "She was under compulsion herself and probably lying. Keep looking. We need to make sure we find all of them. Something more is happening here."

I nodded. Conn's seriousness had cured me of my lust. He joined me in searching, breathing hard through nostrils the size of cannons. Rasmus didn't even flinch when Conn's breath wafted over his skin.

Maybe my magick neutralized the compulsion we found, or maybe Conn breathing on him overrode it. Whatever the case, Rasmus didn't bat an eyelash when I asked him to drop his drawers. He slid them off and down, and I pretended to be a doctor as I searched his nether regions.

When I found the next one, I had Conn put a hand on Rasmus to steady him because I wasn't sure what rubbing something in that sensitive area on his body would do. I sent my magick into the spot and felt Rasmus shiver before hissing.

An image shot out of it with a different brunette demon in human form this time.

She didn't look pregnant, but Rasmus pointed and said, "That's her. That's the one who seduced me."

Conn growled, turned away, and stomped to the wall. He morphed from his demon form into a dog before scampering out of the basement like the hounds of hell were chasing after him.

Chapter Twelve

When a naked Rasmus stood, I patted him on the butt —accidentally. I meant to pat his lower back, but he was so tall that I misjudged when I reached out. "Ya can get dressed now. If I let ya stay out of the cage, are ya going to call Jack?"

"No, I don't even want to. Why did Conn leave when he saw that last demon woman? He didn't leave for the first one."

I shook my head slowly. "I don't know. He'll tell me when he can. Whoever that demoness is, I think he knows her. This sort of reaction has happened a few times before. Conn's immortal. He's seen more than any being should ever have seen in a life. His time with me is simply the latest blink in his timeline."

Since Conn wasn't here to tease me, I watched Rasmus dress. He turned his back for the most interesting parts, but I didn't mind that view either. He looked as good as a man half his age. I tried to imagine him sweating in a gym to get those muscles, but I couldn't bring the visual to mind. Chopping wood maybe? Or perhaps he lifted heavy things for fun.

"I feel... different," he said.

His comment burst my admiration bubble and sent reality crashing through my mind. "Good," I replied. "I'd hate to glue ya to the cot in the cage later because that's yer bed tonight. No others are available. Warn me if ya feel the need to betray me, please. I'll go easier on ya for owning up to it. Compulsions are powerful magick. We can't assume my touch broke them."

Rasmus turned to me. "Aran, you can't think Jack is working with the demons. He's a demon hunter. That would make no sense."

His mind was sharp, and it had made a giant leap already. I lifted one shoulder and let it fall. "I don't know what to think at the moment. There's more to this hunt than finding an open demon portal. I knew something was off when I agreed to help, but now my instinct is shouting it's a cover for something else. This is a time to tread carefully."

"I'll warn you if I start to feel mistrustful again," Rasmus said.

I nodded as we climbed out of the basement. "I think one of yer compulsions had to do with me specifically. My direct contact with that one would break it if that were true."

"That would mean Jack sent me to you knowing full well I would never trust you."

I shrugged. "Or maybe he wanted to make sure ya wouldn't come to like me. Let's go get something to eat. There are several wonderful restaurants within walking distance. Conn will find us later."

Rasmus looked at me. "I doubt Jack ever imagined we'd be working on such an intimate basis."

I chuckled. His comment wasn't even a joke about me patting his butt instead of his back. His gaze was all innocence and shock. Only once today had I glimpsed the real male

Rasmus was. "Things would have been worse if I'd had to put ya to sleep, even though I might have been less embarrassed. Ya might have woken up feeling violated, though."

"Is it really true that Jack never came to see you at the cottage?"

I snorted. "Not once. Fiona came nearly every weekend unless she was doing things with her friends. There was a year or so around fifteen where I barely saw her, but then she got a broken heart over some boy and felt her father had no sympathy for her pain. The only other people I saw were the daily checkers that the council sent to make sure I stayed put."

"It's still hard for me."

I giggled. "I find that absolutely amazing after Conn hovering over yer naked body for thirty minutes. Ya're quite the man if his demon breathing didn't put ya off."

When I glanced up at him, Rasmus was red-faced and smirking. It was a good look for him.

"Well, thank the Goddess ya have a sense of humor. I feared Jack had done worse to ya than he had to me."

"Doesn't it matter about there being a compulsion on Jack too? Maybe he wanted to be with you but he couldn't be because of it."

"I would have broken it eventually, but sex wasn't the breaking point of our marriage. I'm hurt but rapidly recovering from his infidelity."

"Why were you so determined to divorce him then? I still don't know why you didn't hear him out before going through with it. That's what most married people do."

I lifted an eyebrow. "Jack stole my family's property. The divorce was about freeing myself from someone I should never have trusted. I gave Jack what I could in exchange for my freedom back, even though I owed him nothing. After this is over, I don't want to see him until Fiona gets married. We share a child but he will never share my life again." I interrupted and pointed at a restaurant. "Let's go there. The food is excellent."

Rasmus stopped before we went inside. "Wait... I have no money on me. Your demon didn't let me grab my wallet."

He was determined to see Conn as evil. Maybe that would never change. So long as he didn't harm Conn, I probably could live with the suspicions that came so naturally to most.

"Don't worry about yer wallet. I've got dinner tonight. Order what ya want because I'm not destitute any longer. Ya can validate that with my mother. She was certain I was going to be sleeping on the streets and panhandling for change after I got out of prison."

I snapped my fingers and my small cross-body purse appeared. I slung it over only one shoulder for ease of removing it later.

Rasmus smiled. "That's a good trick. Can you teach me that?"

"Maybe. It depends on how much magick ya have in ya. I can tell ya have some. Ma could tell ya for sure how much and maybe where ya got it. Conn could tell ya as well, but he won't. He says magick, like life, is a journey of discovery. He's tightlipped at all the wrong times. I've learned to live it."

"After that full body search, you probably know as much about me as my wife," Rasmus said as he followed me inside.

I thought about the reality of Rasmus being married as I asked for a table for two. After running my fingers over every inch of him, I guess I was feeling a bit of jealousy for the woman he wanted to do it.

I also knew it was only a severe case of lust talking—one of the many advantages of being forty instead of twenty. I would scratch my itch soon enough and with someone safer than a demon hunter, but I wouldn't forget touching Rasmus for a while. He had the kind of body that made a memory for a woman.

We took our seats at a table by the window and I looked over it at him. "Do ya think we can finish a meal together in peace?"

Rasmus sighed as he stared back at me. "No promises," he said.

I picked up my menu and laughed at his honesty. To me, his admission was major progress in our working relationship.

I LEFT an exhausted Rasmus climbing into his cage cot after asking Katie for some extra bed clothes and a pillow. I also left the cage door open but spelled both windows and the door. There was a half-bath down there.

If he tried to leave the building, the spell would let me know it. I informed him of what I did and why I did it. He grunted indignantly but didn't seem to truly mind. My first-time kidnapping someone had gone much better than I could have hoped.

I returned to my room and found Conn curled up in a small ball of misery on my bed.

Sighing softly, I set down my purse and walked to perch next to Conn. The last time I saw him like this, Conn had revealed himself to a human woman who'd run away from him screaming. He'd had to chase her down and mindwipe her to keep her from babbling the truth to everyone she saw.

I'd barely known him then, but the pain of his rejection had been relatable. I'd fallen for a non-magickal person or two before Jack entered my life.

I ran my hand over the short fur on his doggie back. He raised his head and looked sadly at me.

"Who is she?" I asked, not wasting time dancing around things. We both knew it had been the second demoness that sent him into this spiral. Conn was well used to my directness and it saved us tons of time.

He rolled over and changed into the brother form. We could talk telepathically, but I didn't like it much. I preferred using my mouth over my mind, and that was a statement anyone who knew me would agree with.

"Lilith was the first woman I ever loved, and before the Great Rebellion, I had intended to make her my queen. After I was bound to The Dagda, I asked her to come with me. He would have given her the same powers and we would have served his family side-by-side. Lilith refused. It was years before I accepted it was not me she had wanted, nor was it more power. She only wanted the status of being married to the king. Now she carries a child that isn't mine—a child that might be half human and in violation of demon laws, if your hunter is right."

I put my hand on his arm. "I'm sorry ya're suffering, Conn. I'm sorry for whatever dreams ya had about the two of ya that never came true. Did she marry a king after the Great Rebellion?"

"No," he said. "Lilith got mortally wounded when the rebellious demons fought The Dagda and the rest of the *Tuatha de Danann*. My sacrifice was meant to spare her and my kind. The gods obliterated her with all the others who refused to honor the bargain. After she exploded into dust, I assumed I'd never see her again for a thousand years."

"Ya paid a noble price for yer people, Connlander of the Fir Bolg. It must be hard knowing it was never fully appreciated."

Conn sighed in resignation. "Lilith regenerated much faster than I expected her to. I guess it doesn't always take a whole thousand years. She looks exactly the same as she did."

But when she placed the compulsion, she hadn't been pregnant. Or at least, she hadn't been very far along. Her visage looked too normal.

"I thought yer demoness was exquisite, Conn. Do ya still love her?"

Conn rolled to his back and put his hands behind his head. "Not the way I loved Sarah, but Lilith will always hold a place in my heart. We cannot be together because Lilith sided against me in the Great Rebellion. She made a mockery of my sacrifice. No trust is possible between us. This is why a person should never live in the past. Both women I loved are beyond me now."

Sarah had been the only woman I ever heard Conn call "wife". They'd been together for a century or more before she died. I know she was a magickal, but not what kind. He never talked about her to me and I honored his silence. It had always been my policy to allow him as much privacy as I could.

I cleared my throat to force out my next question. I didn't want to even ask it, but we needed to be realists. "Do ya think Rasmus is the father of her child?"

Conn blew out a breath. "I honestly don't know. I understand why he believes it. Lilith can be very convincing when she wants to be. And she's one of the highest of royals."

"Finding the compulsions seems to have broken some of the power on Rasmus. I have my original doubting sidekick back, and yet he's not quite the same arse as he was before. I'm sure I'll be fine if ya want to sit the rest of this mission out."

Conn snorted. "Do you consider me weak for not wanting to confront her?"

I smirked at him. "Do ya consider me weak for doing everything in my power to avoid Jack? Everyone keeps telling me that all he wants from me is a chance to talk. We both know that a bunch of BS. So, no, I don't think we're weak. I think we're both avoiding murder."

Conn laughed at my summary. I smiled down at him.

"The demons are using the hunters," he said. "It could be a game they're playing, or it could be the beginnings of a war, Aran. I can't let you face them without me, but I will walk in the shadows until needed."

"War crossed my mind when Rasmus was telling us his version of his capture," I said, rising from my bedside perch. "I'm here if ya want to talk more about Lilith. I have always wanted to know what ya were like before ya came to serve The Dagda. It doesn't seem fair that ya signed on to serve him for eternity. If I could free ya from yer forever bond, I would."

"My bondage was the only answer, and I entered it with no regrets. Freedom is an illusion. We all serve something or someone, even if it's just our own egos. At least I serve something greater than myself. My people remain as free as I could bargain them to be."

"Which is honorable. Jack serves only his own ego," I said.

"Yes, he always did."

It still bothered me that it took me being jailed by the demon hunters for seven years to see Jack as he truly was. I frowned as I studied my clothes nearly forgetting what I'd been doing. That's how upset I still was over marrying a man who loved his ambitions more than me. But what could I do to change the past? Nothing. There was nothing I could do.

Finally, I snapped out of my mental funk and pulled something out of my duffle to sleep in. "Do ya think Rasmus has the same integrity problems as Jack?"

"Time will tell us that answer. All I can see for now is that his personal wounds made him an easy scapegoat. It would not surprise me to learn your ex-husband paid one of those demonesses to put a compulsion on your ponytail guy. It also makes me wonder if Jack is in league with them, despite what his fellow hunter believes."

"I wondered the same," I said. "And please stop talking about Rasmus like he's my problem. He's not 'my' anything. I barely know the man. Plus, he compared me to his *wife* on the way to dinner tonight. Add in him potentially fathering a demon baby, and the man's a hot mess. I'm not rolling into bed with him simply to irritate Jack nor because he looks like a god chiseled the muscles on his body."

Conn chuckled. "You should have seen your face next to his man parts today. That was priceless. You looked so pained. It was the most fun I've had in years. I'm so glad you're back, Aran."

I snorted as Conn continued to laugh and describe my embarrassment in even more poetic terms. Running my hands over every inch of Rasmus was going to make it difficult to sleep tonight. I kept thinking about all the parts of him I'd wanted to touch more but hadn't dared. Conn reminding me over and over wasn't helping me forget.

Celibacy was a problem for people with magick, and my pent-up situation was getting worse. Repressed sexual energy too often morphed into explosive spells and dangerous magick being accidentally used.

At least my physical misery cheered Conn up. I suppose there was something good about that.

Chapter Thirteen

Katie went to the basement, saw the cage was open, and naturally assumed Rasmus had become a guest. When I wandered into the dining area, he was at her table drinking coffee and listening to her stories. Their shared laughter grated on my nerves.

"Good morning," he said, saluting me with his coffee cup.

"I reserve judgement on the day until I've had a cup of coffee. I'm glad to see my wards failed to alert me ya left the cage."

Katie giggled. "That's my fault. Is he dangerous? Should I have left him in there?"

Rasmus hid a grin in his coffee cup. I narrowed my eyes before I glared at him. "He's not as dangerous as he used to be. We've come to an understanding."

I pulled out a chair. Katie made soothing sounds as she slid the coffee in front of me. "There you go, sweetie. It's not an Irish cuppa because I know ya drink high-caffeine sludge like the regular humans now."

"Blasphemer," I said, sipping off the top of the steam. "Being beautiful doesn't excuse ya."

Rasmus turned to smile at Katie. He even showed her all his teeth, which were as perfect as the rest of him.

I sipped and pretended not to care. Well, I didn't care. But after the restless night I spent tossing and turning over the feel of his abs under my fingers, I wasn't feeling friendly toward him this morning.

"Aran's better once she gets the first cup down," he said to Katie who giggled in return.

Watching them was worse than watching the giggling barista flirt with Conn.

"Will your roommate be joining us?" Katie asked in her singsong way.

"Conn was in the shower when I came down. We're leaving as soon as we can."

"Don't leave because of the fairies. I'd rather have your company than theirs."

I was sullen and silent as a smiling Katie left to fetch our breakfast.

"What fairies?" Rasmus asked.

Katie made excellent coffee. Half a cup down and I was already feeling awake. "She has a fairy family coming to stay here. This house is her bed-and-breakfast business. Back in Ireland, we called this kind of place an inn. Katie's an innkeeper."

"What kind of magickal is she?"

"I can't discuss her powers. She was Conn's friend long before I knew either of them existed. Both of us protect her privacy."

"Is she a witch like you?"

"No and stop guessing. Ya don't have her kind her in America. She's not a demon."

Katie walked back into the room. She looked at Rasmus as she set our plates down. "I'm a banshee. If you're working with Aran and Conn, I don't mind you knowing."

My mouth twisted. "Ya waited six years to tell me what ya were, but ya tell this demon hunter after one tiny conversation. Care to explain that, banshee?"

Katie's wicked grin beamed my way. "Your optimism rubbed off on me, Aran of The Dagda. I'm far more trusting of people now."

"Yes, I'm a contagious optimist. People use that word to describe my pleasant attitude all the time," I said snidely.

Rasmus burst out laughing. "You're so grumpy before your coffee. Have you ever woken up with a smile on your face?"

Katie grinned wider as she looked between us. "That sounds like an offer to me, Aran. Maybe you put the wrong man in the basement last night. You should have made Conn sleep down there."

I grunted at her teasing. "Does Rasmus look like he'd fit in that twin bed ya gave me to sleep in? Conn slept in his dog form after he fell out of his in the middle of the night."

Katie froze. "Is he still in dog form? I don't know if I have any doggie kibble. I made him a plate like yours."

I straightened in my chair. "Conn's choosing to be human for now, but I'll give ya the hundred-dollar bill in my pocket if ya serve him a bowl of dog food."

"No, I can't do that. I value my peace too much to irritate him on purpose," Katie said before returning to the kitchen.

Sighing in disappointment, I dug into my breakfast. I was three bites in before I realized Rasmus was watching me instead of eating. "What now?" I asked when his study got on my nerves.

He leaned on the table. "Are you always like this?"

"Are ya referring to my grumpiness, my love of pranking Conn, or that I insist on protecting my friends?"

"Yes," he answered with a chuckle.

I spread my hands with the fork still in one of them. "What ya see is what ya get, Rasmus. I'm not one of those women who say one thing when they feel another. I've gotten a bit more reticent in the past few years after living in seclusion. Once upon a time, ya would have said that I never met a stranger. I've become the opposite of Katie and more mistrusting now."

"Thanks for not giving up on me then."

"How do ya mean?" I asked, forking in more eggs. Katie's cooking was sublime.

"I remember all our exchanges. My current state feels like I've changed my mind about a hundred things, but I don't think that's the case."

The man still couldn't bring himself to simply apologize for being an arse. A simple "I'm sorry" would have sufficed, but no, he had to analyze it to death and explain it to ya.

I went back to my food. "Demon compulsion is subtle on purpose. They don't want ya to know it was ever done. The urges it sets affect ya slowly, and when dispelled, leaves nothing lingering except a mild form of confusion. Ya did nothing terrible to me, Rasmus. We quarreled, but I don't hold grudges."

"I pulled a stun gun on you."

"Yeah, that was the first time I felt fear looking into yer lap. The other time was yesterday."

His wide eyes let me know that Rasmus totally missed the joke.

"I would have done nothing to you without someone forcing me to. I'm not that kind of man."

I chuckled around a bite before swallowing. "Yeah, I know —I was teasing. After breaking the first compulsion, I realized ya were just a tool."

When his mouth tightened, I realized how he took my words. I couldn't help laughing at him misunderstanding my words. "That's not what I meant. I meant ya were being used against yer will."

Ramus grunted at me like an angry caveman. Why do men do that? Even Conn did it when I stopped listening after too many details.

"I have a recollection of everything that I said to you since the moment we met at the cottage. What I don't recall is being with that woman who says she's carrying my child. That makes little sense."

"Because none of what ya remember with her ever happened," Conn said, sliding into the chair next to me.

"Good morning," I said to him.

He looked into my coffee cup. "Is that your first one?"

"Yeah, but it's strong... and I'm in a good mood. Ya're safe."

"What do you mean it never happened?" Rasmus asked, staring at him.

Conn smiled when our hostess slid a plate of food in front of him and patted his cheek. "Thank you, Katie."

"You're welcome, Conn. Aran tried to get me to serve you dog food."

Conn turned a glare my way. I chuckled, shrugged, and went back to eating. He said nothing to me before he turned to Rasmus.

"You would remember the act. She might have made you forget some of it, but without the compulsion, you would remember details. You also would have permanent marks on your body. I saw nothing like that yesterday. When we find her, we'll discover the truth of the matter."

Rasmus seemed to wilt in his chair. His relief was obvious. He turned to look at Conn as he ate. "I hate to ask this, but I'm trying to understand. Are you a demon or aren't you?"

"Goddess bless, here we go again," I complained, throwing up a hand.

Conn chuckled as he dug into his food. He ate half of it before answering the question. "I'm an imperial demon, which some consider being a lesser life form. Imperial demons tend to be small of stature, and normally can't change their size. I'm not one of those."

"Aran calls you her familiar."

"What she says is true. A witch daughter of The Dagda's lineage currently controls my fate."

"Is that because you're inherently evil?"

"No more so than you. How many demons did you think you were murdering as a hunter?"

Rasmus dropped his head and nodded. "I now think my work was based on falsehoods and delusions. And I don't think you're a lesser anything. You brought me here without harming the building I was in or me. You don't act like any of the demons I've fought."

I simply couldn't leave that one alone. "Are ya wanting to start a boys club, Rasmus?"

Rasmus grinned at me. "No, I'm just having an epiphany."

I was on my second cup of coffee and feeling mellow. "Ya're allowed. Conn doesn't hold grudges either."

"Good. Because I'm grateful to both of you. Whatever you think I can do to move our search along, I'm willing to do it," he said, falling silent before giving all his attention to his meal.

The three of us honored the quiet peace between us to finish breakfast. I finished my second cup of coffee and most of a third before I felt ready to deal with things.

I looked over at Conn. "If we find the ones who put the compulsions on Rasmus, we might find the open demon portal too. Let's start by visiting the first demoness. Did ya know her too?"

"Yes," Conn said. "Her caste is out of New York. By now, she's reported that we found her compulsion. They will expect our visit."

"Are ya up for tagging along? My offer for ya to sit this out is still on the table."

"No, I'm up for it," Conn said. "You need to be prepared to fight."

"I had very little to do for seven years. Keeping up with my fight training killed time."

"So you trained the way any prisoner might. Is that a joke?" Rasmus asked.

I snorted. "Want to step outside and see if I'm lying?"

Conn chuckled. "Are the two of you going to bicker all day? I don't mind."

"Only if we keep trying to talk to each other," said Rasmus, turning his head to look directly at Conn.

Then he and Conn both burst out laughing. I glared at both of them for what they were implying, but neither seemed to care about my feelings.

Chapter Fourteen

R asmus, it turned out, owned a car. It was at his actual home, not the building where the demon hunters had been keeping him. The three of us called for a ride that took us there. The plan was to drive from Massachusetts to New York. By the time we left Katie's and got to his home, it was nearing noon.

While Rasmus packed an overnight bag and gathered some of his things, Conn and I wandered around his living room. We found no photos, no books, and no shoes under the coffee table. There was one sad-looking throw pillow on the end of the sofa. Even the furniture at the cottage had been nicer.

But what I couldn't get a handle on was the total absence of anything feminine. Where was the evidence of the wife he mentioned? Goddess, where was proof that he even had a personality? No one's home was this sterile. It was like a hotel room that got cleaned every day.

"Something's not right here, Conn. Rasmus mentioned a wife. I remember it clearly," I said.

Conn nodded. "Yes. I'm quite sure you do."

"Not for the reason ya think, ya wisecracker. Will ya leave off that?"

My familiar was traveling with us in human form, but he lifted his head and sniffed loudly. "This place doesn't smell like the hunter. It smells like nothing, as if all scents were purposely eradicated. There is the faintest smell of hand soap in the bathroom. The kitchen barely smells of the food trash that was taken out weeks ago. I doubt this place is someone's permanent residence."

I made a face over what that meant. "I went over every naked inch of him. Where bloody else could a compulsion have been hidden on the man?"

"I stopped you before you finished checking his crotch area. There could have been a second or even a third one down there. The man was endowed enough to hide six or seven."

"That's not funny, Conn."

"No, it's not funny, but it's still true. I got startled at the sight of Lilith. You probably stopped searching the moment I left the room."

Sighing, I looked around. No way was I admitting he was right. "Would another compulsion explain this place?"

Conn's only answer was a shrug.

"If we remove any others, whoever put them there will surely know the game has turned again."

"Agreed," Conn said and put his hands in his pockets. "Plus, I don't think you have the willpower not to jump his naked body if we search him again."

I walked to Conn and punched his arm hard. He laughed, but it came out of his throat in his evil voice. It was creepy to hear it coming from someone who looked so much like me.

Rasmus came back carrying a duffle that bulged. He

grinned when he looked at us. "Did I miss another fight between you two?"

"Something like that," I said. "Ready to go?"

Rasmus held up car keys and jingled them.

By now it was nearly two. We were losing the day fast.

After we cleared Salem and headed west to Albany, I cleared my throat to get the driver's attention. "When did ya become a demon hunter, Rasmus?"

He stopped making man-talk about cars, looked at Conn, and snorted. His eyes met mine in the rear-view mirror. "That's a strange question."

"Is it? I was only making conversation, but I would like to know. When I met Jack, being a demon hunter was all he talked about. He'd studied mythology and sociology at university. Then he came to Ireland for his post-graduate work. He said Ireland had more magickal mythos than any other place on Earth."

Rasmus was quiet for a moment. He seemed to wrestle with his brain again. Conn swiveled slightly in his seat to watch him.

"Do you have a headache?" Conn asked.

Rasmus frowned. "My head hurts frequently, but nothing can be done. I was in an accident that robbed me of my memories and gave me a permanent head injury. I can only recall the last few years of my life."

"How terrible," Conn said, offering genuine sympathy.

Rasmus nodded. "Before I became a hunter, they said I used to be special forces in the military. Since I started receiving a monthly pension for being medically retired, I finally accepted the story everyone told me was true."

It wasn't that I felt no sympathy for Rasmus being hurt, because I did, but the first thing I thought of were his amazing abs. No man looks like that naturally past the age of twenty-five unless he works at it. Being in the military would explain his physical condition and maybe some other things.

When I realized he was going on with his story, I pushed away my memories to pay attention.

"One day I woke up in a hospital healing from a fight I couldn't remember ever happening. There wasn't a mark on my body, but I couldn't remember anything. Two members of the demon hunter council came to see me. They said demons had attacked me and I'd barely escaped. They also offered me a job as a hunter. Jack helped me find a place to live and trained me."

"How long ago was that?" I asked.

"Seven years."

I left the obvious unsaid, but Conn, who was riding shotgun in the front, gazed over his shoulder at me. The math wasn't lost on him either.

I stared out of the window. "Witching is just what I do and magick is like breathing to me. I never went looking for normal work. Magickal work like this job always finds me. I was making plans to break myself out of the cottage before ya showed up with yer offer."

"But you would have been a fugitive."

"Magickal authority and legal human authority are very different, Rasmus. Yer demon hunter council had no proper authority over me, and the human legal authorities in the state of Massachusetts have no records of my incarceration. The demon hunters operate covertly."

"You are full of all kinds of conspiracy theories."

I chuckled like he'd said the funniest thing ever. His ignorance of those he worked for was the real joke, but I changed the subject. "Ya also mentioned a wife. Do ya remember her?"

That question earned me another glare in the rearview mirror before he answered. "A sobbing woman ran out of my hospital room after the doctors announced I would never get my memories back. I never saw her again, and no one seems to remember her being there but me."

"Well, that was certainly an odd turn of events after everything else," Conn exclaimed.

Rasmus nodded. "Yes. The military refused to release my old personal information about my marriage because she allegedly divorced me. When I questioned the doctors, they said I imagined seeing a woman, but that she hadn't been there. A couple years ago I finally gave up looking. The military declined all my requests and cited it as a matter of national security to keep my accident details a secret."

Nodding, I settled into the backseat and into my own thoughts. I didn't want Rasmus to feel like I was digging out of disbelief. Conn and Rasmus were back to making light-hearted conversation about nothing. I let the conversation stay there while I sunk into my own thoughts.

So what had I learned since I agreed to this crazy demon hunt?

Conn could laugh like his natural self even while in human form. That was the creepiest thing ever.

Jack had more money than he should have had. My daughter thought I was a criminal. And my mother thought I should be more concerned about keeping a good haircut than I was about my divorce.

I also learned Rasmus had great abs, lived in a soulless house, and had no memory of his demon encounter. I suspected Jack and the council were capitalizing on his misfortune, but that had yet to be proven.

The whole missing wife thing was crazy. What if someone was making sure she stayed away? Why had she given up on him?

This search was getting stranger every moment.

By THE TIME we got to Albany, it was close to six, and the sun was setting. Gas station and truck stop snacks had left me starving for actual food, but Conn said dinner would have to wait until after we talked to the demon caste here.

He would need to shift forms to do his searching and the darkness was helpful. His parting words to me were to watch for a strange dog to appear later.

Honestly? Any dog form Conn took was automatically strange.

He could also be a goat, a cow, and a horse to name a few other animals. His horse form was majestic, but he refused to take me for a trot around the field. He also refused to turn himself into a panda or a llama just because I thought they were cute. We had some fun times back when we first got to know each other. I was twenty-one and carrying Fiona. Baby hormones make a witch quite sassy.

We'd parked on what appeared to be a middle-class street by an abandoned chapel. The streetlamps were in working order and people were out walking their pets one last time before bed. Sure, the location was too cliché for words, but where would ya hide if ya were a creature from the Underdark?

I'd have probably picked a church as well. Everyone else would look for angels in a place like this.

I'd never met an angelic being, but Ma was convinced they existed. Many strange magickal creatures lived in exotic places around the globe, but give me a fairy, a troll, or a leprechaun any day. I understood them better.

It was harder to find demons because they held human forms whenever they walked this plane of existence. Only the royal family held enough magick to shift into their original form up here.

Conn never bragged about being a royal, but he admitted to being a king the night we talked about Lilith. All I knew for certain was that he could take any form he wished. I had never seen another demon do the same. I figured it was part of his deal with The Dagda.

When I was in magickal school, they explained that demon ability was something science-y having to do with slower vibrations and their frequency differing from humans. I don't recall all the details, but even as a teenager I understood not all demons were equally frightening.

Sorting them out in the work I did, though, was definitely best left to magick professionals like me. They were tricky, irreverent, and had skills in the plane that could turn those like Rasmus into their puppets.

"Are we sure this is the right place?" Rasmus asked.

I watched him reach up and rub his ear in the very spot I'd discovered the first compulsion mark. He wasn't grabbing at his crotch like Michael Jackson yet, but it wouldn't surprise me if he did that next. The memories were obviously still in his head. He just couldn't reach them.

"Conn is going to check around to see if he finds any demon trails. He says they shed energy and it creates tracks."

"Effluvium," Rasmus said.

I chuckled in the dark. "That's right," I said.

We waited another ten minutes. An unmarked cop car drove by and turned to make another pass to check us out. I grabbed Rasmus by the shirt and pulled him close. "Boost me up on the car," I ordered.

"What?" he asked.

"We're not moving from this spot until Conn returns. Lift me up and set me on the car. When that cop comes back, I want you to stand between my legs. We need to make him think we're hanging out and flirting."

"What about Jack?"

Yesterday, he barely mentioned Jack's name. Talking about him now was solid proof Rasmus was still under a compulsion. I either missed finding one or the suggestions about Jack hidden in the one behind his ear had returned full force.

"My ex-husband is not here. Ya're the one here. Do as I say."

The cop's lights swung around the building and headed our way. Rasmus saw him, reached down, and then boosted me onto the hood like I was light as a feather. He slid himself between my parted thighs, which made me laugh genuinely and not have to fake it.

"Ya're a big guy, aren't ya? It's been a long time since I spread my thighs this wide for a thrill."

"Hush," Rasmus said, watching the cop instead of me.

His hands squeezed my hips and nearly covered my butt. Everything about this man was extra-large. I laughed and felt sixteen again. I told myself any woman would feel girlish with a good-looking man standing in such an intimate position with her.

The cop car slowly creeped by us, but sped up as he went

by. Seconds later he tossed his light on the top of his cruiser and sped off through the night.

I stayed where I was, enjoying the moment even though the threat was gone.

A regular car rounded the corner shining its lights on us too. Rasmus pulled me across the hood until he leaned into me. My gasp of surprise seemed far too loud to my ears. I hoped he hadn't noticed it.

His head bent to mine and a little shiver passed over me as his breath tickled my ear. "Why aren't we going inside the church?" he asked.

His comment had me blinking, but I snapped out of my lust-fueled daydream when a mongrel dog growled nearby. Rasmus stiffened and pulled me closer. Even a demon compulsion couldn't quite stifle his male urge to shield me from potential danger.

Not that Conn was a danger to either of us.

"That has to be the ugliest dog form ya've ever used," I said, looking down at Conn.

Conn responded with a disgusting doggie sneeze.

I patted Rasmus on the arm. "Down, please." I had to pat harder before he actually did it.

I missed the heat of him when I was standing alone again, but I couldn't be thinking about my needs just yet.

"Are they inside?" I asked.

The dog barked. *There are more of them than I expected and not all from the same caste. You will need the mantle. Draw on me for it.*

I nodded that I heard.

"Are you seriously talking to a dog and nodding when it barks?" Rasmus asked, staring at Conn.

Conn growled at him again.

I smirked a little as I explained. "We're heading in to confront the demons. If ya want to stay in the car, Conn and I won't mind. Going in could be dangerous for ya. There's always a fight before they settle down enough to listen and talk."

"Are you going in there?" he asked.

"That's what I came to do," I told him.

"Then I'm going in as well."

I didn't know what sense that made, but it was brave of him, so I tried not let him catch me rolling my eyes.

Chapter Fifteen

T he door to the church wasn't locked. The inside of it
was lit with candles. Floorboards creaked, no doubt
announcing us. It was like walking into the scene of a creepy
horror movie. Most sacred places felt serene. This one did not.
If I hadn't trusted that Conn was right, the hair rising on my
body would have been a dead giveaway.

Mantle, Conn sent, visualizing it in his mind.

I stopped Rasmus from going forward. "I need to do
something first. Ya might want to give me some room."

He blinked as he stared down at me. It was always about
size with men. I guess Rasmus never watched Jackie Chan
jump up and kick someone eight-feet-tall on the head. No, I
didn't have Jackie's martial arts moves, but I had my own
talents.

I spoke the agreement in the original language of the gods.
Energy instantly gathered on me. It swirled around my body
forming a light-silver armor that glowed like moonlight.
Wearing the mantle was heavenly while it lasted, and hell when

I took it off. I hoped to make this quick and not have to spend all my willpower later to give it up.

We didn't know where the mysterious Lilith was hiding. She could be here. Given their former relationship, I felt like Conn would sense her if she was near, but demons could be sneaky. Alarms went on inside me whenever Jack was nearby.

I stretched my arms and looked at them. The armor never manifested in the same design twice, but today's version was buzzing all over.

"*Diadem*," I called out. Something that looked like a metal headband appeared in my hand. I fit it to my forehead and looked at Rasmus who was staring open-mouthed at me.

"I'm very medieval looking, right? The Dagda said this outfit was a symbol of sovereignty but he didn't tell me of whom. He said I'd discover the answer for myself. He also said only a natural witch could manifest it."

When Rasmus didn't respond to anything I said, I gave up talking to him and walked down the aisle until I stood before the raised pulpit and altar. I stared for a long time, but no one showed up to greet or threaten me.

Did they think I would give up and go away? I was far more persistent than that.

Behind me, Conn barked several times.

"Yes. Don't nag me. I'm getting to it."

Sighing, I moved one hand over the other as I built a ball of energy between my palms.

I pitched my voice as loud as it would go. "Someone better come talk to me before I destroy this place. If yer portal's here, it will pull all of ya back into the Underdark. Is that what ya want?"

I bounced the energy ball from hand-to-hand until my patience ran out. I drew back to let it fly at the wooden pulpit but halted when a line of nine gray and brown demons appeared. They were no taller than me and their horns were short and red instead of black. They had branded the area above their left breast with their caste.

They morphed into nine handsome men as I watched, and one stepped away from the others to walk closer to me. He was a lot taller and standing on the platform six inches above me. I'd never seen this demon caste before and I imagined I looked like a child playing dress up to them.

"Why has a child of The Dagda invaded us? Put your mongrel and human outside so we can talk properly."

I clapped my hands and popped the energy ball like a balloon. The explosion rocked the church walls and all the windows. I chuckled when all the demons raised an arm to shield their faces.

"A demoness from this caste put a compulsion on my human friend. I want it removed and I want to know why she did it."

"It's half-dissipated. The signature is gone. You destroyed your proof."

"We saw her signature before it went away. Which is where the lot of ya will be going if ya don't bring her here to answer my questions. The humans say there are a lot of killings going on. But we know better than that, don't we? Ya wouldn't be standing here so calmly if it were true."

"Our royal did a job for a demon hunter. Look to your own kind for answers."

"Whoever hired ya was most definitely not one my kind," I said, smiling at him. "Someone intentionally kept me busy for the last seven years—too busy to investigate what was going on. As I said, I have a lot of questions."

"Which we don't have to answer," he insisted.

Conn ran forward, barked once, and then morphed into a very large version of himself. He wore a silver mantle as well. On his head sat a golden crown that seemed alive.

"Answer her or you will answer to me," he growled.

All nine men dropped to one knee before him. "Forgive us, lord."

"For what?" Conn demanded. "I've heard nothing but cowardly denials. We saw your royal in the signature. Speak the truth."

A female demoness appeared in front of the kneeling men. "No need to hurt them, my king. I compelled them to say nothing. They are only doing as I bade them do."

"Is that her?" I asked Conn.

"Yes," he answered in his demon voice.

I turned to call over my shoulder. "Rasmus, come here please."

His footsteps shuffled on the floor as he made himself walk to where we stood. There was reluctance in every step. I don't know who he was more afraid of, but he reeked of fear. Even I could smell his adrenalin spike.

"Remove yer compulsion from this man," I ordered.

"But I didn't..."

I held up a sparking hand. "We saw yer signature. It was behind his ear. I broke it but didn't dispel it completely. Remove it before I get testy."

Huffing at being bossed around, she stomped down the steps to our level. Keeping an eye on Conn, the pretty brunette royal went to Rasmus and grabbed his ear. She spoke a command. Moments later, he yelped and backed away.

"Who paid ya to put it there?" I asked.

The demoness looked at me and smirked. "Ask your husband. He knows the answer."

I held up a ringless hand with sparking fingers. "Ya're not keeping up, yer highness. I have no husband—not anymore."

Her eyes widened at the news. I got right to the point. "Did Jack Derringer pay you to put a compulsion on this human?"

"Jack's a good employer," she said with a smile. "He's paid us to do a lot of things for him and his kind."

Grinding my teeth together was all that kept me from screaming. My ex-husband was a demon hunter who paid demons to do him favors. How long had that been going on?

I turned to Rasmus. "Ya heard her tell us a truth about Jack just now. Do ya feel any need to defend him?"

Rasmus rubbed his ear. "No, but I have a right to be confused. I worked as a hunter for years. Why would he pay off the demons we kept trying to kill?"

I rolled my eyes before turning back to the demon princess or queen or whatever they called their female royals. "Where are the missing demon hunters?"

"We don't have them."

"Who does?"

She looked at Conn and swallowed hard. "I am under a compulsion not to reveal her identity."

Conn stepped toward the female. The demoness lowered her gaze. "Mercy, my lord. I was only doing as the future queen ordered."

He lifted her chin with a single sharp talon of his clawed hand that could easily and efficiently slice her head off. The Dagda blessed Conn with the ability to subdue all demons. But this wasn't about subjugation or putting fear into her. Headless regeneration took many centuries. That's why she trembled where she stood. Conn would behead her for no other reason than to make sure his power was never questioned.

His talon suddenly glowed. She gasped as his magick took hold of her. "As your one true king and master, I command you to tell us your future queen's name."

"Lilith," she whispered. "She has returned. The former hunters serve her now."

"We shall see if that is true," Conn said.

Conn removed his talon from her chin, turned from us, and stalked to the rear of the church. I knew it was to keep from doing exactly what the demoness and I had expected him to do. Anger radiated from him.

The demoness stared at me. "I expected him to kill me."

"I expected it as well. Today must be yer lucky day," I said. "Could ya answer one more question for me?"

She stared at the back of the church where Conn stood with clenched fists. "I will if I can."

I pointed to Rasmus. "I found yer compulsion and one other from Lilith. Can ya tell if there are others?"

She looked at Rasmus. Her eyes turned red as they searched him. "Your human is hard to read. His kind did something to him before they asked me to seal the compulsion. They probably chose his ear because it was one of the few areas on him that remained unaffected."

"Are ya saying that humans drugged Rasmus?"

"They made him forget himself. The blockage of those memories swirls around his root and rises to his third energy center."

"So ya're saying the drugs did something to block knowledge of his own body." I turned to Rasmus and studied him. This was certainly a twist.

"It is not my place to guess anyone's intentions other than my own. I have done all you asked, daughter of The Dagda. Return to your kind."

"Stop selling compulsions," I told her. "They aren't fair."
She lifted an eyebrow in challenge.

"And ya better not have an open demon portal here or I'll
be coming back to shut it. Those aren't allowed, either."

"We've been in Salem for as many years as your kind has
witch. None of you ever learned to leave things be."

"I come from Ireland, but I know all about yer Colony
witch hunts. We had them in Europe. Don't be thinking I'm
above putting a curse on yer caste because I'm not. I can stop
the regeneration of yer people for centuries. Ya can continue to
live here in peace, but ya have to leave the humans alone. That
was always the bargain. Nothing has changed."

"Then stop the demon hunters from hunting us while
hiring us. Their actions make a mockery of your words."

I looked at Rasmus who was frowning deeper and deeper,
before looking back at her. "I'll add disbanding the demon
hunters to my to-do list. That's going to be a tricky one."

She turned toward the stage. All the male demons
disappeared when she did.

Rasmus stared at the floor where she evaporated into thin
air. He was probably in mild shock. I babbled to give him time
to get hold of himself.

"Demons call that vanishing act transmogrification
because they disintegrate their entire form and reassemble it
somewhere else. Rumor says there's a finite number of times it
works before they simply crumple to bits and have to
regenerate."

Rasmus looked at me. "What did they do to me? She
insinuated there was something non-magickal going on."

"She did indeed, and I don't have the answer to that
question, Rasmus. We'll deal with it when we can, but right
now, we need to help Conn calm down. He's worked up over

having Lilith's identity confirmed. She's sort of his ex-girlfriend. He's shook up about her."

Nodding absently, Rasmus turned and followed me to the back of the church. I uttered the command to store my mantle away.

Knowing he'd never harm me, I put a hand on Conn's demon arm. "Let's get something to eat and go home. These weren't the demons we were looking for, which means we can cross this place off our search list."

He nodded once before morphing into human form again.

This time when Rasmus talked about cars and other nonsense on our drive, I didn't roll my eyes. He eventually got Conn to smile at something he said, and I was grateful he provided my upset friend with a distraction.

Chapter Sixteen

Dinner ended up being drive-thru because the men wanted to get back as soon as we could. Katie had located a friend with a tiny rental that was available. We jumped on it because it had two bedrooms and futon in the living room. The rental was ours for a week.

When we stopped for gas, Rasmus took the cash we gave him and went inside to pay. I'd had Conn check the registration for the car on a hunch. After laughing at my lack of other detective skills, he'd done as I asked and found the car was not registered to Rasmus. It was registered in a woman's name—Hilda something. She shared the same first name Jack had called the demon hunter council woman Conn had seen him consoling.

I studied Rasmus as he held the door open for a couple of people. "We need to monitor him. He's no fan of Jack's now, but we still can't trust him."

Conn had smirked at me. "If you were sleeping with him, keeping tabs on him would be easy.

"Sleep with him yerself. I got enough problems," I said to my laughing nemesis.

Conn shook his head. "I tried kissing a man once, but it was not enjoyable."

"That is too much information, Conn."

"You said you wanted to know what I was like before I served The Dagda."

"I believe I've changed my mind."

Conn shrugged and grinned. "I'll sleep at the foot of his bed tonight. I'll even wait until he falls asleep, so I don't scare him as badly. If he makes a pass at me, you'll know about it soon enough."

"Thanks for taking this shift. Ya're worrying about nothing. Rasmus is not bi-sexual."

"How do you know?" Conn asked.

"Intuition."

"More like wishful thinking," he said with a smirk.

It was nearly midnight when we got to the place we rented. It had a code activated lock we used to get inside. We blindly chose bedrooms and fell into them. Conn was the only one who wasn't totally spent. He got tired, but it was never the same kind of tired that humans felt.

"Are ya okay?" I asked him before he shifted into a dog.

"No, but I will be once we get to the bottom of things."

I nodded. "I'll call Ma in the morning and see if she knows how to break compulsions without destroying them. Curses are the same, except harder to break."

Conn snickered. "Do you need a hug and tucked in before I go?"

"No. Go away. I'm done being nice to ya."

"Thanks for caring, Aran."

"Ya're welcome, Conn."

THIS IS why I didn't like phones. Ya wasted time calling a person and never getting them. When ya did connect, ya wasted time talking about everything but what ya needed to know.

And talking to my mother over the phone was the absolute worst torment in the world.

"I'm glad ya called, Aran. I think ya should schedule another haircut appointment. It would clear yer mind and maybe ya would come up with a fresh answer to yer problem."

What was her fixation with my hair? Would she shut up about it if I dyed it? I counted to ten before replying. "I just got a haircut, Ma. I don't need another one. What I need is to find a way to break demon compulsions completely. I'm able to disrupt them, but that's not the same."

"Compulsions differ from curses, Aran. The magick driving a compulsion is all about the person placing them and their intention. Some compulsions are so subtle a person can go their whole life never knowing they've got one. I have heard that people sometimes use Devil's Breath to override a compulsion. The herb gets them to talk, but it also knocks them out. This is especially true for humans."

"So ya're saying there's nothing I can do but get the demon to remove it."

Ma snorted into the phone. *"No, child. Ya can go get a haircut and a fresh perspective on things. Stop being stubborn and cheap."*

"I'm being neither!" I shouted into the phone.

"Then go get another haircut. Bye, Aran."

A laughing Conn wrestled the phone from my fingers before I could throw it against the wall. "Your temper is much worse than I recall it being before you spent time in magick jail. Inanimate objects become projectiles now if I turn my head away for too long. You need a keeper until you readjust to society. Take Rasmus with you. It's your turn to babysit him."

I stopped and stared. "Why are ya calling him by his name? Ya've been calling him hunter or demon hunter or human up to now."

"Why are you so suspicious, Aran? This is the second day you've woken up in a foul mood."

I huffed as I crossed my arms. "Ma keeps insisting that I get another haircut. She's refuses to listen to all the demon hunter shenanigans we've been discovering." I pitched my tone to mock my mother. "*It's fine, Aran. Another haircut will give ya a fresh perspective.*" I stopped mocking to snort. "She's being ridiculous and I'm too old to do what she says."

"I don't have an opinion about what you should do or not do. All I'm saying is take Rasmus with you."

"I heard ya the first time," I muttered under my breath.

Conn smiled as he handed me my phone back.

I took it and sighed in defeat. "Okay. I'll text ya. When are we going to track down yer regenerated demoness?"

"Soon. In the meantime, I suggest you do a little digging of your own. Give Mulan my love when you see her."

"Why would I be seeing Mulan today?"

Conn rolled his eyes. "Maybe you need to see her because she's a Wu Shaman and might know a few things about demons that you don't. Your mother was goading you in hopes you'd figure that out on your own."

I felt like the biggest of idiots after Conn spelled it out for me. "Well, she could have just said that instead of harping about me getting another haircut."

"And you could act like you have a clue. She's trying to help without helping. That's always been Bridget's way."

I pressed my lips together and nodded. "Fine, I'll make another appointment with Mulan and I'll babysit our hunter. He can go with me."

"Rasmus talks in his sleep," Conn said. "He and someone spend a lot of his sleep time fighting. He keeps asking them to understand something. But he mumbles it and won't answer when I ask for clarification. Whatever they gave him to make him forget, it buried his old life deep."

"Do ya think he's talking to a demon in his sleep?"

"Yes, but the human kind, which is scarier than him talking to a real one. We haven't really confirmed his personal details yet. I'm thinking his past might shed some light on this whole situation."

"It sounds like we'd be taking on the military to ask those questions. Why would they talk to us?"

"I'm thinking we can get around asking permission. How do you feel about raiding the hospital records first? Rasmus said he woke to Jack. Who else was in the room? Did the military pay his bill? Or the demon hunters? I think the answer to that will be illuminating."

Chapter Seventeen

"I'm willing to pay for an hour of consulting."

Mulan was organizing her hair pins. "What is consulting? I know nothing about talking for money. I do hair, witch. That's money. Not consulting. If you do not need your hair done, go away."

I stared her down.

Mulan chuckled when I said nothing more. "I can make your hair even longer. Do you want it dragging on the floor like a princess in a fairy tale? I can do that."

I held up a hand. "I know you have mad hairstylist skills, but I'm happy with my hair growth speed. What I need from you is the secret to removing demon compulsions?"

"You get hair done and we can talk."

I didn't have time for this nonsense. "How about ya cut his hair?" I turned and pointed to Rasmus who'd taken a chair when I'd started arguing with Mulan.

"He's got bigger problems than needing a haircut," she said.

Laughing at her own joke, Mulan took off.

"Come on," I said to Rasmus, motioning him to follow me.

We traipsed through a room full of giggling stylists who winked at us as we passed through. I rolled my eyes at their amusement and kept on moving. Mulan was not in the rooms with the hair washing stations.

I stopped, snorted at my gullibility, and glared at the emptiness. "The Wu Shaman and her games are annoying me."

"Wu what?" he asked.

Mulan backtracked into the main washing room. "You are slowest person I know, witch. We will do this in my private area. Feel lucky I did not give up."

Swearing under my breath, I followed her down a hallway with a sighing Rasmus following close behind me.

I waited until he was in the chair and she'd started the washing process. It bothered me to watch him close his eyes in pleasure as her fingers moved over his scalp. I knew precisely how good it felt because I'd been in the chair last week. It was a whole different matter to be a voyeur when it happened to something else. Women in hair salons didn't stare. That was etiquette. But I couldn't tear my gaze away.

"Can we talk now?" I said, angrier when I had to clear my throat.

"He has many demon compulsions. They must have had him for a while. He must have been good in bed," Mulan said.

I opened my mouth but only a slow breath escaped me. "Can ya see them?"

"Yes. He has several in his private places—some old, some recent. You only broke one on top of his head. A forty-year-old woman should not fear naked men so much. This one better choice for you than handsome-old-man husband."

I didn't bother to correct her. I just shook my head. "I

broke one of his compulsions but couldn't completely remove it. I made the demoness who sealed it break it."

"Same thing in the end," she said, shaking her hands free of suds. "Come. You rinse out his conditioner while I go get my shaman tools."

"How much is yer shaman work going to cost me?"

Mulan glared. "Bridget was so right. You are big cheapskate."

I crossed my arms. "I am not a cheapskate. I'm frugal."

"Fancier word changes nothing. Do you want help with demon compulsions or not?"

I dropped my arms and stalked around Rasmus. He opened his eyes as I switched places with Mulan. He watched me closely as I turned on the water and checked the temperature. Mulan disappeared without either of us being aware.

"Don't turn my hair purple again. That lasted for days."

A laugh of surprise escaped me. I'd forgotten all about doing that. "No promises," I said.

His grin wrinkled the corners of his eyes. The expression reminded of the rare times he'd found humor in my company. He looked so appealing in that moment that I put my attention on his hair and kept it there.

Even though I denied myself the pleasure of exploring the rest of him, I took my sweet time rinsing out the conditioner and running my fingers over his scalp. When Rasmus closed his eyes, I knew it was because of me and it weakened my knees.

My fingers slowed as the urge to touch the smile on his lips all but shoved my self-control out of the way.

"Stop wasting all my water, witch. You can make lovesick cow-eyes at your new man later," Mulan said.

My fingers gripped his hair too tightly as I wrung it out.

"Sit up," I ordered.

After a low-chuckling Rasmus was upright in the chair, I grabbed the nearest towel and deftly wrapped it around his dripping strands.

I backed away and dried my hands on my pants.

Mulan smirked as she watched me. "I harmed no turtles in the making of my shaman tools. I collect those that die sustainably. Or I buy the shells from wildlife foundations. I buy in bulk."

I started to say something snarky, but then I realized she was wearing an actual vest made of small turtle shells daisy-chained together. In the center of the vest was a much larger shell. All of them had strange writing on them. The Wu Shaman held one shell in her hand as she walked toward us. Her other hand held a plethora of green scarfs.

Rasmus backed into me as Mulan advanced on him. "What do you want?"

Mulan peeked around Rasmus to look at me. "Do your job, witch."

"What job?" I asked, glaring at her.

"Hold him still so I can measure his crotch. One compulsion remains that I see, but it is a bad one. It has many layers. We will use bone oracle to clear the whole spot. It will take big turtle bone to cover everything, but I think I have something that will fit."

"Aran will measure me," Rasmus said. To make sure the Wu Shaman understood, he pulled me around and held me in front of him. "She's already seen everything. She won't mind."

Mulan's mouth twisted as she stared at him. Rasmus was the first to look away. His face was red as could be. I didn't know whether to laugh, be angry, or grin at Mulan because he wouldn't let her touch him.

Muttering what sounded like angry Chinese, Mulan stomped to a room off the one we were in and returned with a big box in her tiny hands.

"Put on gloves and you find turtle bone shell that covers him," she ordered, pushing the box into my hands.

Under a pair of disposable gloves had to be at least fifty empty tortoise shells similar to the biggest one comprising Mulan's shaman vest. They were of varying sizes, varying colors, and all had strange writing on them. It looked more like runic writing than the flowing script of any Chinese dialect. I felt true magick radiating from all of them.

Curiosity overrode all my complaints about her attitude. I placed the box of shells in the shampoo chair, put on the gloves, and gently sorted through them. Rasmus held the towel on his hair in place with one hand while he looked over my shoulder to watch.

"Is all this really necessary?" he asked in a low whisper.

"Apparently," I answered, pretending I wasn't searching for ever bigger tortoise shells in the box. Good for Rasmus, though, for not commenting on my search. None of them seemed big enough based on what I remembered about him, but I definitely wasn't voicing that out loud. "Conn said we need to see what the Wu Shaman can teach us about demons. She casts them out for a living."

"Maybe she simply scares them to death. She certainly makes me want to run screaming out of here."

I chuckled. "I had that reaction too when I first came here. Then she grew my hair six inches. Magick lessons are never comfortable, Rasmus. Ya're a big boy, though. I'm sure ya can handle yer discomfort for a bit longer."

I dug out the only shell I thought might work and held it

up for him to see. "Do ya think this would work as a jock cup for yer man bits?"

He pressed his lips together and nodded. "Yes, but I'm not getting naked in front of her to try it on."

"No one is getting naked," Mulan said, rolling her eyes.

Rasmus shrugged before glaring at her.

She turned to me. "He has enormous problems."

I would have laughed, but I knew her words weren't innuendo. She was reading his energy.

I set the box back down on the shampoo chair but left my gloves on. "We've got the shell. What's next?" I asked.

"Pick long green scarf and tie it around him like putting diaper on a baby. Hand me shell first."

I carried the shell we'd chosen over to her. She plugged in a ceramic knife before fishing a bottle of swirling black ink and a feather from her shaman duffle bag. "I can tell the symbols on the shells are magick. Are they part of your shaman work?"

"It is Ancient Chinese from the Shang Dynasty era. What I have written is my name and my credentials. I will add your long-haired lover's name and question to his shell. Then we will do magick to divine his answer. I give you only information today and not drive out demons. He has other problems that could interfere and make him sicker. I see drugs, but nothing normal. Most drugs turn energy black in humans. This is sticky gray and all over him."

"Ya just confirmed what the demoness told us. Rasmus has some amnesia about his life. We think he served in the military and they did something to make him forget. That's another mystery we have to solve. What's the heated knife do?"

Mulan turned to look at it and then at me. "I write his question on the shell, put magick on it and your lover, and then I take the shell and put the heated knife to one symbol to make it crack."

"I've read about that. The crack is supposed to make symbols that can be deciphered."

"Yes."

"Fascinating," I said. "Tell me about the history of your magick."

"During the five hundred years of the Shang Dynasty, Wu Shamans were female and male. Every shaman had their specialty. There was great respect for shaman magick. Then came the great division."

"There's always a great division when things are going well," I said.

Mulan nodded. "Women became responsible for all religions. Men became responsible for all governments. Eventually, power-hungry emperors decided religion was not needed by their people. They called themselves *Wu* without knowing what it meant. They pretended to divine answers to questions and to heal, but they could do neither. There are few shamans left with my skills. My family made me call myself a 'natural healer' to hide what I was."

"I'm glad ya don't feel the same need to hide yerself here in Salem. We're a city full of witches, but I feel like there's room for all kinds of magickals in this town."

Mulan didn't comment. "Tie scarf like diaper now. I'm almost ready."

I picked the longest green scarf and walked to Rasmus with it. Pressing his lips into a thin line, he crossed his arms and spread his legs. I stared at his crotch trying to decide how to go about it.

"Like wrestler," Mulan said with a gallon of impatience dripping from her words.

"Wrestler?" I muttered.

"Think sumo," Rasmus whispered. "Twice around the waist, and then through the legs until you can tuck the end into the waist band."

"Good idea," I said, and did as he suggested. There was barely enough cloth.

"Here," Mulan said, handing the shell to me. "I added his name and a question asking where the demon compulsions are and how many he has on him."

"Thank ya. Where does it go?"

"Inside green scarf. He cannot touch it. You put it in place."

I didn't dare look at Rasmus when I heard him grunt. "Are ya messing with us?" I asked her.

"What mess?" she demanded, looking around with a glare. "I keep spotless shop. There is no mess here. Not ever. Mess is bad for chi. Do what I said."

Rasmus frowned as Mulan walked to check her heated knife. "If there was a bossy contest between the two of you, my money would be on her. What's she going to do with that knife?"

I laughed. "Well, that was certainly a sideways compliment. Call out if I get this situated wrong."

I pulled out the scarf and put the shell into place with one try. When I raised my head to let him know, he was smirking down at me. I shrugged. "It's hard to miss with a package like yers."

He looked off instead of smiling directly at me. I reminded myself that Rasmus had a missing wife and had potentially fathered a demon baby. My libido didn't care about those things, but I did.

I turned to face Mulan. "Done."

188

"Move away. I need your witchy energy out of his personal space."

Holding up my hands, I walked as far away as the small room allowed.

"Will this hurt?" Rasmus asked her.

Mulan looked over at me and smirked. "Only men ever ask that question. Women lift chin and wait. I don't know how men ever rule over so much." She looked back at Rasmus. "It is like taking a picture with your cell phone. The shell receives imprint of your energy from the place where the compulsion was placed."

She picked up a staff I hadn't noticed before then. An assortment of things were tied on the end pointing skyward. Mulan murmured an incantation and power came out of her. It widened into a bubble that surround Rasmus. He stood inside it looking around in awe as she chanted. Eventually, the bubble left him and got absorbed back into Mulan. Outside of her chanting, the entire process was silent.

"Bring me the shell now," she said. "He can't touch it."

Sighing at her bossy orders, I walked back to Rasmus. I looked up into his confused eyes as I reached inside his scarf diaper. "Is that a hard turtle shell in yer diaper scarf, or are ya just happy to see me?"

His chuckle wafted over me, filling me with a delight I hadn't experienced in years. I held the shell in one hand while I undid the scarf with my other. The gloves took some of the fun out of it but left enough to have me smiling.

I carried both back to Mulan. "Here ya go."

She lifted the hot knife and pointed to surface. "Set it there. Put the scarf back with the others."

When I came back, Rasmus had also walked closer.

Mulan took a seat and held the heated knife over the shell.

She traced the writing in the air above the additional part she'd written, while simultaneously she spoke it all aloud in her own language. Then, very cautiously, she touched the knife to one symbol. The smell of the shell burning filled the small space.

She chanted again then lifted the knife, eased back, and studied the spot it had gently burned. A second or two later, the shell exploded into too many pieces to count. Some pieces disintegrated into nothing but dust.

"What does that mean?" Rasmus asked.

I had the same question, but Mulan's expression was one of confusion.

"The demons don't want him to know what they did to him." She pointed at the pieces. "One just gave his life to thwart my divination. Wherever he or she was, they exploded in front of everyone. It will take centuries for that demon to reform. Your American demons aren't used to dealing with someone like me, so they thought we would not notice failsafe."

"No need for ya to worry about protecting yerself from them, Mulan. They probably think I did that to them," I said with a shrug. "And I can live with that. But now what can we do?"

Mulan stood and sighed. "I will give your man a haircut, and then you go bargain with demons to remove them."

I blinked at her matter-of-factness. "Is breaking their magick beyond yer skills?"

Mulan looked at Rasmus and then back at me. "If we cast out the demons, we might turn him into human vegetable. Better to find other way. I will not charge you for this—just for haircut."

Rasmus turned his back and walked across the room. The towel fell from his hair to the floor. He didn't seem to notice.

Mulan and I both watched him. "Thank you for trying," I told her.

"It's okay. I miss my work," she said. "Maybe you need my help again sometime."

"If I ever go into business for myself, I'll hire ya to help me."

Mulan shook her head. "No, I will stay here. Ireland is not for me."

That's right. I had said I would go home when this was done. Ma must have shared my entire life story with the Wu Shaman because Mulan seemed to know more about my plans than I did.

"Let's go cut his hair," she said firmly, shaking off her failure as she removed her vest.

She put her shaman outfit into the box with the shells we didn't choose and added the scarfs to it as well. When she finished, the only item left out was the now cooling ceramic knife.

"I can't fix your man, but I can make him look good. I will also pray to the ancestors to make your quest to free him successful. They may intercede once they know I failed them."

I shook my head. "Ya didn't fail yer ancestors. The demons won this round, but we'll win in the end."

As usual, Mulan didn't stay to listen to me. She took off at a near run and left us to follow her. I guided a stoic Rasmus to the main room and into Mulan's chair.

He smiled at people and nodded when asked questions but was otherwise silent the whole time... and stayed quiet on our trip home. His hair looked amazing, but his expression was like looking into a void. I'd seen wraiths with more animation.

Confronting Lilith seemed to be the next logical option to free Rasmus from his compulsions. My initial task of finding an open demon portal had grown to include finding out the secrets Rasmus couldn't remember keeping.

But there was also the whole military connection that was unexplained too. That path would lead Rasmus to more truths about himself. And I was pretty sure it would reveal that he was not a demon hunter or a human.

Chapter Eighteen

Dinner was a sullen affair. Rasmus was still upset over Mulan's revelations. Conn was frustrated that he was being lied to by demons under compulsions that warped their version of the truth. We had reached a point where every direction led to lies and more lies.

I'd ordered Chinese food—probably because Mulan was on my mind—but none of us were hungry enough to do it justice. We'd be eating leftovers for days if this moping didn't stop.

"What're we doing?" I asked, breaking the silence. "I made a promise to find an open demon portal, but I don't think that's a real problem. The real problem seems to be the demon hunters and demons potentially being in business together. Are they keeping me busy? Or distracted? Why not just leave me where I was?"

Conn shifted in his chair and looked at me. "That is a good question."

I nodded. "And Rasmus seems at the center of everything. Why?"

"His past is unknown," Conn said.

"His magick is hidden, even from him," I said. "The demon hunters saved him, but they also used him to keep me busy and to cheerlead for Jack."

Rasmus lifted his head to look between us. I guess that question was on his mind as well.

Conn put down his fork and frowned. "They're using you —using us—to find Lilith and her caste."

I shrugged. "Probably... yet it's something we haven't been able to do. Lilith has outsmarted us."

"And now Mulan—the most infamous Wu Shaman in all of China—experienced the second failure of her life because of us," Conn said.

"Second failure?"

Conn nodded. "Mulan failed to remove a demon from her sister and her family publicly shamed her for it. I looked into the situation after we met—her sister was never possessed. She faked it to get Mulan out of the country. Mulan still blames herself because she feels she should have known about her sibling's hatred of her. She should have suspected."

"What happened to the sister?"

"Her faked demon possession caused people to lose faith in her parents as well. The family lost their herb farm, their status as healers, and all their prosperity. Mulan sends money home to them every month. They guilt her into it. The parents now run a laundry and the sister works the counter."

My disgusted grunt was loud. "Mulan's tough on everyone, but it sounds like she's being too tough on herself."

Rasmus jumped in... finally. "The demon compulsion alone isn't why Mulan's divination attempt failed. All she was doing was looking for information, but she couldn't see anything because of whatever else was done to me. A demon gave his life to keep it hidden. What is so important about me that someone would guard the secrets of my past with their life?"

"That's an excellent question," I said.

Conn grunted in agreement. "We have two paths. One is to branch off this quest and look for the secrets the demon hunters are hiding about Rasmus."

I nodded. "Or we could chase after Lilith and force her to remove the compulsions from him. Since we don't know where she is, that path is a little murkier. Splitting up yesterday didn't get us anywhere. Should we flip a coin to choose a direction for tomorrow?"

Conn crossed his arms. "I think I know where Lilith is hiding. She's surrounded herself with demons who led me in a circle. When my search ended where it started, I wondered why that was the case."

"Do ya think she's somewhere inside the circle?" I asked.

"Yes," Conn said. "And she's here in Salem. Her caste may be running a shelter for unwed mothers. How else could she get the medical help she needs for her pregnant human form?"

"That's as brazen as it is practical," I said.

Conn shrugged. "That's Lilith. She's the queen of subtlety when it serves her purpose. It was one of things I loved about her."

I looked at Rasmus who now leaned on the table with his face hidden in his hands. "Ya seem to be the one at the center of all universes. What would ya like to do?"

It took him nearly a full minute, but Rasmus finally dropped his hands. "The Albany demoness said Lilith captured demon hunters and enslaved them. If they aren't dead, we need to go after them. They were my team. I need to know what happened to them and why I was made to believe they were dead."

I nodded. "Are ya okay with that, Conn?"

Conn nodded without verbally responding. We both knew facing Lilith, and his past with her, was inevitable, but I understood why his feelings made him not want to rush that moment. My familiar, friend, and tormentor was a badass, and a truly vicious one when angry, but he had a single weakness that my family had exploited for thousands of years. Connlander of the Fir Bolg was an honorable creature who would sacrifice himself to save all his people, no matter what they did.

"Can ya babysit while I go visit my mother, Conn? She has something of Da's that I need to borrow. I'd take Rasmus with me, but I think it's best to keep our kidnap victim a secret. If Fiona is there, she'll run to Jack without a single thought."

"I thought your daughter visited you in prison. Why is she not on Team Mom?" Rasmus asked.

That was his lame attempt at making a popular joke, but I gave him points for not being a sad sack. "She's on Team Dad because Jack bought her a fancy car just like his."

"Since when are Honda Civics considered fancy cars?"

I looked at Conn. "Does Jack own a Honda Civic?"

"Yes. He owns five cars total, but the fanciest one is the blue Lamborghini. It's too small for my tastes. I prefer his Porsche Cayenne. He bought Fiona a red Jeep Cherokee exactly like the one he bought for himself so they could be car twins."

Rasmus blinked in shock.

I rolled my eyes. "Well, I'm glad I'm not the one paying the insurance on her car and I'm glad he didn't buy her the

Lamborghini. At least Jack gave her something that won't get her ass kicked at university."

"*Five cars?*" Rasmus repeated.

I gaped at the amnesiac demon hunter. How was Jack's love of toys a problem when Jack putting me in prison wasn't?

Compelled or not, Rasmus defied my understanding of males. I'd never met one like him.

I stood, carried my dishes to the dishwasher, and looked at the boys. "Tidy up when ya're done. If Mulan comes to the house, I don't want her finding a mess."

"Is she coming?" Conn asked, looking almost cheerful.

A corner of my mouth lifted. I doubted the Wu Shaman would do anything I asked at this point, but I would invite her along just to keep Conn balanced.

"My instincts are humming," I said to him, not really answering.

A horn beeped outside, which told me my ride to the hotel had arrived.

"I'll find my own way home later. Don't wait up," I told the men.

"You could have driven the car," Rasmus said a grunt.

And risk being tracked to the hotel where my family was hanging out? No thanks. But I smiled at the offer.

"I don't know how long Ma will keep me there. The two of ya might need to make a fast escape before I return. It's best I leave it for ya, just in case."

Rasmus nodded but didn't look happy.

I waved goodbye before the door closed behind me.

MA WAS awake and Fiona had just left. If I believed in guardian angels, I would have said one was definitely looking out for me, but I followed a different path in my faith. Mine stretched backwards in time to before people counted time like they do now. I saw myself merely as the latest servant of one of the many gods looking out for all of us. The work I did was done by many before me and would go on long after my time ended.

"Are ya sure using the ring is a good idea, Aran?"

I nodded to Ma's question before putting it into words. "I don't need to use the ring in the literal sense. I'm hoping the mere sight of it resolves things peacefully. Seven years away has lessened all demons fear of me. They see me as weaker instead of stronger because I let myself be put in prison. I need an edge so I don't end up wiping out an entire caste simply to remind them of who and what I am."

"Alright then, violent daughter. Ya were the one who was chosen by The Dagda. I have faith in yer intentions."

"Yes, but I don't serve the power of the ring, Ma. We both know Da was chosen as the backup guardian. They always pick someone of another faith to do so, and I don't think I'm the proper candidate. I will return it to ya for safe keeping after I've settled things down. I can't believe the ring hasn't drawn another champion to it yet. Da's been gone for a good while."

"An angel will bring someone here when the time is right. I'm more concerned about other things. What if the power of the ring doesn't work like Celtic magick? What if it conflicts with yer witching spells? Ya might encounter bigger problems than if yer bluff fails."

I laughed at her concerns. If ya needed to put a label on what I believed, I suppose I was a modern pagan. All I knew about other beliefs was what I'd learned in school. The ring belonged to the mystery schools of Arabia. Da's explanation was that the ring belonged to King Solomon of Israel by a god who gave him not one ring to control demons, but two of them. I guess Conn and the version of me at that time didn't travel globally.

I smiled to reassure my mother. "If anything bad happens from my plan, I guess I'd head to Rome to have a talk with the new owner of the original ring."

Ma huffed. "You'll not find that person in Rome, girl. People there would slit the person's throat to get at its power. Judgers don't accept that such power only can be used by the one chosen to use it. While walking on this plane, the original ring's guardian is reduced from being an angel to being a human. He's going to be as vulnerable as ya would be without The Dagda looking out for ya."

I thought of The Dagda and the years he trained me. It made Ma's theory even more believable. "I humbly accept that neither of King's Solomon's rings would ever work for me, Ma. Hopefully, the sight of it will scare the demons out of their secrets, even though I'm starting to think the evil behind all of this is totally human. We both know evil humans are a far worse problem than demons making mischief."

"Yes, we know that. Alright, then. I'm done trying to talk ya out of it using it."

Ma reached into her shirt and pulled out a polished silver chain with three precious rings on it. The first was Da's wedding band, which she put on there after he was cremated because his energy lingered on the gold still.

The second was a ring Da's mother—my paternal grandmother, and as I learned, Conn's previous keeper—had given Ma when I was born. I didn't know what my grandmother's ring did, but as a child, I used to ask Ma to let me wear it. Ma always said she'd let me wear it one day. That never happened back then. I figured I'd get it the day my mother left this world for the next, along with her and Da's wedding rings.

I couldn't bear to think about that day, so I simply didn't think of it at all.

The third ring, though, did not belong to our family and never had. The third ring Ma carried was one Da had been paid to protect during his lifetime. His magick from The Dagda hadn't blossomed fully in the same way his mother's and mine had, but Da's pure heart and kind soul had qualified him for a holy task few walking the Earth were ever deemed worthy of doing.

Ma, whose greatest magickal gift was laying curses, was still in awe of the being who carried the original of the ring Da guarded. She always said ring's true keeper was an angel come to Earth for this one purpose. Angel or not, I knew someone powerful came to Da shortly after I was born and asked that he protect the ring's twin.

It lay inert and had remained so all the years Da had worn it. There was no doubt in my mind, though, that the ring had latent power. Nor did I doubt that a magickal transference would occur if anything ever happened to the original. My instincts alone informed me of this, but I also saw the shining white light of its aura.

No matter what belief system ya followed on this planet, there were objects that were holy and those that were a threat to mankind. Both had to be respected and I took that wisdom to heart.

Ma unfastened the chain and removed two of the three rings. "I've been meaning to give ya Mother O'Malley's ring for years. She meant for ya to one day have it, but I didn't trust yer husband not to talk ya out of it. That's yet another thing I suppose I should have told ya sooner. Maybe I should have sent the ring to ya by Fiona when she visited ya in prison."

I put my hand over one of mother's. "Let me save ya from uttering apologies every time ya tell me something ya've kept from me. I'm grateful ya kept our family stuff from Jack. I'm sorry I didn't see his true self sooner. Just say yer piece when ya need to and I promise not to get offended. Every story simply reminds me that I'm human and can be fooled."

"Goddess, Aran... no one is ever going to be harder on ya than ya are on yerself. The man was yer husband. Of course, ya wanted to trust him. Now hush yer self-effacing diatribe and put on yer grandmother's ring."

I took the ring from Ma's outstretched fingers and slipped it onto the ring finger of my left hand. It filled the spot where my wedding ring used to sit. The delicate band sized itself to my finger as I watched. The cluster of stones vibrated against me in recognition.

"Look at it glowing on ya. I know how ya love shortcuts, Aran, but don't use any harsh jewelry cleaner on those stones. They're natural. Just use water for the dirt and cleanse it on a cluster of amethyst once in a while."

"Yes, Ma," I answered. There was no reason to fuss back.

The day Bridget O'Malley stopped fussing at me would be the day she passed on. With my luck, her ghost would stand beside me for the rest of my life complaining about how I did things wrong or didn't do something right.

"Are ya sure about giving me this ring, Ma? Ya've had it a long time. I know how bereft ya can feel without something ya've had for a lifetime."

"Yes, I'm sure," she said softly. "But thank ya for asking. It never glowed for me, which is a sure sign of a rightful owner."

She held out the other ring and shook it until I finally took it. "Maybe if ya wear this for a while, the angels will come to stop ya. Then we'll both be freed of the responsibility."

I laughed at her teasing. "Are ya saying they might fear I will be a bad influence on the ring?"

Ma laughed at my words and shrugged. "I would never say that to yer face because I'm yer mother, but an angel would probably tell ya the truth. I hear they're brutal."

My grin was wide as I slipped the quiet twin of King Solomon's Seal onto my right hand. Like my Grandmother O'Malley's ring, it also sized itself to fit my finger, though my hands were much smaller than Da's. As the metal warmed to my skin, I felt a bolt of unfamiliar energy shoot through my hand and travel up my arm. Once that energy rested on both my shoulders, the energy traveled up to my head and also across my chest until it settled around my heart.

I didn't feel more powerful after all that movement, but I felt like it was talking to me. The message seemed to be one of relief. Had it not felt safe hanging around Ma's neck? Or had it been worried for her?

Conn's mantle of power had always felt sentient to me. I definitely could command it, but it also advised me in ways I couldn't explain. Finding out King Solomon's second ring possessed its own sentience was a surprise I hadn't anticipated.

Rather than sensing the hibernation of its power, I felt it striving to accomplish something and knew I was a means to an end for that goal. I could hardly be mad since I was planning to use the ring to scare the demons into answering my questions, but I was too tired to consider all the moral implications tonight.

Bending to kiss my mother's cheek, I hugged her to me. "Thank ya for loaning me the ring Da guarded. I promise I'll be careful with it. Do ya know what Grandmother O'Malley's ring does?"

"No. It was only a pretty bauble on my hand," Ma said, patting my cheek. "I'm sure ya will learn its intention one day. Be safe going back."

"I will. I'll be taking one of the taxis in front of the hotel. The boys are waiting up for me. Conn sent a text that they were watching sports on TV."

"Conn missed ya something fierce, Aran."

I nodded as she walked me to the door. "I missed him too, but I'd do it again to keep Jack away from him."

"Jack's magickal arrow wouldn't have killed Conn, but he would have had to kill Jack to get away. Being widowed in that manner would have created a much worse situation than yer divorce has. Ya made the right decision in waiting for Fiona to grow up some. I'm proud of ya for doing the harder thing."

"Thanks, Ma. It helps to hear ya say it."

Ma held the door open for me while she said the rest of her goodbye. "Stop looking back and wondering what might have been different. I swear on Goddess Danu's good name that Jack Derringer was leading ya to yer current dilemma since the day the two of ya met. Turn loose being angry that he disappointed ya and do the spell to call yer powers back before ya tackle the demons. It will improve yer clarity."

"Okay, Ma. I'll do the spell before I face them. I promise."

"See that ya keep that promise to yerself. Ya need the practice," Ma said, closing the door in my face.

Chapter Nineteen

R asmus noticed my rings the moment he stepped into the kitchen. "Did you remarry while visiting your mother last night? If so, he has terrible taste in wedding bands."

My first thought was Rasmus woke up on the wrong side of the bed this morning. Letting his snarkiness slide, I held out my left hand where my grandmother's ring rested. Seven years ago, I'd removed my wedding band the first night at the cottage and cried myself to sleep afterward.

I had kept the simple gold band Jack gave me only because ya didn't throw genuine gold away. Plus, it had Jack's energy on it. In a pinch, I could use my old wedding band to put a curse on him... or ask Ma to do it. She was more precise.

I had no idea what Grandmother O'Malley's ring did other than look pretty. I knew for sure that Ma was going to miss wearing it. Any woman would miss a gorgeous ring with beautiful stones. I'd have to buy Ma a replacement one day.

I looked up from my musing and smiled at Rasmus. "This ring belonged to my paternal grandmother. Ma gave it to me last night when I visited her."

Rasmus stared at me for a long time without blinking. "Did she give you the man's ring too?" he asked, nodding to my other hand.

I glanced at the incognito artifact. Instead of showing the elaborate symbols of the Seal of Solomon, the top of the ring had turned solid gray while I slept. As its wearer, I still felt its latent power, but it looked like a common man's ring now. Why was it hiding its identity from Rasmus?

I couldn't guess its motivations, but it was my nature to honor such things in all magickal creatures and artifacts. I'd gone against enough of them during my training with The Dagda to learn the penalties of defying their wishes. Magickal sentience was not to be taken lightly.

My curiosity about the seal was roused further by its stealth, but I enjoyed playing it safe when I could. Smiling, I told Rasmus what truth I felt I could safely share with him. "Da got this ring shortly after I was born. He wore it until the day he passed. Ma was feeling sentimental last night and loaned it to me. It makes me feel close to him, but it's not mine to keep forever."

Nodding, Rasmus finally lowered his tense body into a chair at the table. "Sometimes I wonder what my life was like before I forgot everything. Did I like my parents? Why haven't they come to see me? I see children and their parents together, but not a single warm feeling rises inside me. It's like my childhood never happened at all. Wouldn't the feelings still be there if I'd ever experienced them?"

My gaze softened at his story. I got a cup and poured him coffee. "I can't imagine what it's like to not remember ever climbing a tree or riding a bike. That would be traumatizing for me."

"It's maddening," he said.

Conn came into the kitchen and halted. "I see Bridget finally gave you Murieann's ring."

"Ma gave me two rings last night," I told him, and held up both hands.

Conn scooted out a chair and sat. "Did that granite ring belong to your father?"

The penultimate demon had no reaction to it at all when he should have been cussing me. Okay. Now, I was really curious. I ran a finger across the top of the gray stone in the ring. The carved symbols of the seal were definitely not there any longer.

I stared at the ring for a long time. When Conn concluded his observation had upset me, I let him think it.

"I'm sorry you still miss him so much, Aran. I promise you that the feeling of loss lessens in time."

I smiled at Conn. He should have been screaming bloody murder over me wearing King Solomon's Seal. Instead, he was yawning and trying to wake up.

Smiling, I poured my oblivious, non-frightened demon king a cup of coffee. The ring's incognito act totally ruined my plans to use it to threaten Lilith's demon caste.

What choice did I have, though, except to keep its secrets until it was ready to reveal itself? I still wasn't sorry I borrowed it. A magickal artifact this sentient was too dangerous for Ma to be carrying around her neck.

Maybe Ma was right. Maybe now that I had it, a true guardian would show up for it. Surely by now the original caretaker knew Da has passed on.

I made omelets while I thought about both men's reactions to the rings. After setting food in front of them, I carried my own plate to the table.

We'd fallen into an odd camaraderie since breaking that one

compulsion on Rasmus. All talking ceased as we ate. When the meal was finished, Conn rose and took our plates to the sink. I'd never seen him be so domestic before. Ma must have insisted he clean up after himself during the last seven years. Grinning, I wondered how often Conn had stayed in dog form just to avoid doing so.

I stared at the table to hide my smile as I sipped my coffee. "I have some spells to do before we search for Lilith. I'll do them this afternoon."

Rasmus frowned. "Spells? What kind of spells?"

I moved my gaze to his. "Spells are serious business to witches. And *my* spells are *my* business. Ya don't get to ask a witch that."

He ran a hand through his hair. "Sorry. I didn't sleep well last night."

"So I gathered," I said, sipping my coffee and practicing my calm. "Ya sound ready to explode this morning."

Rasmus nodded and cupped his hands behind his head. He stared at the ceiling. "I'm restless and taking it out on you. That's not fair. I'm truly sorry."

Well, look at that. The man actually could apologize without anything bad happening to him or his tongue. I smiled at him. "Ya're forgiven, Rasmus. And I'll be sure to put some sugar in yer next cup to sweeten ya up."

His snort was soft but the corners of his mouth did lift a little.

I kept on talking. "While Conn's out looking for our demons this morning, I'm going back to talk to Mulan. Ya can entertain yerself here or tag along with me, but I want to talk to her alone. It should only take me five minutes so long as Mulan's not with a client."

"What are you planning?" Rasmus asked.

"To ask for her help again."

"Which explains nothing," he replied.

"Ever hear of winging it, Rasmus? Or going with the flow?" I sipped my coffee and stared at him over the cup. "My instincts are singing about Mulan. I can't turn my back."

Conn poured himself a refill and leaned against the counter drinking it. "If the Wu Shaman comes along with us, she will see my true form."

I sipped my coffee and nodded. "It will be good for her. Never hide yer true self from someone ya like, Conn. They figure ya out anyway."

"Is it still my job to locate Lilith?"

He sounded depressed about things, but I couldn't let his reticence sway what had to be done. We all needed answers— me, Rasmus, and Conn.

"If ya can find Lilith that would help us," I said, swiveling in my chair. "Even a general direction of the caste would be helpful. If ya can't find them, maybe Mulan can. Her magick operates differently. I doubt the demons living in America will be prepared for her. She will be our element of surprise."

His nod was short and brief. I felt terrible for putting him through this, but he'd insisted on helping. "If ya want, I'll tell Mulan ya have a block because of yer history with this caste. I'll use ya as my excuse to talk her into coming with us."

Conn's chin lifted into the air. "No need to fabricate a story to spare me. I'm too old to mourn what was never truly meant to be mine. I'll find her eventually. I'll find all of them, even if some have to go away for a while when I get done with my search."

Which in Conn's terms meant he'd rip them apart and force them into a regeneration cycle. If that level of violence helped us get to the bottom of this mystery, I was all for it.

"I'll drive you to see the Wu Shaman," Rasmus said.

The granite ring grew heavy as a stone. "Let's not take yer car," I said. "Let's call for a ride. It might prove less of an adventure."

Rasmus frowned even deeper. "Why? Do you think they're tracking me?"

I shrugged, but the ring grew warm against my finger. Apparently, it had decided to help my cause. "I think they're tracking one or more of us. Or keeping track of us. We don't want to lead them to Lilith and her caste if that's what they're after."

Rasmus straightened. "Why would they want Lilith?"

"I don't know that they do yet," I said carefully. "I think what they want is leverage over a demoness the largest caste considers their next queen."

"The child," Rasmus spat out. "They intend to kidnap her child when it's born."

I kept my gaze from his. I knew a lot of things about demons that I wasn't going to share with Rasmus. But I would share what I could.

"Demons—the former *Fir Bolg* ones of Irish legend—don't bear children often. When one comes every few hundred years, it's because they are a gift allowed by the same gods that gave me responsibility for keeping them out of trouble. If Lilith is pregnant, she will protect the child with everything and everyone under her power, as any mother would."

Rasmus rose from his seat, slammed both hands on the table, and then walked out of the kitchen.

Conn sighed and crossed his arms. "You may have lost your travel buddy this morning."

"It's a matter of honor. He may not remember who he was or where he came from or even what his life was supposed to be like but doing good drives him anyway. He's feeling about the demon hunters the way I'm feeling about Jack. The only difference is that I've had seven years to get used to Jack's treachery. Rasmus has only had a few days."

"You like him," Conn said.

I shrugged. "I lust for him a little... and I feel for his dilemma. Neither of those are the sort of thing a woman should let her guide her decisions about a man."

"Are you forty or a hundred?"

I snorted. "I admitted to feeling lust, Conn. What more do ya want from me?"

"I want a sign that Jack didn't break your heart so badly that it will never mend. Not only did Murieann never marry again after her husband left her, but she never dated either. Handsome men would come along. I could tell she found them tempting but none were ever tempting enough. Sometimes a physical connection is all that makes our lives tolerable. She died alone with no lover saddened by her loss."

"And then ya came to serve her naïve grandchild who was too busy carrying her own child to think straight."

"You were full of light and life. You still are. I was grateful for you."

I got up from my chair and went to put my arms around Conn's waist. He released a wistful sigh and hugged me back.

"Caring is not a weakness. It fuels magick of all sorts," I told him.

"I know. I still want to kill him for what he did to you."

"Rasmus or Jack?" I asked.

Conn answered with a wicked grin. "Take your pick. I'll see you this afternoon."

"Good. I need ya to keep an eye on Rasmus while I do my spells. He's edgy today and I can't tell why."

Chapter Twenty

Rasmus opted to wait for me in a coffee shop a few doors down on Mulan's block. I gave Rasmus my phone so he'd have something to do.

The coffee shop was one Conn and I used to frequent. And to think that a Wu Shaman was running a business so close to us and we never knew it. Or at least, I didn't know. I suspected Conn knew. He'd probably been keeping an eye on Mulan since the day they met.

She was with an older client when I walked inside her shop. I waved when she saw me and took a seat. Ten minutes later, the woman was rolled up and under a dryer. Ma got that done when she came. Ma liked a fluffy heat style set on rollers that "made the curls last" as she put it, while I settled for a damp blow dry on the best of days.

At the length my hair was now, I didn't bother to dry it at all most of the time. I used a curling iron for special occasions or simply twisted it up. Fixing my hair every day took too much time. I was not one of those women.

My daughter, though, was a girly-girl like her grandmother.

She'd fiddle with her strands for hours until she was satisfied they looked artfully chaotic. She'd gel her hair into submission and then shoot it with something called a freeze spray to make sure it stayed in shape.

I used to wonder what Fiona would have done with power like mine. Would she have refused to fight if it messed up her hair? The thought had me smiling.

"Where is my biggest failure today?" Mulan asked by way of greeting.

I intended to teach that woman to properly say hello even if it killed both of us. "If you're referring to Rasmus, he's having coffee down the street. I came alone to ask ya something. With those compulsions still in place in his pelvic area, I don't trust Rasmus to hear this conversation."

"I have quit Wu Shaman work. This is hair shop only. Do you need shampoo and set? Or styling lessons for your unruly curls?"

I motioned to the shop door and outside. The reluctant Wu Shaman sighed heavily but nodded before following me out.

"I think you know why I'm here, Mulan. I need your Wu Shaman services."

"No. I am failure. Find another who is success."

"There's not another Wu Shaman in this country, much less in Salem."

"There is no Wu Shaman here. There is only former one who should retire in shame."

I crossed my arms and glared. If I didn't give Mulan something bigger to feel than her own self-pity, she wasn't going to help me.

"Ya need to quit whining about what happened to Rasmus, which is still unexplainable, and help me figure out his bigger problems. To do that, I need to locate a demon caste and constrain them if they get fight-y with me. Conn is too compromised to be of any use, which is why I need ya so desperately."

As impossible as I found it, Mulan's frown deepened. It was like watching a total eclipse of her humanity. The darkness on the Wu Shaman's face scared me and I wasn't easy to scare.

"What is wrong with high demon?" Mulan demanded.

"High demon?" I asked, smiling at the term.

Mulan waved off my question. "This is what my people call demon king."

"Oh," I said. "Well, the queen of the demon caste I need to find is an old girlfriend of Conn's. He seems to be letting her slip under all his radar. Maybe he's doing it on purpose or maybe he's not. I can't tell because he gets depressed at the mention of her name. I know Conn has a thing for ya and I was hoping ya might distract him."

"High demon has thing for many women. I'm a short nothing in his eyes."

"It's true that he enjoys them," I said, because it was true. Conn did not practice celibacy. "But he sincerely likes ya, Mulan. He respects ya. He was married once and that lasted a century. He is a loyal lover when motivated to be one. I think ya could be competition for his ancient interest in Lilith."

"This Lilith is now demon queen?" she asked.

I nodded. "And she's very pregnant with what could be the first demon-human hybrid born in several millennia."

"Who is human father?"

I blew out a breath. "Rasmus. Or so he was told."

Mulan rubbed her forehead. "Such a child would have rights in both worlds—maybe power over both. Maybe villains have plans to use demon baby for big mischief."

"All that could be the case, but there's more happening here."

"Nothing is simple with you."

"Ya're not wrong," I said, smiling at her. "I suspect demon hunters want to steal the child. Or at least, that's what I'm thinking. The demon queen is as old as Connlander of the Fir Bolg, but not as powerful because she declined to serve out Conn's bargain with him."

"What is plan?"

I shook my head. "I don't know yet. All I know is that I have to disrupt what I do know even when I don't know what it means."

Mulan shook her head. "You talk complicated too."

Smirking was unavoidable. Not many could juggle my life. "I also think they're using Rasmus to track me. I think they want me to lead them to the Lilith which is why they let me out."

Mulan dropped her hands and stared. "Do you intend to save demon baby?"

"Yes... and the mother too. The problem is that Lilith has enslaved a bunch of demon hunters for reasons I don't know yet. So I have to free them from her. Ya could say that all of this is a hot mess to sort out, and ya would be right. It's not even clear who needs to be chastised and who will need to be destroyed. Also, there's a level of corruption within the demon hunter group. My ex is knee deep in it."

Her jaw dropped open. "You lead VERY complicated life. How do you sleep at night?"

I chuckled as I shrugged. "Here's one last thing. The demon hunters imprisoned me to keep me out of the way for seven years. They let me out just in time for that demon child to be born. I don't believe their timing was a coincidence."

Mulan turned her back to me and paced. People walking toward us saw her and crossed the street instead of passing by. The Wu Shaman must have quite the reputation in this neighborhood. Why did knowing that make me smile?

"Who is paying for this work?"

I blew out a breath. "No one. I have no client."

"Rasmus is client."

"No. He's merely a pawn in the game," I said.

"Then *you* are client. Or maybe *Connlander of Fir Bolg* is client."

I burst out laughing. Conn's expression would be priceless if I announced that Mulan considered him her client. "Given that I want ya to distract Conn from his old girlfriend, I guess Conn is sort of yer client. Personally, I'm going to consider ya my partner-in-crime."

"A Wu Shaman does not commit crimes, but I will not mind a temporary partnership with such powerful witch. If there is profit, we will share equally the wealth of it. Do you agree to my terms?"

I couldn't imagine what profit there would be in anything I had to do, but if thinking there might be some got Mulan on board with my plans... so be it. "If there is profit, we will split it four ways."

Mulan shook her head firmly. "Rasmus only get victim share of ten percent—no more."

I badly wanted to laugh again but didn't dare. The Wu Shaman took money too seriously. "Fine. Rasmus only gets a victim share. We will split the other ninety percent between the remaining three of us."

Mulan sent her dark hair swinging as she shook her head. "No, I should get fifty percent of ninety because high demon is my client and you come to me for help. I am most valuable person in our temporary partnership."

I crossed my arms, fought my mouth twitching in amusement, and glared back at her. "Do I look like I just got off the fecking boat from Ireland yesterday? Ya'll not be getting me to give ya a fifty percent share, Mulan. Ya'll take yer thirty percent of the remaining ninety and that's final."

Mulan held up her hands. "Fine, witch. You win this one. We will split our profit in thirds."

"*Unless* I have to recruit other magickals to help me," I added just to annoy her.

"Do not twist your panties. I will be all help you need," she assured me, and stuck out her hand.

I smiled back and nodded as I shook with her.

Mulan thought I was smiling was over the deal we'd just cut. What I was really smiling about was that I'd spent ten minutes standing on the street bargaining with a money-grubbing Wu Shaman over some imaginary profit that didn't exist.

"This needs to get done right away. Can ya help me today?" I asked at the end of our handshake.

"After last client—maybe mid-afternoon I help."

"That would fine. I have to go prepare, which takes several hours. We plan to follow some leads early this evening. Conn and I typically find it best to deal with demons in the early evening. Like us, they all have day jobs. Ya have to catch them after work."

She motioned me to follow her back inside and got me a card from beneath the welcome counter. She wrote a number on the back. "Text me address of where to meet you."

"Thanks. Conn or I will be in touch."

Chapter Twenty-One

I couldn't stop staring. Neither could Rasmus or Conn. Mulan's appearance had rendered all of us mute.

Her dark hair gleamed and her makeup cleverly kept yer attention focused on her red lips and lined eyes. The short red dress she wore ended several inches up her slender thighs and had cutouts in several other clever places, all of which indicated she wore nothing at all beneath the dress because there wasn't room for more clothing.

I looked absolutely ragged standing next to her in my snug jeans, white blouse, and denim jacket. The heeled boots Fiona gave me were my one saving grace. I wore no makeup at all because I had yet to purchase any. And worst of all, I'd pinned my mostly gray hair behind my head with a simple clip because I was too lazy to fix it. After frowning at it, Mulan never spared my hair or me another glance.

Every time Mulan smiled tonight, she aimed the full brilliance of her red lips and white teeth only in Conn's direction. Her efforts to hold his attention exceeded all my expectations. Conn couldn't look away from her.

We were all standing on the street waiting for him to tell us which way to go. I think Conn was still too stunned by Mulan to speak.

When she got tired of waiting on him, Mulan turned and narrowed her eyes. "This way," she said, heading off in that direction.

Conn followed her swinging hips without uttering a single word of protest.

I rolled my eyes at his weakness and glanced at Rasmus who was rubbing his mid-section. A memory of his abs rolled through my mind, but I pushed it away. "What's wrong?" I asked.

"Her presence makes my stomach hurt. It also makes me want to run away."

I smiled and took his arm to make him walk with me. I didn't want to lose sight of Mulan and Conn. "I think Conn has a similar reaction to Mulan."

"Yeah, but he chased right after her."

I smirked. "I thought all men loved the thrill of the chase."

"No man in his right mind would chase that woman. The Wu Shaman is dangerous."

"So am I," I reminded him.

Rasmus turned his head and stared down at me. "I have a different reaction to you."

"Oh, I'm quite aware of that. Mulan has all the attention tonight, but that was my agreement with her," I said with a laugh.

"No, you don't get it," Rasmus said, tugging us to a stop. He stared down at me. "I'm attracted to you."

"Okay. Well, I guess I'm flattered," I said, pulling gently away.

"That's not good enough," Rasmus said. "I want to make you aware of me. I want to make you lose sleep."

I glanced ahead where Conn and Mulan looked back. I held up a hand to signal for them to wait for us.

Rasmus put both his hands on my arms. "I dreamed I flew away from you last night. The moment that happened, I had a massive panic attack. It was worse than the one I had when I woke up in the hospital and couldn't remember anything. I don't want to fly away from you, Aran. I don't want to forget."

I studied his face. "Is this why ya were so grouchy this morning?"

"Yes," he said. "The idea of never seeing you again scares me."

I reached up and stroked his jaw. That was as far as I could reach.

"The magick holding ya captive has weakened. On some level, ya probably credit me with being the reason, but that's not necessarily true. The process will not be pleasant when the rest of yer compulsions get removed. Our bodies adapt to everything, even bad things. I can't spare ya the trauma, Rasmus. I truly wish I could. Ya're going to have to tough it out to get to the other side."

Rasmus tightened his grip, heard me hiss, and then softened his hold. I kept hold of his arm. I couldn't let him run away.

He turned until he could stare down at me. "Don't let me hurt anyone when it happens."

"Oh, I won't," I promised.

"Good," he said, bending his head until his lips grazed mine.

I stumbled away from his grip in shock. Before I could

recover, Rasmus linked our hands and dragged me along with him.

When the four of us were standing inches apart, I was still blinking like someone slapped me into a stupor. I hadn't been kissed by a man in over seven years, which explained my surprise, but that didn't explain all the magick streaking through me when his lips met mine.

There was something else happening between us.

I glanced down at my new rings while the others were talking. Grandmother O'Malley's ring shimmered on my left hand, warm and comforting. The twin of King Solomon's Seal on my right had turned the color of deep green jade. The energy in it thumped against my finger like a heartbeat. Had it recognized Rasmus? That would be extremely odd. But then so was that kiss out of nowhere.

Maybe the ring had been reacting to my reaction, which was definitely one of surprise.

We traipsed to a building with a sign that read "Sanctuary of Salem" on the front. Next door was a converted building that had been turned into residences. At the front door of the second building, two armed doormen stood guard.

Mulan's chocolate eyes turned golden. She turned to look at me. "There are many demons inside the building."

I nodded to show her I'd both heard and agreed. "How many more tricks do ya have up yer sleeve, Wu Shaman?"

She looked at her bare arms. "What do you mean? This dress has no sleeves. Do not confuse me with your misleading observations."

Conn covered his mouth to hide his smile. I looked at him. "Are ya doing okay there, Mr. High Demon?"

"Better than I imagined. Thank you for asking, Aran."

I smirked at his gratitude. "Shall we ask to see the queen?"

Conn held out his hand. "Mantle first," he suggested.

I nodded and took several steps away. I bowed my head as the familiar energy spread over me. It coated me in a translucent armor that could be seen through, except for the outline of a small golden shield resting over my mid-section. Any magick thrown at me would be returned to the thrower three-fold.

The doormen felt me change and looked in our direction. Everyone was in human form, but wearing the mantle of The Dagda, I could see all demons in their natural state. The two posing as human doormen were a dull red color with black horns curving back over their heads.

Like Conn, they were members of the imperial caste, or "imps" as we called them.

I walked around my posse and up to the doormen. "Tell yer queen that the daughter of The Dagda wishes to have a word with her."

They looked nervously over at Conn.

"Yer one and forever king is waiting to see how I'm received. Do as I ask and everything will be fine. We're only seeking information... for now."

"Our queen is refusing all visitors," one finally said.

I looked his way. "I can understand why. Being so close to giving birth, though, I figured she'd want the father of her babe to be with her. If the rumors are true, she's going to need him to prove the babe's parentage."

Their panicked gaze went to Conn again, but I stepped in front of my posse to block their view of him.

"Gentlemen, ya both know Connlander of the Fir Bolg is not the father. Lilith betrayed him and he hasn't forgotten that nor forgiven her. Now, I'm losing patience with ya, so call her and tell her I'm here." I nodded to them and pointed. "When ya get yer answer, I'll be right there waiting."

He was gone for three minutes and then came back. "You and the conflicted one can come in. The priestess and demon king must wait out here." Then he turned on his heel and went back to his post at the door.

"She's not a priestess," I said, yelling at the doormen. "My friend is a Wu Shaman from China and a master at casting out demons. I would recommend ya act respectful around her."

"Am I supposed to be the conflicted one?" Rasmus asked quietly.

I nodded. "Ya're the only one left, so I think we can safely assume that, yes. On the plus side, if ya were the father of the queen's babe, they probably would have used a more descriptive moniker for ya."

"Is going in there safe?"

"No," I admitted. "But if they attack us, Conn will transport in there before I could say his name. He's tied to the armor I wear. I'm literally wearing his energy."

Rasmus soberly nodded. I didn't blame him for having reservations. I had them every time I dealt with demons, but this had to be done. There were too many secrets and I wanted to reveal all I could.

We walked to the doormen who nodded to us. I looked over my shoulder and nodded to Conn. He transformed into a demon, but a much larger one with a golden crown that went over his horns.

Mulan's squeal of surprise was followed by a dancing fit punctuated with stream of that language she spoke when stressed. I snickered and waved at Conn.

I faced the guards. "Ya both should keep in mind that ya will ultimately answer to yer true king for yer actions. Since ya did what I asked, I have no fight with ya. In fact, I'm grateful for yer cooperation."

Rasmus and I walked into the lobby with the doormen glaring at our backs. Inside, we ran into a crowd of demon hunters with glassy eyes. They noted our presence and stiffened. Maybe they sensed my magick. Or maybe it was Rasmus hissing in recognition beside me that snagged their attention.

I reached out to ground him with my grip. "Are these men the ones ya thought died?"

Rasmus's eyes blazed with anger as he nodded. "Yes. Are they still living?"

"Yes, they're being compelled to be our welcome committee. I'm sure this was intentional."

Rasmus growled low. "Are they supposed to be a threat? Or are they a trap?"

I turned to stare up at him. "I know ya're angry and I don't blame ya but try to keep a cool head here. I'm choosing to see the presence of these missing men as a show of good faith. I suggest ya do the same. If ya lose yer temper, we lose our advantage."

His tight nod was the only answer I got. The demon hunters lined up on either side of us forming a path that led only to the elevator. If we'd tried to go anywhere else, I'm sure it would have been a struggle to do so.

"Come on," I said to him. "Let's go talk to yer alleged baby momma. I'm guessing this is the last time I'll be able to tease ya about it."

"I pray you're right," Rasmus said as we stepped into the elevator.

Chapter Twenty-Two

The elevator opened directly in the middle of the top-floor suite. Suddenly, a large man—maybe one of the compelled demon hunters—wrenched Rasmus from my grasp and held him in a chokehold with a curved knife pressed to his throat.

My eyes blazed as I pulled on my magick. Conn's demon form popped into existence beside me. The demons fell to the floor, but not the man holding Rasmus. He had a strange energy and his size was far too large to be a simple human.

To use my witch magick, I'd have to drop the mantle. Dropping the mantle would make me vulnerable to great harm. I decided to try what I usually tried, which was to talk my way out of this situation first.

"Is that how ya treat one of yer own?" I asked, letting him assume I thought he was human. "I'm glad I never let my ex-demon-hunter-husband talk me into joining yer affiliation."

"If anyone tries anything, I will slit his throat."

"Yeah, sure. We all believe ya. And once he's dead, one of us will slit yers. There will blood everywhere and dead bodies and…" I stopped and shrugged. "What would be the point? All I want is to talk to yer pregnant mistress."

"The demon queen isn't here and you know it," the man said, drawing a thin bloody line across Rasmus's neck.

Moving too quickly might cause the man to increase the pressure. Rasmus had hold of the man's arm but couldn't seem to move the knife safely away. The man had to be something supernatural.

I flicked my hand in their direction. "If ya keep on like ya're doing, ya're going to kill yer shield. Trust me, ya're not going to want to do that because Conn will dismember ya before ya can blink."

"If you value this man's life, you will do as I ask."

"I do value his life," I said as casually as I could. "But he's one of yer own kind. He's a demon hunter. He's been my hostage until now. I was planning to use him as a bargaining tool."

"He's no demon hunter. He's a coward in hiding from his true self."

"Well, that's an interesting take on things. I didn't know that about Rasmus. Can ya explain it to me?" I asked.

Mulan chose that moment to bust through the doors in her party dress and kick-ass knee boots. In her hands was a wooden staff decorated in symbols that glowed. She'd somehow hid the weapon in that tiny dress with holes, and for a moment I was lost in wondering where in the world she'd stashed it.

Like an Asian action heroine, Mulan scanned the room before her gaze landed on Conn, who gave her a full-sharp-toothed smile. Her lined eyes narrowed to slits in her face as she stared back at him. I would have loved to watch them angry flirt with each other, but I had other concerns.

"This man is a guardian, *not* a demon hunter," the man said.

I snorted. "Well, he believes he's a demon hunter. Someone must have convinced him that he was," I argued once I was paying attention to the dire situation again. "I kidnapped him because I believed he was a hunter out to trick me. Feel free to enlighten me if I was wrong."

"Your job was to find the demon queen. She's been missing for weeks."

I held out both hands palm up. "Well, what in bloody hell do ya think I've been doing? Why do ya think I came here? I was in the process of searching for her. But what's that to ya? The demon hunters were the ones who hired me."

Lilith was here. I felt it because Conn felt her. His demon magick could connect with any demon he chose. The problem lay in what it took for him to get to the point of it working. For whatever reason, The Dagda hadn't made it a foolproof thing. But we both felt Lilith clearly. We felt her fear. Not much made a demon afraid.

"Are ya a demon hunter?" I asked.

"No. I am a guardian. You know what I am."

I tilted my head and stared. Then I looked over at Conn. "What's a guardian?"

"I have no idea," Conn said in his low growly voice.

The compelled demon hunters surged up the stairs and out of the elevator like zombies. They moved glassy eyed into the area. The man with a knife to Rasmus's throat had to move to avoid the horde crushing in on him and Rasmus.

Amidst the chaos of demon hunter zombies, Ramus managed to push the knife away. Both his hands were cut and bleeding. He fell to the floor and tried to roll out of reach.

Conn streaked through the demon hunter zombies like a

bowling ball knocking down pins. Before I could blink, he had the man by the throat. The curved knife fell to the floor.

Conn expanded his demon form until the man dangled in the air.

Mulan stomped over to me. "Can you do something about these moaning people? I can't pay attention to what's happening."

I shook my head. "No, I can't use my regular magick while wearing Conn's energy mantle. It doesn't work that way. I only use this to fight demons."

Mulan snorted. "Next time I get bigger cut of profit."

The Wu Shaman shook her weapon in the air, which I noted had twenty or more tiny turtle shells hanging from the top. She murmured in her secret language, shook it again, and then she banged it on the floor. All the demon hunter zombies fell down and did not get back up. I even heard snoring.

Unfortunately, all the demons had fallen under her spell as well. Mulan's magick didn't discriminate.

"That's a very cool trick. I have a quickie spell that glues people in place. It's one of my favorites," I said to her, while I surveyed her handiwork.

"They will sleep for one hour—no more. Get busy. Earn your keep."

I went to Rasmus who was holding his neck. "The wound is still bleeding. Are ya feeling light-headed?"

"I'm fine," he ground out through clenched teeth. "Find out who that monster is that nearly killed me. He's as strong as Conn."

"Not really, but I know why ya would think that," I said, pointing to the side. The man still dangled in Conn's chokehold. His face was turning blue from lack of oxygen. "Let up a little, Conn. I want to talk to him."

The man continued to fight.

"Who are ya?" I asked.

When he didn't answer, Conn shook him.

"Unless ya want yer neck snapped, I suggest ya start talking to us."

Out of the corner of my eye, I saw Mulan stoop to pick up the sword the guy had used to cut Rasmus's throat. I lost my train of thought and turned to her. "What are ya doing?"

"Collecting spoils of war," she said.

"That's not..." I stopped. If it kept her happy, what did I care?

I turned back to the guy. "Who are ya? And what are doing here?"

He gripped Conn's enormous fingers and shoved against them. "I do not recognize the sovereignty of the daughter of The Dagda."

My face scrunched up. "Is that supposed to hurt my feelings? Am I supposed to care? Explain this to me because I don't really care what happens to ya. I'm looking for the demon queen."

The man glared at me in disgust. "You will show the demoness mercy. You will save her because you are weak."

I fisted both my hands on my hips and glared at him. "Ya don't even know me. This situation is like walking into the middle of a movie. I don't know what's happening or who the bad guys are. Why aren't ya jumping up and down to explain it to me?"

"Because you control a demon."

I snorted while I pointed to Conn. "How can ya be so sure? Maybe Conn controls me. Maybe we take turns controlling each other. I still don't see how my relationship to

Conn is a problem for anyone walking the planet. We're like the police of demon kind. We're the good guys."

"You are not worthy. You let them all live," the dangling man said.

My sigh was loud. "No, the gods let them live. I could easily obliterate every demon I encounter, but it wouldn't stop them from returning. Surely, ya know that, if ya know anything at all about demons."

"You lie," he said, renewing his fight.

"No, I don't lie. Trust me, I wouldn't be in trouble half as much if I could lie effectively."

Conn turned to growl at me. "This is getting us nowhere. Let's kill him so he won't be a future problem."

"Let's see if we can compel him," I said, but then I had a thought and looked at Mulan. "Got any tricks to make him tell us what he knows?"

Mulan gave me what I was beginning to call her "ya-lazy-shit" look. Every time she looked at my hair, I got glared at with a similar expression.

"No. Do your job, witch."

Rasmus, despite the blood oozing down the front of him, chuckled at our discussion. But with Conn using most of his strength to hold our hostage, dropping my energy armor was definitely not a good idea.

"I need a cage to hold him first," I said, voicing my wish out loud.

A very pregnant woman waddled into the room from some hidden passage. I looked at her and smiled. "Ah! Queen Lilith, I presume? Hello, I'm Aran of The Dagda."

Lilith turned and looked at Conn, whose massive head swiveled toward her. "I would bow and ask your forgiveness,

Connlander of the Fir Bolg, but I fear I would never be able to get back up."

"Lilith," he said softly in his deepest demon voice. "I'm glad you finally regenerated. It's been a long time."

"A very long time," she said. "Let me finish my apology so I can help you. You were right, Great King, to make the bargain with the gods. I should have listened to your wisdom."

"Our people live. I still have no regrets," Conn said.

"Strangely, neither do I," Lilith said, smiling up at him. "Doing what I did was the only way I could learn the true value of your sacrifice. I was not able to be the female you needed. Did you ever find a demoness who was?"

Before Conn could answer, Mulan stomped over until she could glare up at the woman from two feet away. "Know that I may take him as a lover and I do not share."

Lilith tried to laugh at the threat, but in the end, clutched her stomach in pain. "Connlander certainly deserves you, Mighty Wu. He also has my condolences."

Conn's rumble of demon laughter shook the room and woke the sleeping demons up. They looked at their queen holding her bulging front and then realized a giant Conn was staring down at them. They stayed on the floor, probably not knowing what to do.

I understood their confusion. Mine was as great, but about different things.

Conn used his free hand to bonk our attacker on the head. The man sagged in Conn's fist. Without him struggling, we could at last talk to Lilith without him hearing us.

"It's a pleasure to meet ya," I said to her. "Do ya know who the man is that attacked Rasmus?"

Her gaze flicked to Rasmus. "He should recognize him.

He's the same as him. They call themselves guardians. They want my child."

"Why? Is it a human hybrid?"

Her gaze dropped to the floor. "I do not know who the father is."

She knows. The assurance blasted through my head. The bigger Conn was, the louder he telegraphed his thoughts. If I were in her position and facing an old lover who was still angry, I'd probably lie as well.

I looked around and saw Rasmus slowly climbing to his feet. Mulan, having made her claim on Conn, walked over to let him use her staff as a prop.

Then I realized she was carrying the guardian's curved sword in her other hand. I didn't know whether to laugh or be afraid. It was half her height and the tip was dragging on the carpet.

"Did ya hear all that?" I asked Rasmus.

He nodded, wincing at the pain the head movement cost him.

Lilith reached out a hand to me. "Help me walk to him," she ordered.

The demons on the floor gasped as I took her hand. I smiled down at them. "I intend Lilith no harm. I came only to find answers to my questions and to make sure no one took her child."

"I heard you defending me to the guardian who attacked," Lilith told me as we moved slowly toward Rasmus and Mulan.

"Yer signature was on one of Rasmus's compulsions in a very sensitive spot. I found it when I checked him for them. Conn recognized you... and here we are."

"What is this conflicted guardian to you?" Lilith asked.

"A tormentor. My kidnap victim. Perhaps my friend. We're working through the details."

"He is not the father of my child. I never lay with him," Lilith said, speaking to me instead of Rasmus. "I was paid to lie and I did so. I was paid to place the compulsions. I also was paid to lie to your ex-husband, whose hands are no cleaner than mine. He pretends to be a demon hunter, but he works for the guardians. He aspires to be one."

"Who are the guardians? And what are they?" I asked, truly baffled by my lack of knowledge.

"They are a group of extraordinary humans who plan to rule all creatures. They killed many of my people in a way that will require centuries for them to regenerate. We remain uneasy business partners, but I did not understand the depth of their evil natures. Now I hide from them to protect my child. The guardian you captured was here spying on us."

"Given how unreasonable the man acted when he saw us, I can see why you're in hiding. Was he here to report when you gave birth?"

"Yes." We stopped close to Rasmus. "Bend down, guardian. I will heal your neck. Your blood is staining the floor."

Rasmus looked at me and I nodded. He bent and she pushed his fingers away from the wound. "Grit your teeth to bear the pain," she advised.

Seconds later, the smell of burning flesh filled the room. To Rasmus's credit, all he did was grunt.

"Done," she pronounced as she pulled her fingers away.

"Do ya know any more about the guardians?" I asked.

Lilith shrugged. "I hear some are like gods, but I don't know the source of their power."

I held her hand in both of mine. "Rasmus has at least one

compulsion I wasn't able to break. We need ya to free him from it, please."

Lilith ignored my plea as she looked at Rasmus. "Remembering will not bring you what you seek, guardian. It will take everything peaceful about your life away."

Rasmus frowned down at her. "Any knowledge is better than knowing nothing."

Lilith snorted. "Your energy is different from the others. I don't think you were ever fully one of them, but I only know what I was told. They did something to make you forget yourself. Aran's ex-husband became your keeper."

Jack being his keeper made a lot of sense to me, but I knew Rasmus still had trouble believing Jack had betrayed him.

"Free him," Conn said.

When I looked at Conn, the guardian was hanging limp in his hands. "Did ya kill him? I thought we were going to question him."

"He's not dead—not yet. We don't have a cage. This was easiest."

I looked at Lilith. "We'll take yer guardian spy with us, but they'll probably send another to replace him once the word gets out."

"Take him and I will do what you ask."

I looked at Rasmus. "We want ya to remove the compulsions from him."

Lilith looked at Conn. "Will you forgive me if I help the conflicted guardian?"

"My forgiveness is not a worthy goal for a demon queen. Do what you must, *Lilithia of the Fir Bolg*. You made your choice back then. Make a better one now."

Lilith nodded. I could tell she got something out of what Conn said to her that went beyond his words. I would never ask for details and Conn would never tell me. This level of privacy is what I allowed him. I really did see him as part of my family. It was always about trust. That was something Jack never understood.

"I will remove the compulsions from the conflicted guardian, but not here. We need more room for it to happen. Meet me at Gallows Hill Park at nine. There are many demands on him and ripping them away will not be pleasant. There is also what his kind did to him and that I cannot undo. His mind's survival is not certain."

I looked to Rasmus for confirmation that he still wanted them removed and got a brief nod.

"We would appreciate it greatly," I said to her.

Lilith found my eyes and held my gaze. "I mended my ways long before you were born, daughter of The Dagda. My people want to live in peace without the need for wars and regenerating. We serve humanity in exchange for being left alone. Is this not the kind of peace the gods wanted between us?"

"Yes. That's what The Dagda wanted. It's probably what the Goddess Danu wanted too."

"But what do humans want?" Lilith asked me. She motioned the prone demons to get up and help her. "They have committed the kind of atrocities that make even demons wince."

"If ya wanted to scare me, ya succeeded," I told her because she wasn't wrong.

"I don't think you fear much," she said.

"Is there an open demon portal?" I asked.

"There might have been if my child were truly half-human. The child is not." She held out her arms to Conn. "Do you wish to check my words?"

When Conn shook his head, she said something in demon language to several of her people. They ran out of the room.

"I have a set of handcuffs that might hold the guardian. They once kept a powerful witch I know from breaking free of them."

My eyes flashed, remembering the cuffs I'd worn, but I managed to hold the scream of rage that wanted to burst out of me. "How long was Jack doing business with yer kind?"

"With my caste? A decade or more. With others, from the very beginning. His loyalty is to no one but himself. I'm surprised you never saw that truth in him."

My shoulders rose and fell. "I had a child with him. Everything I did was to protect her."

Lilith nodded. "That's understandable," she said.

Two of her people rushed back with the cuffs. I took them in my hands and clipped them around my wrists. Lilith watched me with a stunned expression.

I muttered softly and the handcuffs popped open. I removed them and handed them to Conn and Rasmus to lock onto the wrists of the mysterious guardian.

When I felt the future demon queen staring harder me, I lifted an eyebrow at her curiosity. "Everything *I didn't do* was also to protect my child."

Chapter Twenty-Three

It seemed no one had heard of guardians. I couldn't ask Jack or Fiona, but I asked Ma and whoever else in the family answered their phone.

I would have asked Mulan, but she'd taken her curved sword and left us.

My biggest regret about the evening is that I'd forgotten to ask Lilith about my cousin, Liam. Hopefully, Lilith would continue talking to me, even though everything I'd learned only confused me more.

The cuffs successfully subdued the guardian, but they also kept him knocked out. We locked him in one of the rental home's bedrooms.

After a shower, I went to grab some food and fix some tea. I found Rasmus sitting at the table with his head in his hands. It was nearly eight and we'd have to leave in a few minutes in order to make it there on time. I'd already scheduled our ride to drop us off at a bar close to the park. The plan was to go back there afterward and order a ride home.

Why wasn't Rasmus happy? Everything happening was exactly what he said he wanted.

"Rasmus?"

"What if Lilith is right? What if I am like that sword guy we captured? She called me a guardian."

"Are ya afraid Conn and I will have to subdue ya once ya remember yerself?"

He snickered without humor. "I'm more afraid you'll hate me and that I might also hate myself."

I scooted out a chair and sat down across from him. I stuck out my hand—yes, the one with King Solomon's ring on it. He laid his large hand across mine.

"She called ya *the conflicted one,* which means ya aren't a total bad guy. This means I will never hate ya completely. We're frenemies."

He snorted and tightened his grip. "You have to be the strangest woman in the world."

"Yes, so ya've said many times. I'm not trying to be strange on purpose. If ya perceive that I'm different, it's because I'm following my witchy destiny. What would happen if ya discovered ya were a demon?"

"I don't know."

"Right. That's my point. None of us ever know what we'll become when life exerts the pressure of big changes on us. But the fundamental stuff never goes away. Think of yerself as a good guy and see what happens. Ya're a good man inside but also a grouch who sees the worst in every situation."

"Says the woman who can't say a nice word in the morning until she's had two cups of coffee."

"Ya're loyal when ya think ya have reason to be. A compulsion can only magnify what is already there. Ya had to have some good feelings for Jack for them to be able to compel ya to support him through thick and thin."

"You are a nutcase, Aran. You're playing matchmaker for a Wu Shaman and a bound demon."

"Imp—the proper term to describe Conn is imp. He's an Imperial Demon."

"You only use semantics when it suits your argument. And you wield humor like a weapon."

I pushed out my lip and pretended to pout. "I've run out of faults to comment on. All I got left is that ya kiss like a man who knows what he's doing. I really like that about ya. We might do a bit more of it if ya survive."

Rasmus rolled my hand and thumbed my knuckles. "You're fearless when it comes to doing what's right, no matter what it costs you." He lifted my hand and held the back of it to his lips for a kiss. "I'm afraid of what's going to happen. Part of me wants to tell the demoness to leave me like this. But... I can't. If I turn evil on you, what will happen?"

"I'll put ya in a cage in Katie's basement until I can talk some sense into you. That's what friends do."

"I thought you said we were frenemies."

"Well, we are, but every friendship has to start somewhere."

His head dropped. "I'm glad you went through with the divorce. If you were still married to Jack, I wouldn't be able to admit how nice it was to kiss you."

I giggled... and lied. "That little lip brush was a kiss? Goddess, I barely remember it."

Rasmus smirked and tugged me tight to the table as he leaned forward. "Next time I'll do better."

"How about this time?" I asked. "I mean... next time seems a long way off and we don't know what surprises tonight will bring."

His lips found mine with an ease that surprised me. He must have been thinking of kissing me again as much as I had thought of kissing him. My left hand rose to one side of his face to keep him where he was. His mouth was hungry, exploring, and yet gentle as he pulled my bottom lip between his teeth.

Yielding to my desire to really kiss him, I opened my mouth to let him inside just before he pulled away. I blinked in shock, and then noticed Conn stood in the kitchen doorway smirking at me.

"I know we were all having a good time—you two kissing and me watching—but we have to go. It's eight-thirty."

I nodded and pulled my hand away from Rasmus. "Alright." A horn honked outside the house. "And that's our ride. Let's go then."

We gathered our things and went outside to the car. Conn sat up front with the driver. Rasmus and I sat in the back. His hand sought mine and held it tightly.

Was this the beginning of something? It didn't feel like it. It felt more like a desperate goodbye.

We walked to the park from the bar and found Lilith sitting on a park bench waiting for us. Ten or more of her guards surrounded her on all sides.

Rasmus stopped in front of her. "Did you do what you did to protect your people from me?"

One of Lilith's eyebrows arched. "Does it matter?"

"Yes. It matters to me. I don't want anyone to see me like the guy who attacked us," Rasmus said.

Lilith gazed at him for a long time. "When a female carries a child, she is vulnerable. That is true no matter how powerful she is. The expectant mother will compromise much to deliver her baby safely. The same mother will later prostitute herself and her morals to keep her child safe. When humans could not siphon power from demons to improve themselves, they found an even older source and stole its power. You are connected to that source. If I knew its name, I would tell Aran and Conn, but the truth eludes me."

"Am I a thief who stole some ancient creature's power?"

"I don't know what you are. All I know is that even your demon hunter keeper feared you. They destroyed many of their own trying to create beings like you. I can't explain why they kept you alive or how they did it."

"Did they fear me the way all demons fear Conn?"

Lilith shook her head and laughed. "We do not fear Connlander of the Fir Bolg. We love and loathe him equally. He gave away his freedom so we could all keep ours. He is our savior whether we like that fact or not. He will command all our kind as our one true king forever."

Rasmus looked over at me but spoke only to Lilith. "Will I remember talking to you? Or to anyone?"

"You will remember what the gods wish you to remember, *conflicted one*. It is the same for all of us. However," Lilith said, turning to smile at me. "No one forgets crossing the path of a child of The Dagda. Even when she's a witch with poor taste in men."

I grinned at the demoness. "Are ya throwing stones from the window of yer glass house?"

"Only this once, Aran of The Dagda. Remember you asked me to do this."

"I won't forget," I said, bowing my head.

"Undress now," she said to Rasmus.

"Is that necessary?" he asked.

Her eyebrow arched again as he questioned her. "Either do it or wish you had. It doesn't matter to me if you ruin your clothes."

"Fine," Rasmus said, stomping a good distance away from us.

"Is it *truly* necessary?" I asked in a whisper.

Lilith chuckled. "You two are the most unlikely pairing I've ever seen."

I crossed my arms. "Well, I guess ya have a right to yer opinion. I feel that same way about the Wu Shaman and Conn."

One of her minions motioned to Rasmus until he stood about thirteen feet away. This was the distance of her magickal reach while carrying the baby. When I inherited Conn, it was the first thing he explained to me. The female demon body splits its energies between growing the fetus and performing magick. The baby always won. A distance of thirteen feet was the maximum during later stages of pregnancy.

Smiling, Lilith rubbed her hands and chanted until a red glow surrounded her. *"Infectum fieri." Be undone*, Lilith had commanded in the old language.

Conn and I watched the seal on the compulsion we found explode in the air in front of Rasmus's man parts. His manhood withdrew as far as it could from the damage as he swore loudly. No one watching laughed at his pain. We all winced, even Lilith's entourage.

"Poor bastard," Conn said in sympathy.

All I could do was nod in agreement and hold my breath for the rest.

Lilith waited until he'd recovered enough to listen. "There are thirteen other compulsions and all of them are tied to your navel. They run in many directions and cover a variety of commands. It took thirteen separate demons to put them on you. Those calling themselves guardians obliterated all thirteen demons when they were finished because they still believe we die. All I did was seal the compulsions. The guardians let me live because they knew no demon dared break my seal. A blast of my power to your third energy center will free you from all demon holds, but the truth may harm you more than the compulsions did. This is all the warning I can give you, conflicted one. Are you certain you still wish to be released?"

"Yes, I'm certain," Rasmus said.

Lilith formed an energy ball in her hands, the same way I did when wearing Conn's mantle of protection. It was the energy I used in a fight.

Maybe the magick Conn taught me was demon magick. Maybe all magick was similar in nature. I knew an energy ball that size could easily mean the death of Rasmus.

Was this what his dream had been about? Was he going to die?

When the energy ball was the size of a grapefruit, instead of throwing it, Lilith passed it over to a demon that Conn whispered to me was her second-in-command.

Several others helped her back to the bench to sit while her second-in-command carried the ball of energy to Rasmus who stood a foot taller than him.

"Do whatever you have to," Rasmus said.

The demon drew back and slammed the energy ball into those outstanding abs I'd admired so much. Rasmus screamed as the energy penetrated and spread through his center before spiraling up and outward.

Lilith's second turned and ran.

Thirteen lines linked to compulsions lit up flowing from his navel to his feet, his head, his chest, and all places in between. I could have traced them with my finger.

His screaming made me take a step to go help him, but Conn held me back. "No. I feel danger. Let me go."

Rasmus had one hand on his abs while the other grasped at air as he stumbled in a circle. Then a rumble started in the ground under his bare feet.

Conn halted mid-stride and then turned and ran back. *"Everyone down!"* he ordered.

I stared at Conn, not comprehending his command. He pulled me to ground as he went down himself. The demons all did the same. A huddle surrounded Lilith.

Rasmus screaming was all I heard until there was a loud ripping of flesh and bone. I peeked up to see the man I knew being pulled apart by magick until his body reformed itself into a different man—a different creature.

His eyes glowed blue as he looked down at his hands. His gaze swept around the field and landed on the demons, including a pregnant Lilith sitting on the bench.

His body drew in energy until he was charged up like a lightning bolt.

I suddenly knew what he was planning to do and I had to stop him. I wrestled free of Conn's hold, jumped up, and ran.

"Rasmus, no! They helped ya. They're not your enemies. Don't hurt them."

His blazing gaze switched from the demons to me. He lifted a hand and I knew that lightning he'd stored was headed my way. My right hand flew up on its own to shield my face. King Solomon's ring buzzed madly on it.

Rasmus saw the ring, reflected its glow, and then raised his own arm to shield himself from the sight of it.

Surprised, I lowered my hand and looked at the ring. It glowed now with the same blue of Rasmus's transformed eyes. He didn't recognize me—that was obvious. I doubt he even knew himself yet. But Rasmus recognized the ring, or at least, he noted the power it held.

What did that mean?

I had one angry thought about what I would do to Jack when I figured this all out, but then the creature Rasmus had become seized in place where he stood. His mouth screamed silently like he was in some sort of terrible pain. I took one step toward him before a giant pair of wings burst from his back. They were a gradient dark gray with feathers that looked translucent.

He launched himself into the night sky, his wings flapping one time as he shot up like a rocket. I watched him fade from sight and then lowered my hand. The ring instantly turned back to solid gray stone.

None of what happened to him made any sense to me, but Rasmus was gone now no matter what I believed or thought.

Conn walked over and turned me to face him. "Why did you run to him? He could have killed you."

I held out my hand with the ring. "He was going to hurt Lilith and I couldn't let him do that. Da's ring stopped him, Conn. I think he recognized it."

Conn looked down at it. "Is the gray stone magickal?"

"It's a holy relic in disguise," I whispered.

Conn shook his head. "No, Aran, look at it. The ring is just a plain stone and you're probably in shock. I saw you kissing Rasmus in the kitchen. I know how you must feel losing him that way. His total change into that creature was a brutal ending to your flirtation."

I could see I wouldn't be convincing Conn—not today, at least. And once I did, it would only worry him to know the truth of the ring I wore and how it cloaked itself. Once again the ring had chosen to hide from all the demons I knew. Yet it had showed itself to the creature Rasmus became. That had to mean something. I just had to figure out what.

"Is Lilith okay?" I asked.

Conn nodded. "She is weak from the magick she spent, but fine."

"Do you have any idea what that creature was, Conn? What Rasmus transformed into looked like the angels Ma always talks about."

"You were never slow," Conn said vaguely, not really answering my question.

I walked over to Lilith. "I don't know what happened, but I appreciate what it cost ya to free Rasmus from his bonds. Call me if the demon hunters or guardians return. Conn and I will protect ya as best we can."

The demoness looked up at Conn. "You saw what he turned into. If what we saw is true, you know what the humans have done. Tell the daughter of The Dagda what you know, Conn. Her gods are different. She might never guess."

I looked between them. "What are ya talking about?"

Conn looked in the direction the winged Rasmus flew off in. "The humans may have trapped a Nephilim, which is a human-angel hybrid. They may have made a serum from his blood that gives them a boost of power. That would explain the near insanity of the fake human guardian threatening Lilith's caste. Humans aren't meant to wield that level of power, Aran. Most Nephilim weren't able to handle it themselves. They succumbed to madness and had to be killed."

I shook my head. "Rasmus never acted insane. His reaction to his change seemed more like one of total confusion."

Conn shook his head in disagreement. "The Rasmus you knew was only a vessel for his true form. The man we knew was never real."

I refused to believe that the Rasmus I knew was no more than a shell with a magickal ghost inhabiting it. Like most paranormal and supernatural creatures, Nephilim had once existed on our planet, but they died out during the great flood.

But what were guardians?

The creature Rasmus became seemed to be something far more mysterious than a human-angel hybrid. I felt it in my bones.

LILITH LEFT to return to her home and one of the demons drove us back to the rental house. I couldn't stop thinking about what had happened. Rasmus had been nothing but trouble, but I was going to miss him something fierce.

Fire engines and police cruisers greeted our arrival. Someone—or something—had set the house ablaze and torn most of the roof off.

Conn wandered away to find out what he could. I stared at the mess and made a list in my head of all the possessions being burned to cinders. It wasn't long before Conn reappeared.

"No one was in the house when they arrived. The man-made guardian we captured is gone, handcuffs and all. They're saying the furnace in the attic exploded. It's the only answer that made sense to them with all the debris scattered around. The guardian that attacked us either did something to cause this or he was rescued by others of his kind."

I nodded absently. At least Conn hadn't concluded that Rasmus flew over here and released him. I think we both believed that the tormented creature we saw Rasmus turn into was too confused by his pain to take such an action.

"Well, it's not like I had a lot to lose. I'm going to miss my witch kit for sure, but it's all replaceable. The only true loss for me tonight was Rasmus. And I still have hope he somehow survived his transmogrification."

Conn reached out and patted the top of my head. "Your naivety is showing, but I'm going to let you float in denial. You deserve it after today."

"I'm being hopeful, Conn. Come with me. I need to show ya something." I took Conn by the hand and led him to the side yard.

"Look down," I ordered, putting my own gaze on the ground. There was a trail of feathers leading from the front of the house to the backyard. "I think Rasmus is still transforming. He may remember himself yet."

"It doesn't matter if he remembers being human or not, Aran. Nephilim don't have feelings and emotions like humans do. That's part of what makes their immense power so destructive. Their creation was outlawed by the gods for the good of the world."

"Are ya saying Rasmus is some kind of Frankenstein monster?"

"I'm saying, that if Rasmus is Nephilim, he's the child of an angel-human relationship. It's the most prohibited relationship in all of creation. Eons ago their existence prompted the gods to wipe out all of mankind just to get rid of them. The guardians, whoever they are, are playing with things that could end all life on Earth again."

"But we don't know his story for sure. Rasmus himself told me he didn't remember anything about his past."

Conn narrowed his gaze. "Give it up, honey. You cannot save that creature. You tried to save the vessel he dwelled in and that didn't work. There's nothing to be gained by wishing for a different outcome. You know I would never lie to you about something this important."

My sigh was loud enough to drown out the sound of more sirens. The closest fire engine was still pumping gallons and gallons of water onto the roof of the house.

I nodded to let Conn know I'd actually heard his lecture and taken it in. "I liked it better when all we had to worry about was a cheapskate troll stealing sheep from local farmers for his dinner. Life was simple back then. Ireland was simple. Why does everything in America have to be so freaking complicated?"

Conn smiled at my complaints. "Go talk to the owner of the rental. She wants to know we're both okay. I told her we were out for the evening and came home to find the house on fire."

I nodded before Conn walked off.

When he could no longer see me, I stooped to pick up a feather. It glistened gray in my hand and turned to white while I watched. Fascinated, I stooped and gathered up a few more. All of them did the same as I held them.

I could use them to scry for Rasmus and keep track of the creature he'd become. Would that be considered stalking? Would Conn gripe at me over it? The answer to both was yes, but I was feeling rebellious.

I gathered up all the feathers I could find until the pockets of my clothing bulged with them.

As I turned to head back to the front of the now sopping wet house, I felt the wind lift my hair—except the wind wasn't blowing.

A naked man with glowing blue eyes and dark gray wings floated gently down to land until he stood in front of me. His hair was long and black with white at the temples. He bowed his head to me slightly. The Nephilim's physical body—if

Conn was right—looked enough like the human version to be a blood sibling.

I more than suspected the Rasmus I met was still in there... somewhere. Since I was afraid to speak aloud and break the moment, I merely repeated his head bow. Finally, my tongue got the better of my mind. "Are ya okay, Rasmus? Did the change hurt ya? I was worried about what happened."

His body changed from gray to white until it glowed like the feathers I'd gathered. Instead of answering, he bent his knees and launched himself like a rocket into the night sky again. His wings wrapped around him, shielding the rest of him. He looked like a shooting star as he moved.

Had the feathers been a message for me? Conn would likely call them a warning. Perhaps they were both. But given the fierceness of Conn's fight with the man-made guardian we captured, I think if the new Rasmus creature had wanted me dead I would have been.

I studied the sky, looking for signs Rasmus was flying around up there, but I saw none. I hadn't imagined that whole thing, though. He'd come to see me after his change and left me some of his feathers for proof.

One day soon, I was going to have to tell Conn about the creature's visit, but not tonight. Right now, I needed to call Katie, tell her what happened to the house, and see if she had a room for us. I also needed to reassure our rental house host that none of this was her fault.

Tomorrow, I would need to shop and replace the things I lost from my witching kit. When I wasn't sharing Conn's energy, I needed a full witch's toolbox. I could do simple spells without those things, but I couldn't scry or do the more complicated ones.

I suppose things could have been worse. I couldn't see how yet, but it would come to me. It always did.

What still depressed me was that none of my numerous goodbyes to Jack had been good enough to banish him. Now, after losing Rasmus, my only option to discover the truth of things was to track down my devious ex-husband and torture him until he answered my questions.

I'd rather kiss a fish-lipped leprechaun than deal with Jack again any time soon, but a magickal life tended not to give ya a lot of options. Would I be paying forever for my decision to marry Jack? Goddess, I hoped not.

I followed my heart when it came to love and my head when it came to witching. Both led me into trouble and more trouble, but there had been plenty of good times too. Twenty years ago, they'd led me into marriage and motherhood. Maybe one day in the near future they would stop leading me back to a man I never wanted to see again.

At least turning forty wasn't as terrible as I feared it would be. And I'd survived the last seven years of my life, which validated my optimism for what lay ahead. Conn and I had freed some sort of ancient creature from captivity. That counted in my favor, right?

Maybe I was officially a midlife witch, but the biggest adventure of my life seemed to be just getting started.

— THE END —

Ready for more? CLICK HERE to get Book 2 or visit my website at donnamcdonaldauthor.com.

Note From the Author

Hi. I hope you enjoyed reading *40 Ways to Say Goodbye!*

If you enjoyed this book, please consider leaving a positive review or rating on the retailer site where you purchased it. Reader reviews help my books continue to be valued by resellers and help new readers make decisions about reading them.

You are the reason I write these stories and I sincerely appreciate each of you.

May thanks for your support!
~ Donna McDonald

40 Ways to Lose a Guy

TALES OF A MIDLIFE WITCH, BOOK 2

Click to pre-order Book 2 today!

Book Description

My bad luck with men is a joke in my family.

The two other women in my family think I attract only bad guys. Rasmus morphing into some ancient winged creature and flying away convinced my mother she was right. Working with Colonel Benson and the sexy elf Conn recruited to guard my daughter is worsening her opinion. Can you believe my daughter at twenty thinks I'm the naive one? Well, the joke's on both of them.

Turning forty didn't make me extra picky, but they need to stop judging me for saying no. Colonel Benson is happily married, and I turned down the sexy elf Conn dangled in front of me on principle. I don't have time to deal with ancient winged creatures, eccentric fairy folk, and back-stabbing demons. The last thing I need is another man determined to ruin my life. Jack Derringer did a bang-up job of that already.

Speaking of my ex, and I really wish I didn't need to, but it seems Jack is involved in something extremely shady. It turns out that the reason Jack sent me to prison was to line his wallet. Should I be flattered that my absence was worth so much to someone? Finding out Jack betrayed me for money is why I informed my daughter that I couldn't promise to not kill her father when I saw him.

No one's paying me these days, but I still need to sort this out, find a way to permanently lose the guy I divorced, and maybe find the one that flew away from me before he gets captured again.

Chapter One

W e chose a booth at the back of the bar and sat facing the door so I could watch for our visitor. I chose seats as far away from the music and pool tables as I could get us.

If Father Peter Landerman was wearing his hearing aids this evening, we'd be fine here. If he wasn't wearing his hearing aids, I would ask the waitperson to move us next door to the restaurant where we could be sure to hear each other. If he was wearing his collar, which I fully expected him to be doing, I'd have to seat the priest where he wouldn't draw attention.

Why would I go to such extremes merely to talk to an old family friend? Because I planned to shamelessly pour Peter's favorite booze down him until he told me what I wanted to know.

I turned to Conn, my demon familiar and the caretaker of my not-so-great wealth to ask about our finances. Fresh out of magickal prison, I had no idea if I had any money or not. Every time I asked Conn about it, he told me not to worry and started throwing around financial terms like safe money market accounts and high-risk high-rewards investments.

There was usually a bit of bragging in his comments as well, which I also tuned out. Anything more complicated than negotiating payment for work confused me.

I admit I took a more practical approach to my earnings. Either I had money to spend on something or I didn't. Tonight, I wanted to be sure I could spend it as freely as necessary

"Are we solvent enough to pay for top shelf liquor tonight?"

Conn grinned at me and chuckled at my question. "Yes. I cashed out one of our money market certificates. Renting the house for a year took most of what I converted, but I know you need the stability."

It was good not to have to explain to Conn the reaction I'd had leaving the cottage for good. I hated what the place meant the whole I was there, but it had been all I knew for seven very, very long years. Jack's house was just that—his house and not mine. It wasn't stability I needed so much as it was to establish some other place as a my sanctuary. I'd jumped at the first house whose energy felt right.

Conn hadn't offered me a single argument against it. What mattered more than a house we didn't have to leave was that we were together again. Finding a new normal would be easier with a place to call home for a while.

I smiled at him. "I'll look for a normal paying job after this is all over. My 'after prison' plan was to move home to Ireland but that's not going to be possible for a while yet."

"You're just wanting to be away from Jack."

I considered it, and then nodded. "True, but now I'm not sure one ocean between the two of us is going to be enough. How would ya feel about not staying here in America? Ya have a stake in where we live as well. Are ya done with America yet?"

"I go where you go, Aran. That's the deal between us. I would only miss one person here in Salem, and it's not Lilith. Seeing her has reminded me that she never truly returned my interest, not even when I loved her madly. Besides, there are too many females in this world to every believe only one will do."

"I won't move back unless we both can see it working. We're a team. We always were and always will be."

"Which is why I choose to imitate you. No other keeper has ever given me so much freedom."

I snorted. "If I hadn't treated ya well before I got out of prison, I've certainly would now. That was a hard lesson learned about the ability to move around this world freely."

The waitress interrupted our serious discussion when she brought our drinks. It was a dark beer for Conn, which was his usual drink of choice. I didn't drink much so I didn't have a usual. I ordered a rum and fruit juice drink that wasn't very strong.

Conn chuckled low. "Being here and waiting on a priest to join us feels like we're setting up a joke."

I laughed as I shook my head. "This is no joke, Conn. Father Landerman's knowledge of angels is renown. He even knows about the ones not recognized by his own beliefs, including djinn."

Conn took a sip of his frosty beer and smirked at me. "A witch, a demon, and priest walk into a bar. The witch asks, 'Have you ever heard of a friendly Nephilim, or at least one not looking to destroy the world? The priest, fearing the creature his god once destroyed, runs out of the bar screaming in terror. The demon laughs at the irony of a creature made by the gods who's scarier than him."

He stopped talking to smirk at me because he knew I'd

have to know. When I broke, I broke hard. "Okay. I'll bite, Conn. What happened to the witch?"

Conn's grin stretched wide. "Fearing neither gods or the creatures created by them, the witch was shocked that her question caused all hell to break loose." He snapped his fingers. "Wait... you're right. This isn't a joke. We're talking about your normal life."

"Shush," I said, elbowing him as I chuckled. "Peter doesn't know ya're a demon and he can't tell. He also doesn't know I'm a witch or that I wield the power of a child of The Dagda. So *ex-nay* on the *emon-day*."

Conn's nearly spit out his beer laughing. *"Pig Latin?"* he asked.

I grinned at him. "It's the closest to real Latin a pagan like me can get."

Grinning back, Conn took another sip. "That's blatantly not true. Some of your favorite spells are in Latin. The druids turned their Roman conqueror's language against them. That was a superb historical irony."

I waggled a finger at him. "No druid talk either, Conn— nothing pagan at all. We won't mention any other religions to Peter unless he brings them up. Father Landerman is a respected family friend. He and Ma talk about angels together. I'm hoping he'll talk to me about them. Who knows? Maybe he knows about the guardians."

Conn laughed as he studied me. "I can't imagine anyone talking to you for five minutes without realizing you're a far more powerful person than they have ever imagined existed. Your witch powers don't often show, but The Dagda's power in you always makes itself known."

I sipped my rum drink. "Is that a compliment? Or are ya saying I suck at fooling people?"

"Both," Conn said. "I guess I'm here keeping your company because the priest believes I'm your brother."

"Not this time. Father Landerman thinks ya're my cousin because he knows Ma only had one child. No imaginary love children are allowed in this conversation, either. Ya're here because I need a second pair of ears to hear what he has to say."

Despite being in human form, Conn gave me a toothy demon smile. "How can you broach a real topic with the man if you're constantly filtering reality for him?"

"That's what the top-shelf booze is for, of course. I intend to ply him with liquor to loosen his tongue, as well as his religious affiliations."

Conn's deep, masculine laughter drew the attention of the woman serving at the table closest to us. The way he tossed his head to move his thick hair out of his eyes was enough to have to staring. He smiled back at her when she smiled at him but then looked quickly away. He looked too much like me to be my date and he knew it. That meant there was only one reason Conn was playing things so cool.

I smirked at his actions. "We can't talk about the Wu Shaman tonight, either. Her magic is too tribal."

Conn smiled but kept his gaze on his beer. "I'm obsessed with her—I admit it. It's very limiting to my social life."

I smiled as I sipped my drink. "Limiting for you? What about me? I haven't gotten a haircut in two months. Do ya know why? Because I refuse to listen to Mulan ranting for hours about you in multiple languages. I'd rather waste my long distance minutes listening to Ma lecturing me about my poor grooming habits, and ya know how much I hate that."

Conn rattled off something in a Chinese dialect. I didn't understand a word, but I didn't have to. I wasn't the person meant to understand.

"Good goddess, ya learned her language to impress her." I shook my head in shock. "I sure hope she appreciates yer efforts."

His smile was wide. "Not yet, but she will. And that reminds me of something." Conn pulled an envelope out of his pocket with my name on it.

I took it, opened the flap, and saw a stack of money inside. "What's this?"

Conn's smile was wicked. "It's thirty percent of the ninety percent profit, which ended up being one thousand three hundred fourteen dollars and change, which she generously rounded up. I know this because the Wu Shaman told me that several times. She also said to tell you she invested the ten percent victim's share into an account which at the end of one year if left unclaimed will be divided among the three of us. She agrees with me that the Rasmus we knew is never coming back —hence the investing."

"That woman is crazy, Conn. She hocked the scimitar the guardian used on Rasmus. *That's* what she's calling profit."

His pleased and proud chuckle had me grinning.

"Yes, I believe she sold it online to a collector for a very heathy sum. Leaving the blood on it would have brought a higher value, but she didn't want the responsibility of some random person coming into contact with guardian blood and turning into an evil, man-made guardian monster. She cleaned the blood off, burned the cleaning rags to keep prevent it from spreading, and totally removed the guardian's energy before she shipped the sword to its new owner."

Conn's wickedly happy grin told me volumes about how proud he was to tell me that entire story in precisely that manner. The Wu Shaman was one of a kind—part medicine woman and part opportunistic thief.

I stared at the envelope of money for a while before shoving it out of sight in my new purse. We'd had to replace all our belongings after the first in our previous rental house. It had taken a second visit to the coin dealer just to buy new clothes. Hopefully, we wouldn't end up losing everything again. A year's worth of rent was a hefty investment.

"Tread lightly with the Wu Shaman, Conn. I've seen her power and I may not be able to stop her from casting ya somewhere. If ya break her heart, she also might capture ya, stuff ya, and sell ya to a collector to buy her family's herb farm back."

Conn snickered at my warning. "The same thought already occurred to me. That's why I bought her family farm back before Mulan got any ideas about making a profit off me."

My mouth fell open before I laughed. "Tell me ya didn't. Does she know?"

Conn rubbed his nose. "Her father does, but he promised not to tell her. She's been sending money home for that purpose for years. He told her he got a good bargain and thanked her profusely for helping him restore their family's honor. Her sister is still complaining about her, though. I thought about cutting out her sister's tongue but feared that might make Mulan mad."

"Do ya think?" I exclaimed, knowing he was not joking— not in the least.

Conn looked serious for a moment. "Mulan doesn't need me, but she wants me."

"She needs ya more than she realizes. Mulan needs someone strong enough to deal with her crazy. And I need ya to woo her, because I refuse to be the only one dealing with her. Ma is determined to make Mulan and me the best of friends."

Conn's laughter filled the bar. One of his most winning traits was the deep masculine laughter that so easily rolled out of his throat whenever he was amused. He caught the female server's eye earlier, but now every woman in the bar turned to look longingly at him.

I appreciated it too, but all too often, I was the cause his humor. He laughed at me more than he should. There were plenty of times Conn's teasing made me want to cut his tongue out.

And that's how Father Landerman snuck up on us.

"Is this a private party or can an old man join in on the fun?"

"Father Landerman!"

"Now, Aran, you know my name is Peter. That Father stuff is for parishioners," he scolded.

"Okay. *Peter*," I said with a smile, scooting from my seat. "It's so good to see you."

I hugged the elderly man and helped him arrange his robes to sit in the booth. I waved over the wait person. "Bring us two more dark beers and two top-shelf whiskeys—one single and one double, please."

"I feel spoiled," Peter said with a smile.

"Thanks for the refill," Conn also said with a smile.

"Ya gentlemen are both welcome." I saved introductions until the server ran off to get the drinks. "Peter, I don't think ya've met my cousin. Conn is from Da's side of the family. He's here staying with me for a while."

The priest nodded to Conn but didn't offer his hand. Very few people did. Women had no fear of touching my familiar, but males instinctively kept their distance. Conn said an ancient male instinct warned them away from him because an imperial demon was an apex predator.

Passing for family was never hard for Conn and me, but sometimes we had to get creative in labeling our connection. Brother. Cousin. We changed it to suit ourselves.

We'd gotten strange looks from the other bar customers when the robed priest sat down with us, but it wasn't because Conn was a demon. No, I was the one who got the stares, especially when I hugged him and helped him sit. Maybe a confirmed pagan like me didn't put off the right vibe to be entertaining a man cut from Catholic cloth.

But Peter was a family friend and I didn't care what others thought. Peter knew Ma and I didn't share his faith… or really any faith he could readily explain. I never asked Ma how many details she'd shared with Peter. He didn't seem to be ashamed about knowing me, so I refused to be worried about being seen with him.

"Your mother said you were interested in talking to me about angels. Bridget and I have had many wonderful talks about them. I wish she'd stayed in the states with you. I miss her."

I smiled and nodded. "I miss Ma being here too. Next time she comes for a visit, I'll make sure she looks ya up."

"Thank you, Aran. You're a good daughter. What was it you wanted to know about angels?"

I smiled again. "What can ya tell me about the Nephilim, Peter? I read they were the hybrid children of angels and humans. I also read they were more evil than good. Does the very mention of them make ya want to run screaming from the building?"

Peter laughed at my dramatic teasing. "You joke, but they affect certain people that way. God considered them to be abominations and outside intended creation. Along with the bulk of humanity, most of the Nephilim were destroyed during the Great Flood."

"Ya said *most* of them, Peter. What happened to the Nephilim who survived?"

"Many ancient texts claim those that didn't die hid from God's sight. In the years after the Great Flood, I believe that the ones who remained alive got called 'giants' and even 'heroes' sometimes. I think many of the famous myths about alleged demi-gods were based on them. Some scholars think the tales of Hercules were about a Nephilim because he was a hero who went insane and killed his family. Insanity from having too much power is their fatal flaw."

"Are they evil to your religion then? Tales I read of them didn't paint a pleasing picture."

Our wait person chose that moment to slide our drinks onto the table. I indicated for her to put them all in one place and moved them around while I waited for Peter to answer.

"I disagree with the view that Nephilim were abominations. The reason I disagree so strongly is that scripture states God instantly regretted the flood and the earth's destruction after he lost his temper with humans and Nephilim. What is evil anyway? Often, one person's evil is another's salvation. That's why there are so many scriptures warning us not to judge each other. I believe the actual issue with the Nephilim was that they refused to take sides. They didn't dare because their side would always win. The immense powers they inherited from their heavenly parent were far more than their earthly side could handle. Insanity was inevitable."

I nodded and sipped my drink, thinking of Rasmus changing into a being that flew like a rocket through the skies. "What would ya say if I said I was fairly sure I'd met a Nephilim?"

Peter's eyebrow arched upwards. "Hold that thought until I can hear it better," he ordered.

Then he drank the single shot of whiskey straight down without stopping. There was no coughing or sputtering. Instead, Peter simply took a small sip of the dark beer I'd ordered for him and sighed in pleasure.

Still without speaking, Peter picked up the double and took a healthy sip. I feared with that sort of drinking he would become incoherent before I got the first real question out of my mouth.

"Let's get some food too," I said with a smile.

I waved our server down and ordered a variety of appetizers. Keeping this casual was hard when I was impatient for answers.

After the wait person scurried off to place our food order, Peter found his voice again. "So you think you met a Nephilim and lived to talk about it?"

I smiled at him and shrugged. "I did him a favor. Or at least, I believe that's how he saw things."

I pulled a feather out of my pocket and held it out between two fingers. "He left me this as a souvenir of our encounter, which is the only reason I don't think I imagined him. I will admit that I haven't told Ma yet. She's got a soft spot for angels. I didn't want to alarm her if my encounter turned out not to be with one."

I laid the tiny feather in the palm of my other hand. The feather instantly changed from dark gray to brilliant white.

"May I?" he asked, reaching out to touch it.

His ancient fingers lifted the feather up after I nodded. It immediately turned gray again. He sucked in a breath. "It wasn't a Nephilim you met, Aran, but that was a very good guess about the being you saw. The being you ran into has similar powers."

"What was it then?"

"You met a custos, a praeses, a defensor—they're known by many names. In English, we call them *guardians*."

Conn stiffened beside me but stayed silent.

"What is a guardian? I heard that term before, but I couldn't find anything written about them."

Peter drank the rest of his double shot before he answered me. "There's nothing to find because no one knows what they really are. The Church quietly recognizes them as part of heaven's army, but we don't know enough about their powers to talk about them with confidence. They show up in dire times and do things to correct the balance of power in the world. Or that's what we think they're here doing."

"How long have they been here?" I asked.

Peter spread his hands. "That's also something we don't know, but they appear at troubled times in history. Even when they take human form, I've heard they don't give many explanations. We concluded they have no little or no power while walking the earth in human form. Or this is what we believe based on the few stories we have. It's hard to find someone who talked to them and remembers what was said. Making people forget them is only one of their many talents. Your mother said forgetting everyone sounded more like a curse to her."

I refused to believe Rasmus could ever make me forget him. "Are ya saying that a guardian is a shapeshifter?"

Peter nodded. "Yes, but not like one of those fictional creatures people make up to tell a good story. Think of him more as a Skinwalker like in First Nation legends. A guardian will take on whatever form they need to in order do whatever it is they intend to do—animal, human, maybe even a god. I've studied them all my life, but I've never seen one in person. People who see them only tell me about it during confession, especially if they believe the guardian was an angel."

Maybe Peter would think my question rude, but I had to ask it. "If ya've never seen one, how did ya know what creature this feather belongs to?"

Peter snickered. "You're a sharp woman, Aran. The reason I know is because I saw a feather like that once before. The person who showed it to me said he'd gotten it from a *confirmed* guardian. That person knew more about them than I did, but he refused to give me details. He said it wasn't allowed but refused to tell me by whom. He was a completely reliable source, and I have no reason to doubt his story."

We stared at each other for a few moments. As usual, I was the first to break. "Are ya going to tell me who the person was?"

Peter crossed himself making the symbols of his faith, then linked his ancient fingers together in front of him on the table. I expected the rosary to appear in his hands soon, but it hadn't yet.

"I don't really want to tell you, Aran, but I will if you insist."

I held his gaze. "He left me this feather on purpose. I believe I need to know."

"Fine. It was your father who had the other feather," Peter said finally.

"Da?"

Peter nodded and pointed at the feather. "Either that feather in your hand is the same one he had, or you both were visited by a guardian. And I have to tell ya that the latter worries me sick. Seeing a guardian is not a good sign based on what happened to your father. He was in perfect health and should have lived as long as I have. After his encounter with the guardian, his death came sudden and far too soon."

Conn straightened beside me. "It was my understanding that my uncle died of age-related illnesses. Sometimes the solitary burdens we keep secret age us beyond our years. Don't you agree, Father?"

Peter nodded. "Yes, I do. That was well said, young man."

Those profound words were the only ones Conn spoke in the priest's presence. Church officiants weren't his favorite people. I always figured the animosity between demonkind and humankind had its roots in a lack of empathy. But I'd given up trying to change that many years ago. Inspiring compassion in all creatures for each other was a bigger job for a better person than me.

On the way home that evening, I couldn't shake off learning that Da had met a guardian too.

It also intrigued me that the version of Rasmus I met and had been attracted to could be only one form of the creature he'd became after Lilith broke the demon compulsions on him. What other being could he masquerade as?

Wondering if he had taken the form of some random stranger and kissed some other woman who turned out to be a witch upset me, but I couldn't help it thinking about it. I felt deceived somehow for believing his human form was indeed him.

I twirled the feather the creature left behind in my fingers and wondered which side of the good versus evil fight I had landed on with my own supernatural talents.

Both as a witch and a child of The Dagda, I felt I was doing well in the world. That said, I'd dispatched magickals in the past with no more regard than Jack had shown when he'd imprisoned me. Was I right to think I knew who was good and who was bad?

Ya could have said I was having a true mid-life crisis and not be wrong.

CLICK HERE to get Book 2 or visit my website at donnamcdonaldauthor.com.

Want more? Join my mailing list!

Also by Donna McDonald

NANO WOLVES SERIES (PARANORMAL)

Ariel: Nano Wolves 1

Brandi: Nano Wolves 2

Heidi: Nano Wolves 3

Reed: Nano Wolves 4

CYBORGS: MANKIND REDEFINED (SCIFI)

Peyton 313

Kingston 691

Marcus 582

Eric 754

William 874X

Nero 1000

FORCED TO SERVE(SPACE OPERA/SF)

The Daemon of Synar

The Daemon Master's Wife

The Siren's Call

The Healer's Kiss

The Daemon's Change

The Tracker's Quest

The Siren's Surrender

BABA YAGA SAGA (LITE PARANORMAL)

How To Train A Witch

How To Date A Dragon

To Yaga Or Not To Yaga

Baba Yaga Saga Collection

BABA YAGA ADVENTURES (LITE PARANORMAL)

Whole Lot of Shifting Going On

Witch's Guide to a Magical Life

Party Like A Witch

Baba Yaga Adventures Collection

ALIEN GUARDIANS OF EARTH (PARANORMAL/SF)

Bad Panther

Mad Panther

Dad Panther

MY CRAZY ALIEN ROMANCE (HUMOR/SCIFI)

Tangling With Topper

Touching Topper

Timeless Topper

Topper's Magical Christmas

The Topper Collection

ALIENS IN KILTS (HUMOR/SCIFI)

Matchmaker Abduction

Nate's Fated Mate

Shades Of Darcone

Want to hear about new releases and planned books?

Join my mailing list!

About the Author

USA Today Bestselling Author Donna McDonald published her first novel in March of 2011. Many multi-genre novels later, she admits to living her own happily ever after as a full-time author. Addicted to making readers laugh, she includes a good dose of comedy in every book.

Here are some easy ways to learn more about me...
www.donnamcdonaldauthor.com
email@donnamcdonaldauthor.com